T0003725

Brandy,

You're a Fine Girl

Dee DeTarsio

Brandy,

You're a Fine Girl

Addison & Highsmith

Addison & Highsmith Publishers

Las Vegas ◊ Chicago ◊ Palm Beach

Published in the United States of America by
Histria Books
7181 N. Hualapai Way, Ste. 130-86
Las Vegas, NV 89166 USA
HistriaBooks.com

Addison & Highsmith is an imprint of Histria Books. Titles published under the imprints of Histria Books are distributed worldwide.

This is a work of fiction. Names, characters, places, and incidents are the product of the author's imagination. Any resemblance to actual persons, living or dead, business establishments, events, or locales is entirely coincidental.

All rights reserved. No part of this book may be reprinted or reproduced or utilized in any form or by any electronic, mechanical or other means, now known or hereafter invented, including photocopying and recording, or in any information storage or retrieval system, without the permission in writing from the Publisher.

Library of Congress Control Number: 2021952715

ISBN 978-1-59211-139-8 (hardcover)
ISBN 978-1-59211-284-5 (softbound)
ISBN 978-1-59211-288-3 (eBook)

Copyright © 2023 by Dee DeTarsio

For Elliot Lurie, such a fine guy!

Chapter 1

Crum, England, Mid-1800s

"'Brandy,' he told me, 'you're a fine girl,' he said. 'You'd make a good wife.'" I spat over my right shoulder, a new superstition I was trying to start to ward off evil arseholes. "Besides those empty words, all he ever gave me was a chain that turned my neck green and this." I rubbed my little belly. I lifted my chin ever so slightly, bit my lip, and clocked Mrs. Gladys's reaction.

"Oh, you poor, brave girl." Bullseye. "Why, whatever will you do?" After Sunday services, good Christians might say that Mrs. Gladys had the keenest eyes for detail, but the rest of the week, they'd be calling them out for the bulgy toad-like orbs they were. Believe it when I say that comparison did a croaking forest of witches' ingredients no favor.

I pressed my fingers to my lips and bobbed my head like I had seen ladies of quality do when they wished to pretend something inappropriate had not actually happened — some fancy French word I expect, like etiquette. Well, I don't know about that, except to say I once "et a kit" of chicken at the pub, meant for the Sunday crowd that hadn't shown, and been blasted. The privy had served as my confessional as I vowed before God and turds alike to never be a greedy-guts again. But, needs must. I fear I have been eating for two.

As I hoped she would, Mrs. Gladys then waddled from me to the seamstress (who sewed a fine seam but whose nimble fingers had nary a dance on her loose lips), who told the butcher, who told the baker. Our town's not fancy enough to have a candlestick maker, but you can plot the rest of the tale if we did. Jesus wept. This saga could have been a child's rhyme.

Randy Brandy chased after the navy,

All so she could get some gravy.

'Twasn't her fault that she got caught,

Gave it her all and ended up with naught.

Aye. That last line needed work. I'd like a little hearts and flowers imagery there, with a grandiose ending, something-something, bequeathed the happiness that she sought sort of thing. I sighed. "Not for the likes of me."

Pfft. That kind of thinking would not do. I'd been feeling pretty low these past months, yeah. I might have thought about ending it all a time or two, but Jesus, it's not as easy as you would think. In fact, it's nigh on impossible to cark it whenever you want — difficult enough to make a doubty Christian believe there may be some secret purpose to what the bible thumpers go on about.

If you think walking into an angry, cold sea will do the trick, think again. Lest you're possessed with the bravery of a hero. Or perhaps simply possessed. I just wanted to have my options at hand. For no reason, or any reason at all, I waited until one twilight on a moonless night last February when all the plonkers were gone home and huddled together around their miserable fires and bowls of gruel, amid pitiful prayers of redemption.

A few months before that, I had found a great rock, larger than my head and heavier than a small keg of mead. I placed it right outside the horses' stall near the gate, giving me an additional reason to smile every time the barkeep stubbed his toe. As he was too lazy to move it himself and too ignorant to know it was mine, I bided my time. I tossed off my cloak, which doubled as my blanket on those cold evenings, and petted the rock, my friend, because that's how I had begun to think of him. If you promise not to think less of me, I even named him. Sir Stone of Rocky Bottom by the Sea. Now, where do you think we met? Christ. He was a good and true friend, with a stern craggy profile that let me know if I was out of hand in my complaints.

Daft, right? How dare you? I'm fully aware of how this looks, taking advice from Sir Stone when he never even presented his credentials, but you try getting through this life with nary a family member or friend and nothing more than your wits and tits to help you survive.

A fair limestone rock, he was, bestowing benevolence and disappointment in equal measure. He was that proud of me when I didn't sass the master (and he didn't need to know that was only because my mouth was full of cheese). And he practically glowed when I went to church. I didn't bother to correct him and tell him that the only reason I even went there was because it was one of the only acceptable excuses not to be at work. You bet I volunteered to put away prayer books for the vicar and sometimes even got another half-hour reprieve if Father Sweaty Hands prayed for a bit of slap and tickle. What my fine Sir Stone didn't know couldn't hurt him.

Back to that one night. "Feeling like a little fresh air, Sir Stone?" I asked politely. I spread my apron and gently placed him in it, tied it up, and hoiked him up on my back, the better to carry him. "I bet it's beautiful down by the dock this time of year." I didn't want to alarm him, you see. "Wooh, you do weigh a goodly amount, friend." I was glad he couldn't see my grim smile. Obviously, my tale has no happy ending since I'm still here and my friend is not. Thanks to the one-armed man.

I was in the cold drink, shivering up to my nethers when a giant splash behind me sent me to my knees. I gulped a lungful of the nasty cold waters as Sir Stone bade me, pressing down, down. And then, he was gone. I was pulled up, gasping for air like a sinner for redemption. A strong, muscled arm that felt more like a tree trunk embraced me and tugged me up on the rocks.

"What do you think you're doing?" His deep voice scared me. The timbre of his voice was enough to shiver my timbers had I not already been shaking.

"You yell at me?" I screamed at him. "You nearly killed me, jumping behind me like that. You made me fall. Are you trying to drown me? I should call for the constable." My teeth chattered.

He put his cloak around me and tried to rub me dry. "Shush, shush. There, there." If there are four sweeter sounds on this earth, I've yet to hear them. For one brief moment, I nestled in that one-armed embrace, searching for the solace that had just been denied me. "I'm afraid your rock is gone, though," he said with a faint smile. The light of a flame in its torch up by the dock allowed me to make out his profile as he pulled me further up to the walkway.

I thrust him his cape and made haste back to my room, tucked behind the horse stable near the back door of the tavern. I tossed over my shoulder, "Don't be bragging to all and sundry that you saved me — because you didn't!"

"Be well," was all he said, his one (and only) hand lifted in the dark night.

Grief at my role in Sir Stone's ignominious end nearly prevented me from getting out of bed in the morning. Since then, I try to remain positive. I am positive I will miss Sir Stone until my dying day, a day which can't come soon enough. I am positive I will always be hungry. Always tired. Always cold — except when I am always hot in the hellish midsummer when my misbegotten underarm stains would belie me as a stevedore. My greatest shame was the dirt. I washed and I scrubbed almost every day, stealing soap from the barkeep's wife, who didn't seem to ever notice it missing. Based on the critters encircling her, she wouldn't recognize the need for a bar of soap if a fly harvested the potatoes growing in her ears. I was positive I'd never feel clean enough.

So, if I was stuck living for the next, please-God-no-more-than-five-years, how could I rig it? I set to thinking. An English bugger had taught me to read, both a blessing and a curse. I hated learning about things I would never have, but damn me if the pretends weren't sometimes an idyllic surcease. (And how else do you think a wench like me knows words like surcease?)

"Curiosity is the antidote for sadness," was what the toff told me as he lifted my chin with his long fingers and exclaimed over what he called my "woebegone eyes." He then lifted my skirts, and I vouch for nothing except to say I learned my letters in one day.

That the English bloke also made me learn what gents really like is only a bonus. Ask my sailor.

Our puny port was a funny kind of place. For once, the hierarchy of sin tilted in favor of the poor. The daughter of the mayor couldn't get up the duff without secrets and shame and being sent away for "consumption" to the continent, but a good-natured slattern who worked at the saloon? What else was to be expected? Bring the bastard to call, and he better make good — and marry the poor girl.

Christ on a cross. This was going to work. I sloshed water in the pail and went to my back room off the saloon to wash. "Out." I kicked at the chicken that had managed to sneak into my room and sent it off to torment the horse. "There's not even room for me to turn around, let alone entertain poultry." Times like that, I missed Sir Stone and his quiet counsel. The water felt like a blessing on my face. I had selected a new twig to work against my teeth and followed up with splashing my breasts, which are perfection. I shimmied myself dry and pulled on my dress. I set the bucket back outside by the trough and enjoyed the attention of several blokes.

"Hey ho, Brandy? Do you step outside to cop a handy? Suck my dandy?" He made a rude gesture.

"If I did, Colin Andersen, I fear I would need spectacles to try to find the needle in your haystack." As Colin Andersen was indeed a hay farmer, that was truly funny, as his companions would attest.

I waved those gits off and went back to work. I waited as the townsfolk's grapevine served my purpose: to shame the sailor who sent a charge up my skirt into marrying me. The few bits of coin I earned were barely enough to keep me in mash and beer, let alone soap, and a girl has to think on her future. If I couldn't end it, Lord knows, somehow, I had to begin it. Lordy, was I tired of serving the great unwashed, day after day, the same weary lot of miscreants, only differentiated by their suffering. That clod couldn't stop coughing; this one couldn't see straight. Him? He lost his beloved daughter, a babe, to as fiery a fever as I'd ever seen. It put me in such a foul mood when I bothered to feel sorry for their woes.

Winter was here. Again, and as always. I had no more hope to keep me warm. It would be my nineteenth season of despair, and one way or another, my last.

Chapter 2

Even though the babe wasn't yet, the idea was born. The owner's wife didn't notice the extra cream sipped straight from the bucket every chance I could. And I felt obliged to snatch unsanctioned bites of cheese and beef before I served the plates to the hefty blokes who wouldn't miss it.

I applied myself with virtue to prepare for my future, as one supposed a clerk bent to his books. I enjoyed my "studies" and found no great hardship sussing out ways to snatch extra butter here, savory fat off the bone there, and once, I gave myself high marks for lifting a sack of hazelnuts off a squire. I was well pleased with myself. Occasionally my belly still grumbled, but my mission gave me purpose.

My ship had finally come in. My sailor, the one with eyes as blue as his blasted sea in the miserable month of February when nothing good ever happens, had finally come home. It was an icy morning in that frigid month, as cold as a witch's tit when I spun my web, cast my rod, and set out to ensnare my one true love.

Who would never leave me.

I believe "never" is a French word meaning the gods'll take that wager.

I looked fair glowing that evening. I had on my best gown, though if one only owns two, "best" is nothing more than a rat race. Due to a month or two of the richest, creamiest comestibles I could snatch, I was in fine form. I yanked down my dress showcasing my décolletage, another of those fancy French words that I assume means two pillows. Two perfect, plump, bursting-at-the-seams pillows, practically begging a gentleman to rest his weary seafaring head. Take your pick, one or two, or better yet, come in for a docking right between them both. My sailor liked that, he did. My skin was soft and smooth as freshly churned butter, with nary a blemish. I tweaked my nipples and bowed my greeting extra-low. He could not take his eyes off me and spent coin for a quiet room upstairs for our reunion. He was so handsome when I cozied up to his room with a mug of warm mulled wine and dessert. Dessert being me, of course. His hands and kisses told me how beautiful he thought me. He wasted no time. Afterward, my favorite part, he held me against his chest and rocked me, back and forth in the rhythm of what I imagine the waves felt like on his ship.

He whispered his sailor stories into my ear and held me close, which nearly cast me into sleep until I remembered my purpose. I caught his hand and pushed it to my belly. He caressed me and kissed my hair. "What a fine girl," he said.

"What a good wife I'd be," I whispered back.

"Aye," he said.

I gasped. "You mean it? You'll marry me?" I sat up and made sure to aim my tits at his face.

"Brandy."

I clutched his hand again at my midsection. This time I did the caressing, moving his hand over my generous belly. I nodded my head and refused to decipher the look in his eyes.

"We'll figure this out," he told me kindly as he kissed me goodnight. He was such a gentleman; he had me wrapped with him in his cape to see me downstairs to my room. I smiled at the sound of his tread on the stairs as he left and hugged myself tightly. I was sailing on seventh heaven.

I yawned. I'd never be hungry. I'd never be tired. I'd never be cold. And all I wanted for a wedding gift was a bar of the violet soap he had once brought me from France.

The next morning, early even for the seagulls, calls from the harbor and the ringing of bells reached through my dreams. I stretched, for once eager to begin my day. I peeked around the partition — even the goats were still asleep — and tiptoed through the straw to the door. The periwinkle light was as beautiful as I'd ever seen, though as I'm not a morning riser, I am an unreliable narrator. I yawned again and wondered what ship it was that was leaving. At the tavern, we half kept track of seafaring schedules as they affected our supply and demand. Ah well, I thought. I'd be among the first at the market to get some crusty loaves of bread, and wouldn't Mrs. Meade be pleased, for once.

I quickly reached the docks and blew a kiss at the departing vessel, knowing my man, soon to be lawful and wedded, would be sailing with me by his side into our own new world. (Not literally, of course. I was sure he'd set me up in a snug little cottage where I would keep the home fires burning for him. Try to keep up.) I stopped so fast some stinker from behind plowed into my shoes, nearly lifting my heel clean out. "Mangy, plume-plucked varlet." I barely spared him a glance because, in front of my eyes, my world began to shrink. The ship skulking out of the harbor was The Looking Glass. I fancied I saw him there, on the stern, the witless coward. Cad. Cur.

"You yeasty, flea-bitten miscreant!" I grabbed a melon from a passing cart and heaved it on the ground before me, enjoying its smash. I stomped my foot, clenched my fists, and bellowed with rage. "You sniveling, rat-faced two-timing mutton-fucker."

Tears burst from my eyes, and I continued screaming invectives with the occasional "I hate you" and "I hope you get scurvy and rickets" and that "all your teeth fall from your lying head." And I may have said something about his cock being a gimpy joke of a worm.

I shrilled like a fisherman's wife. Truth be told, the bilious volume was more like the vicar's wife, reaching levels I'm fairly certain the cowardly crew of the scuttering barge that made haste across the harbor could very well hear. In any event, it caused a nearby horse toting a kingly conveyance to shy.

A most unmanly scream roiled out the window, followed by a frilled lacy arm clawing for purchase at the frame. A nuns' tatting competition would be so lucky to have so much fine lace. The driver steadied the beast without, while within, the consternation of some fierce lord was apparent. "Dear heavens and alack, what is happening?" he cried. The shuddering wheels of the coach stopped as a giant, ridiculous confection of felt, feathers, and leather popped out, held up by a wobbly head, which sported as disdainful a look as I've ever seen. (I would practice that look in front of the serving tray I had occasion to polish at the tavern.) His nostrils flared as if to inhale the rotting guts of a squished rat to make sure it truly smelled as horrid as one thought.

I saw his look and raised him a sneer before turning my invective on him. "What's ado with you, you mealy-mouthed gobshite? Never saw a sailor desert his lady love before?" His eyes bulged out of his sockets. "What are you looking at, turdy-guts?" I said with a curtsy to the fancy man in the carriage. "Pardon my French."

He shaded his hand, dripping lace over his face.

"You do know I can still see you, sir, right?" I recognized the bloke. He'd been to the tavern a time or two.

Jesus, Mary, and Judas, his horse had fancier plumage than I've ever seen. I directed my ire square at the pretty chap and the horse he rode in behind and yelled at him in an exaggerated cant, as I did have quite the gift of parody. "Wot's the ado to you, my fine and mighty blighter? Ya never seen a scurvy sailor scurry off leaving his lady love filled to burstin' with his seed?" I cradled my little belly and fondly patted parts southern.

"My poor babe shall grow up fatherless and perhaps motherless too in this shitten' world." I kicked at a rock, stubbing my toe, which fueled my fire. My voice amplified so mightily that in different circumstances, I would have admired the results. "Don't know what foul boil of a god would take a look at the likes of you and grace you with all that," I waved my hand, "and think, this poor pussy of a sot seems like a deserving recipient of my bounty. Tell me, sir, have you ever even had to wipe your own arse?"

I stared long enough to clock the horror in his eyes as the rest of his face was covered by his fine gloves — silk, suede? I do not know. How would the likes of me determine the fabrics necessary to pull together an ensemble like that? All I know is that in my crushing despair at the shrinking view of the backside of my true love, my devastation hadn't quite set in. I ran to the fancy man's horse and plucked a frothy white feather straight from its headgear. (A simpleton like me can't even begin to guess what a hat for a horse is even called.) "Jesus," I let out one final screech before stomping off.

I ran to the edge of the dock, tore the silver locket from my neck, and threw it to the waves. Virgin Mary, do you really believe I'm that stupid? Or rich? Of course, I kept it. "What kind of rotter scratches his own name on a locket to give to his lady love?" I sank to my knees. "It was supposed to be my name. I'm your lady love. What a fine wife I would have been." I held the broken chain clenched in my left fist and hurled the feather from that fancy horse with all my might into the drink, followed by all of my dreams.

Have you ever thrown a feather? You're as big a fool as I. The wind tossed it aloft without a care. Frustrated beyond belief, my rage had no outlet.

I finally stood, feeling twenty-five years old, and slowly turned my back on the sea and the bobbing toy-sized barge of betrayal, about to fall off the horizon. I walked back down the dock near the fishmonger and reached into his discard basket, destined for fertilizer and animal feed, and came up with the ripest, mushiest fish to still retain its form. I took a quick hop and hurled it at the carriage with all my might, as the toff inside ducked with as womanly a shriek as you would ever hear.

"And ne'er the twain shall meet," I mumbled as his coach set off in one direction, and I turned toward the tavern. How was I to know?

Chapter 3

I lifted my skirts and set off at a run toward the tavern. I wouldn't call it a home because a home should have a warm fire, a sound roof that doesn't leak even before it rains, and a clean blanket that didn't require fleas to hold its weave. But that could just be me.

I shivered with misery, contemplating a pitiful life of penury, so abject my morning's breakfast of stale bread and skilly gruel made me pause in thanks. I looked at the silver locket and missed Sir Stone more than ever. When I had shown him my treasure months ago, I slipped it upon his craggy brow. The bottom portion of the oval had snagged on a roughened protrusion and triggered some sort of hidden catch. The locket sprung open in half. Embedded inside was a piece of parchment with teeny tiny numbers written upon it, which made no sense. I pried out the scrap of paper and hoped for I don't know what? A lock of that rotter's hair? A nugget of gold? All I had gotten for my troubles were a few letters on the reverse side. "IS AZ" was printed in the same small slanted script. Sir Stone and I had meticulously examined the inside of the locket and searched for clues. Nothing. There were no clues to life. Shove off.

I pried the locket open again in despair, hoping to find a link to my sailor. Or better yet, that the charm would prove to be a talisman. That there was something we'd overlooked. I honestly thought the universe owed me a magical spell to make up for the hand I'd been dealt. "IS AZ." Forwards, backwards, up, down, that's all there was — a torn scrap of parchment. I could make no sense of it, nor of the few scribbled numbers that added up to nothing more than a rotting miasma, a reminder that my life IS AZ miserable as could be.

Back at the inn that I had fully expected to be shot of once I married my sailor, I shoved my broken heart, along with the locket, into my pocket.

The day was a repeat of drudge and despair — the usual crowds filled with the stench of the miseries of their unmet needs. Nothing would ever change. I would never be content. I would never be full. I would never be warm. I would never swallow without knowing I was a deeply flawed woman missing the best part of herself. I've always been alone. But now I was lonely.

"If one more of the lot of you says sorry to me, you'll be the sorry one when I piss in your beer." Work was unbearable but better than being alone. I had no care serving those yokels. I cried with reddened eyes, and snot dripped all the way to my wrist as I poured their quaff. Not one complaint was made. (Ah, don't think they're gentle souls at heart. One time, I did piss in Scabby Stephen's ale, but you'll have to ask Dumb Pete for the moral of that story.) I thought the night would never end.

The door flew open with a bang. One Lord Fluffernutter sashayed in, his perfume so strong it could kill the rats and put the house cat out of business. "Your lordship." I sniffed as if I had been crying, which I had, but dear Lord, even a wretch like me knew you could catch more flies with honey than a powder keg of Eau de rotting corpse cologne. I have a very sensitive nose.

Of course, his name is actually Lord Elliot Pfeiffer-Mondragon, which I can't spell for the life of me, as I will never figure out what strange hex that P is doing with all those Fs. Nor can others more gifted than I in distributing nicknames.

He was the one at the dock that morning who witnessed my ultimate humiliation. I hadn't paid close attention to him due to my preoccupation with my sailor legging it. Come around for another look, I expect. And a laugh. He's an odd duck. He hadn't been around in a while, though perchance, I was preoccupied with perfecting my scheme and hadn't noticed him before. He was nice enough, I suppose, in that he never bothered with the likes of me. He always seemed to take a keener interest in the stable boy, often questioning him about the grooming and training of horses or methods for brushing. I guess he loved horses.

That night, Lord Fussy-budget flourished his cape, because what else would a fop like him do? He swirled it off his own shoulder, only to accidentally enwrap its black velvety folds around the poor blighter who sat behind him, minding his own business. Bad luck for poor little soused Ned Porter.

Worse luck for the gent, since Ned Porter, who had once been trapped in a coal mine for seven days had, one, a fear of the dark; two, a bigger fear of enclosed spaces; and three, the biggest passion in our whole berg for hating the privileged gentry. Mayhem then ensued as Ned Porter roared and grabbed the cape, pulling the toff along before cracking him on the table, which collapsed. Since fights were welcome as part of free entertainment, it was some moments before Beer Barrel Bob Meade, the owner and my illustrious employer — I'm not being disrespectful, he wore his appellation with pride, like a mum about to birth twin calves — stepped into the fray. Ned Porter was applauded as he lumbered out the door toward his home, and the gent was clean knocked out. I grabbed a rag from behind the bar and dipped it into a water bowl, and went to kneel by his supine form. I squeezed water upon his face and saw his eyes twitch. Lordy, look at them eyelashes! He opened his eyes fully and stared straight at me. His lips smiled, revealing the straightest and whitest teeth I had ever seen.

"I was looking for you," said my future.

I helped him sit up, convinced Beer Belly I would clean up, and he could go, and focused on the bloke. You are not going to believe what happened next.

He pushed the rag out of my hands and held them, cracked and rough as a sow's arse. He winced, from pain or something else I was to ask myself, and slowly moved as if to stand. He surprised me and maneuvered onto his knees. His torso was quite long, and he towered above me as I was seated before him. The great unwashed audience of drunks surrounded us.

"My dear…lady," he paused. "Will you," he cleared his throat, "do me the greatest," his voice cracked then and there, I'll tell you, "honor of becoming my wife?"

I don't think I ever have before or since, but I guffawed. "Oh, kind sir," I said, still laughing and trying to catch my breath. "I fear you have taken a blow to the head and lost your senses." I even reached up to run my fingers over his noggin. It was quite knobby, so who's to say? His lace-draped arm revealed a soft, white clean hand that caught my wrist.

"I've never been more in my right mind. Our paths are predetermined, our love star-crossed, our fate to be feted…you are my destiny."

"Destiny is two blocks over, my good man. It's to me, Brandy, you are incoherently babbling. I assume that is poetry of some sort, but 'tis muddle to me." I may have had a twinge that it wasn't my own dear sailor declaring such sentiment. I rather enjoyed the star-crossed part. I confess to feeling a wrench. That Destiny was a lucky gal. I wasn't above a tumble with one I fancied — have you seen my missing sailor? But I wasn't yet forced into the oldest profession. Yet. Was that a tear in my eye? I brushed at it, knowing it was probably just soot from the dying embers in the fire.

He leaned back then into a more comfortable seat. "No. It is you. I saw you this morning." He glanced over my plump shape. I see your predicament, but more, your possibilities. I see you. And I want you for my wife."

"Why?"

He laughed then, tittered rather. Oh, the elite effete, I remembered thinking.

"The heart desires what the heart desires."

"A fool and his money are soon parted."

"Ah, yes, and I am to have much with which to part. Surely that is an enticement?"

He looked at me, peered at my grimy face, though not without wafting his linen and lace. Again, with the lace. I was beginning to suspect his drawers contained such fussy embellishments, perhaps due to a lack therein?

"You do have the most lovely eyes. Our child will be beautiful."

"You take liberties, sir."

"Oh," he stumbled. "I just meant…it is possible," he cleared his throat. "It is not unthinkable." He tossed his head, his bouffant hair sported spikes of a day ill-done. "I had hoped this proposal to be a mutually beneficial one."

"For someone like me, you mean? I'm expected to jump at this miraculous proposition?" Gents, have to warn you. Ladies are capable of the most capricious calculations of all time in the blink of an eye. Our thoughts are many, fierce, fearsome, and fabulous, but alas, fatalistic. "What's your end game, sir? Sell me into slavery? Murder me for sport? Wager me off to your friends?"

"Dear God! Do people around here really do that?"

He was so shocked it was endearing. Apparently, his coin bag exceeded the size of his brain.

He looked around the moldy room. I followed his gaze, seeing what he must. Smelling what he must. Grime and soot beneath a sagging roof. Splintery benches that one would think would be worn smooth by now from all the great arses riding there. He leaned his elbow on the table corner, which rewarded him with a teeter.

"My home is perfect," he said.

"I believe you."

"I need a wife, a chatelaine if you will, and mother to my future heir." He wiggled his eyebrows at that as his eyes traveled down my form. What a twat.

"You need something, alright, sir, but I wouldn't mark a wife at the top of that list. More like a romp and roll in the hay," I told him. The men in the pub cheered at that. Ah, well. Needs must. I'd be a fool not to listen to his proposition. "Go on."

He stood up. "Dear Lord, you are a pretty one." I jerked my head back to look up at him. "I shall write you an ode," he declared.

"Owed? I don't want anything to be owed, my fine sir. It will be coins on the barrel for me." The men hooted again.

"No. Ode. Ode. It's a paean, a hymn, an homage…to you."

"Odd, odd." I taunted him back. He just laughed.

"Would you rather a beer-drinking song for sailors?"

Oh, how my fickle heart leapt to hear of my sailor gnashing his teeth as my name is sung, far and wide. I clasped my hands at my heart. "Could you do that?"

"Oh, my dear. Your name will be famous, sung by lusty lads near and far, drunk on spirits and dreams of you."

I sniffed. If something seems too good to be true, it's more like than not to be a golden biscuit crawling with maggots.

I put on a slatternly accent. "And I need a home, please, sir, care for me, feed me, wrap me in linen and lace." My sarcasm fell flat, as it all sounded rather nice. "What about your own peers? Fish from your own damned pond, man."

He sighed and placed his hand over his heart. "Ah. There was someone once. The love of my life, the one that got away, that I shall never forget." He sighed again; what a sop. "But you and I? I think we could bump along quite well together, don't you? I have what I have, and you have..." He waved his lacy sleeve at me, encompassing my assets — my bosom, of course, straining out the top of my tight best dress, my apparently fine eyes, and the fact that he was so sure I could be had for this wondrous enticement.

You know what? He was right.

I tossed my apron off then and there, left my second dress, which was hanging in the back to dry next to the horse feed, and didn't even bother to tell the proprietor I was leaving. He'd wonder for half a second when I didn't have his oats ready for the morning, then spend the rest of the day cursing me for legging it. Not that he'd ever claim, or I'd ever admit, that he might be my father. But then again, he might not.

I held out my chapped knuckles for my lord to kiss. I curtsied. And then I told him I loved him.

To my great surprise, the fool-born drunkards gathered in the pub, who bore witness to that touching tableau, and who had known me as a baby, started to clap to a man. My throat clenched shut, and I couldn't speak, so I didn't bother to favor them with a response other than a weak smile that I feared was mistook for a grimace of pain.

The frilly-willy tucked my arm through his and raised his left hand high in a victory salute. The drunken clodhoppers lifted their empty cups, cheered, whooped, and whistled as Lord Fluffy escorted me out of my life once and for all.

Chapter 4

Sir Embroidered Britches took me to his home that night. I had never ridden in a carriage before, and I tell you this: I will never walk anywhere again — what a mighty conveyance! My favorite part is knocking on the panel and barking out orders. "Go there! Faster! Halt!" This is what I was born for. I couldn't see much out the window, for it was dark as Satan's lair, but I clicked my tongue against the roof of my mouth in tempo with the galloping horse. It was great fun. Until my great lord bade me quit.

It was darker still when we arrived at Mondragon Manor. These fops and their noblesse oblige. It wouldn't startle me one bit to discover they were obligated to name their toenails. I tripped at the stone steps that led up to the entry, with a stained glass arched window atop the apex at its very front door. "Is it a church?" I asked.

"Bless you," responded my intended. At least the man is quick to appreciate a joke. For someone who relished the thrice-yearly new straw in my mattress, the hall was magnificent. Except for the creepy, gormless statue of a woman missing her arms that held court in a niche right inside the entrance. I had never missed Sir Stone more.

"Come," my fiancé urged, guiding my elbow. I pretended offense when the buffoon called for hot water for my bath, especially seeing how the second Sunday was only a day shy of a fortnight away. While I glowered at him, I acquiesced. And rejoiced.

The head of his house was a short, short man with very little hair. I'm being kind. I practically had to shield my eyes from the reflection of his great glistening dome that bounced flickers of the flame from the candle he held. He showed absolutely no surprise at his lord and master, arriving home little worse for wear, bearing one extra package, me, looking ridden hard and put away wet.

"My fiancé!" My newly betrothed gushed to his man. "Brandy." While I was trying to figure out whether I should bow or curtsy, though I knew well enough not to scratch the itch that tormented my backside, my fiancé clapped his hands in his glory, breathing in the rich air of his estate. "Gordy," he said to his man, "is my fiancé's room ready?"

My affianced touched my elbow. "His madre calls him Cabezo Gordo, so we call him Gordy." And to the man with the fat head, he added, "Turquoise room, correct?"

"Such assumptions, sir," I said, as I wondered if I had jumped from the frying pan directly into the fire. Imagine my relief when I entered the room with great trepidation, only to find no Turks.

"Gordy," I said timidly at my audacity in using his rude name as introduced by my fiancé. And as I didn't have the cut of his jib just yet, I feared the worst — that he would snarl at me. "Why do they call this room…" I hesitated.

"Turquoise, miss. 'Tis a color. And one of my favorites." He held the candle next to the curtain of the bedstead. "The best parts of blues and greens, as serene as the Caribbean Sea on a sunlit afternoon. That'll soothe your very soul."

"If you say so," I said, having never seen a Caribbean Sea, and having nothing but quivering doubts about the existence of any soul. I took a gander at the rest of the room. If only given one word to describe it, I'd have to say it was soft. Rugs on top of rugs on the floor, drapes that I felt as soon as Gordy left, to verify that they were indeed velvet. A padded bench here, an embroidered linen runner atop a dresser there. Good Lord, the rich even worry about keeping their furniture warm? The textures in this room could swallow me up whole. I began to thaw.

"Mrs. Catarrh will be here shortly, or as long as it takes her, to supervise your bath."

"No. No, thank you." I bobbled a curtsey, for who knew how to act around these folks? "I don't need anyone's eyes on my altogether. That'll cost you extra. I am quite capable."

Gordy looked like he understood. He nodded his head at the tub. "Two pails of heated water will be brought, and if you're real quick-like, you'll be tossed, washed, chivied, dried and already dreaming, or pretending to be," he raised his eyebrow at me to be sure I understood, "by the time she gets here, understand?"

His mouth cracked what I assumed was meant to be a reassuring smile. "The master has a few things here for you to wear and will no doubt take you shopping in the morn to complete your trousseau."

Too tired to ask. But hoping trousseau was as nice as turquoise. A knock-knock-knock-knock-knock on the door jamb preceded the energetic entrance of one of the handsomest lads I have ever seen. He looked to be about my age or a little younger. He wore a plait of healthy, shiny, bouncy brown hair with a most attractive widow's peak in the middle of his forehead, which pointed down to two exceptional blue eyes. Turquoise, the thought hovered in my head. He carried two steaming pails of water. He executed a tricky maneuver, part bow, full twirl, and poured the buckets into the copper tub.

"Atsuko was sleeping, Gordy, so I volunteered." He lifted the pails. "Wanted to be one of the first to welcome our lady to our humble abode." He pointed his right foot this far out and bent at the waist nearly all the way to the floor. "Please call me, RayRay," he said. "Rafael von Rachmond at your service."

He rose and clocked me full on. "Pretty. Very pretty. You'll clean up rather well, I suspect. Enjoy." I might have liked him, but then he whistled. I'd be on the lookout for that one. Experience has taught me you can neither trust nor abide he who whistles. 'Tis the one sin that oddly enough, while I could do it on a whim, woe be unto others who tried the same. "Whistle, whistle, whistle," he danced out of the room.

"I'll leave you to it. Tomorrow will be a big day." Gordy closed my door.

I won't detail my hot, steaming bath, filled with lavender and rose petals, nor the soap that lathered with bubbles so large I nearly floated away. (I hid the barely used bar under my pillow, lest you think I'm some country rube.)

Rich folks are incredible. They have special clothes. Just for sleeping. I could go on in raptures — yet another word Gordy had introduced to me — about the fine weave of the most amazing gown I had ever seen. I assumed it was woven by blind nuns in some sacred cave, its weave spun out of the hair of fairies. I never wanted to take it off. I stood on the footstool (that dripped with golden fringe) to get a better vision of myself in the ornate curlicued (a word I had never before had occasion to use) looking-glass above the fireplace, and let me tell you, vision was the word. My freshly-washed hair was drying in waves and dipped low on my back. You'd want to see my silhouette outlined in those fine threads by the flickering firelight, as my new best friend Gordy would most likely emote, considering his soliloquy on the color of turquoise. My so-called fine eyes were drooping with exhaustion, but nothing could quell the shard of hope that stabbed me in the stomach. The only fear I had was that this would all be snatched away.

I heard a rich, juicy death rattle of a cough followed by the sound of footsteps that slowly dragged over the carpet in the hall. I had a frightening thought that it was a ghost come to call. The crackle of the fire had nothing on the lungs of the crone who finally managed to knock upon and open my door with one spent effort. I jumped off the ottoman and held my hands demurely in front of me while she coughed her greeting.

"Ah, Mrs. Catarrh, I presume."

"Aye," she wheezed. "Miss Cunt, I presume."

"Takes one to know one," I said.

"Girlie, my cunny's forgotten more men's clobbers than yours will ever know."

That took me a second. I thought back to a vicar who tried to tutor me, if you know what I mean, before replying. "Who can find a virtuous woman, for her price is far beyond rubies." I clasped my hands at my heart and looked as innocent as I could manage.

"And so it is." Her mangled laugh turned into a cough so wretched I felt pity and fetched her a glass of water from the table by my bed. (Let that sink in. There's a table by my bed, with a porcelain pitcher of water and a cut-glass goblet. Let the record show, that goblet was worth something, either as a weapon or pawn.) Her cough was alarming. I gave her the water and patted her back while she drank.

She jerked away from me. "Stop hitting me."

I stepped back.

"You can rub my back."

So I did, feeling the bony knobs of her curved spine.

She left.

I dreamed that it was all a dream.

Chapter 5

That morning, I heard a soft tap at my door that then clicked open. I saw the small frame of a woman with shiny black hair cross the room to open the curtains. The streaming light told me that I could get used to living like this. Heretofore I would have had half a day's work done — dishes washed, oats cooked, eggs gathered, cheese bargained for, and bread set to rise. Oh, and don't forget barrels of mead huffed and puffed and rolled into the back if I didn't feel like kissing the delivery man. Seeing's how he was missing several teeth, most likely because even his own molars couldn't stand the smell of his breath, I rolled the barrels myself most mornings.

She opened a wardrobe and pulled out a dress fit for a queen. It was the color of the blue part of turquoise, thank you very much, with a stomacher stitched in gold-colored threads. I forgot to pretend to be asleep and bolted upright.

Then I forgot the dress because the woman, Atsuko, as it turns out, was the most beautiful creature I had ever seen. "Oy, you are a sight!"

She bowed her head. "Where are you from?" I asked. My feet dangled over the side of the bed. "I've never seen anyone who looks like you." She looked back at me, seemingly as curious.

"Nor I, you."

She spoke the queen's language, just like my fiancé, yet her voice was as soft and harmonious as, ah, let me be rich for a while, and I'll get back to you on what rich folks think is harmonious. I was about to say, as the sound of an egg sizzling in the fry pan when you haven't eaten for two days, but that's so peasanty. And not right at all. It was more of a coo from a dove. I want to add a dove in love, but I will spare you from my poetry. Her voice took Gordy's love for the color turquoise and turned it into a lullaby.

"Where are you from?" I repeated.

She laughed, the perfect laugh for the perfect amount of time. "Japan."

"Jesus-fecking-Christ. What is Japan?" She could have said the far side of the moon, and I would have bought it.

"An island far from this one. Gordy rescued me."

Once she helped me dress for breakfast, I sashayed into the dining room. I beamed with how well I knew I looked, and my stomach growled with hunger. I smelled pork!

"Whoa, Nellie. Look at you, Brandy!" Elliot, my affianced, stood and clapped. Gordy, who sat at his side, sent me a nod, and RayRay, who was on the opposite side, let out a whistle. Of course.

"Mrs. Catarrh, whom you met last night, will be your chaperone, but she's sleeping in this morning. Late night and all. Sit. Sit. Atsuko, help get my darling's plate, would you, and join us."

I sat next to Elliot, and Atsuko put a delicate plate the size of a hog trough in front of me. It was filled with pork (I knew it!) and potatoes, and toasted bread, and oh, Lord, eggs, more than I could eat in a year, but sure, I'd give it a go.

"Eat up, miss," RayRay addressed me. "Mrs. Farfuddle, a woman who should be as far from food as possible, is your betrothed's latest acquisition and our esteemed cook."

"Hush, RayRay," the lord and master declared.

RayRay, of course, couldn't seem to help himself. "Oh, Elliot. If there were a title for collecting sad sack strays like the lot of us, you would be king. King Misfortune of Mondragon, rest your weary soul." He looked at me. "There's bound to be a few misfires, though, don't you think?" He saw the look on my face. "Oh, dear God, not you. You very well could be the trophy in Elliot's collection. Pièce de résistance."

Which I assumed was French for scraping the bottom of the barrel.

Gordy picked up the tale. "Quiet, RayRay. Mrs. Farfuddle does her best. We all eat a hearty breakfast because when it comes right down to it, there's not much you can do to mangle potatoes and toast." He took a sip of his coffee. "The best you can do is not be too hungry at suppertime."

"And I quite like my bacon extra-crispy, almost burnt," said Elliot.

Atsuko made a sound, and everyone changed the subject as Mrs. Farfuddle entered the dining room. She twisted a towel in her hands. "Git enough, then?"

Everyone bowed their heads and made positive remarks, "Aye, mm, well done." Their forks clanged against the plates excessively loudly. As I was using my fingers to shovel a piece of toast scooped with eggs and a mast of bacon into my mouth, I looked her over. Had I met her on a moonless night in a dungeon, I would have guessed she was a cook. She was as wide as she was tall. Given the warning though that perhaps her talents lay elsewhere, I surmised she must consume the copious leftovers. I smiled at her. In my book, anyone other than myself who produced comestibles was a desirable acquaintance worth cultivating.

She shot me a look that had my mouth not been so full, I'd have put that roly-poly piece in her place. Elliot squeezed my hand and offered me the rest of his potatoes, then nudged my elbow to bump it off the table.

My fiancé pointed at my cup. "Try the coffee. It's from South America. Put more cream in it."

As I'd never had coffee before, and for all I knew, South America was next to Japan, I gave that a go, too.

I made a face. The group laughed. "Just wait," said my husband-to-be. "When faced with a choice of sleeping the morning away or getting up to have coffee…" As a whole, they raised their cups and drank. As I've had much, much worse, I followed suit, and within a period of five minutes, I felt the glorious pounding of my heart as blood marched through my veins. It was a drum beat geared to battle, ta-rum, ta-rum, ta-rum-rum-rum. Anything's possible. Everything's possible.

"So, my trusted friends and allies. This lovely woman, Brandy," he sipped his coffee, "has agreed to be my lawful wedded wife. I did well, don't you think?"

They agreed as he continued, "But we have much to do, don't we?" He looked at me with as friendly a smile as you could want. "God, I hope our child has your eyes."

Curious. I smiled back at him. Sure. He was a perfect gentleman. He was solicitous and kind.

I would hide his cologne and evade his sweaty palms. Since he gave me a pair of fine gloves, that would help considerably. We would have a whirlwind courtship. He would clean up my manners; I would clean up his condescension. I have witnessed worse betrothals.

And the gods laughed.

Chapter 6

"My parents are coming next week, so we need to employ Operation Dandy Brandy immediately. Brandy, I'm assuming it's fine by you if we marry sooner rather than later, say, tomorrow? Tongues wag, and towns talk, you know. While we have the illustrious Mrs. Catarrh as your chaperone, it's for the best, don't you think?"

I drained my coffee cup. Dandy Brandy thinks Mr. Pins and Needles is quite eager. "Yes, my lord."

"Ah, she's as quick as she is beautiful. My mother is going to ab-so-lute-ly hate you!"

"Miss, don't be alarmed," Gordy said.

As I was not even remotely alarmed, I paid him no attention.

"We are all here to help you. You will be a great lady, a member of one of the finest families of the land. However," Gordy said with a raised hand.

"Good Christ. There's always a catch." I jumped up from my chair. I'd dare anyone to pry the bacon out of my fist.

"No," Gordy said. "The 'however' is in concern to the expectations and traditions to be followed. Believe me when I say you will have no problem whatsoever in learning all you need."

Elliot agreed. "Atsuko and I will help you with your dress and hair. Mrs. Catarrh will tutor you on deportment, RayRay on dance and music, and Gordy, the ins and outs of being a lady of the manor. And all of us," he nodded at me, "will help you with your speech."

My lower lip trembled, and the old me was straining to give him the what-for. But my tummy was full, and my dress was beautiful, and I was so warm before the fire and this queer group of folk. Sir Stone would have suggested I proceed with caution.

My lessons began anon. "What? No profanity for any reason? But what about when catastrophes occur? Surely that's acceptable?" I wrinkled my brow.

Gordy laughed. "Never. Under any circumstance." Atsuko pled his case. "Calm and demure," she said, hypnotizing me with her soft tone. "A lady is always understanding and kind — most especially in the face of calamity."

"That is easy for you to say," I told her, but as I had imitated her cadence, I was rewarded with claps all around. "That's it, my dear," said Elliot. I sopped it up like I did that morning's gravy.

The day flew by. After my lessons followed by luncheon — not lunch, the rich have nothing but time to add extra syllables to their verbiage — Elliot showed me around his estate. He tucked my hand in the crook of his arm and led me about as if I were a lady.

"Watch your step, Brandy. Come. I have something to show you."

"I believe I know my way around barns, sir."

"Not this barn, trust me."

I swallowed my distrust and reasoned if the bloke was about to ravish me, at least it would most likely be inside, atop fine linens in front of a roaring fire. "Careful, sir, you don't want to sully your ensemble."

"Well done, Brandy. I accept your tease and double you an entendre. I care greatly for the state of your soul," he said with a wink as he led me away from a muddy gash in the path before the slippers Atsuko had given me could be ruined.

"You are looking quite lovely," he added.

Beauty is in the eye of the beholder, Sir Stone used to tell me.

"And you are beautiful, Mr. Pfeiffer." I quite liked the sound of his laughter. "Please, just Elliot." He looked down at me, considering. "It's what my friends call me."

"Oh, Elliot." As we entered, I could not believe what I saw. "What is this place?"

"My laboratory. Here is where I conduct my experiments." There were no animals in this barn, rather long tables piled high with plants and buckets of soil. Dried herbs hung from above.

I inhaled.

"What do you smell then?"

"I smell horse shit."

"Mistress."

"I mean, manure," I said with a curtsy suitable for the queen.

"I'll allow it."

"And earth, and death, and spring?"

He clapped once. "Perfect. You understand?"

I inclined my head like I supposed a lady would, but what I understood would fit on the head of the pin that jabbed my braid into the base of my brain.

"I'm working on ways to improve our soil to grow better crops for all of England. This is potash." He pulled up his sleeve and sunk his clean hand in a bucket of black, loamy dirt. "I have a new way to compost old crops, plants, weeds, and trees into a rich fertilizer."

Rows of pots lined the tables; there were hundreds, with different plants sprouted in each. He had mounted glass windows in the roof and on the south side of the barn, with a fireplace roaring.

"As our population grows, we need to feed our people. By making the best use of our land, we can create healthier corn and potato crops, which will last longer once they are harvested. Look at this cabbage. Feel how heavy it is. I harvested this one out back more than a month ago."

He steered me toward the back of the barn, away from the fire. "And look. Here I've been puttering with farm implements." I picked up a strange-looking small shovel with hooks on either side.

"Looks like a murder weapon. You could gouge a punter's eyes out with this."

"Darling," he cautioned.

In a breathless voice, I amended my comment. "Oh, whatever can this be?"

"You are priceless! Sometimes, the universe provides. Yes, indeed." He was quite pleased with me. "That, my dear," he said, taking the implement from me, "is a combination tool for planting and sowing, clearing weeds, digging if you must. And yet look, small enough and light enough for a woman or children on the farm to use if need be."

I caught his passion. He stood tall with his chin raised. His eyes sparkled as if he were about to pose for a painting in the Bible, one that showed him teaching a serf to plant. He waved his hands.

"Can you imagine if a farmer could increase his crops by even five percent? Better soil, easier-to-use implements. His own table would be heavier, as would his coin purse."

I saw notes he had written atop his workbench.

"Crop rotation?"

"Very good. So many farmers keep growing what their grandfathers and fathers used to grow, but by changing crops in fields, nutrients can be replenished, and the stock made hardier. Plant potatoes where the wheat and barley used to grow."

"Under all that lace resides the soul of a farmer."

"Guilty." He cleaned his hands with a rag. "Maybe my workshop is like you and me. Do you think we can produce a strong and healthy crop?"

"Don't tell me; let me guess. I'm the potash in this scenario?"

"Dear God, I hope so."

Chapter 7

At dinner, Elliot talked about babies and heirs and spares. Why, exactly, the heir is expected to have a pair (of bollocks) is beyond me. It's been my experience that the fairer sex can run circles around any bull in the paddock, all while wearing skirts, tending children, and pretending solicitousness while swapping in the better course of action to take. I suffered a pang but went along and lifted my glass high along with the others at the table. What a good wife I will be, I thought. I set my crystal goblet on the table and ran my thumb over the cut glass pattern.

Gordy drew the attention of my loquacious betrothed. "She's tired, Elliot." My face crumpled as I lost the battle to hide a yawn.

"Come," Atsuko said. "I'll take you."

It was my wedding night eve — Ode to Joy indeed. I got to wear another gorgeous gown; Atsuko told me it was called a peignoir. I plugged my nose and gave it my snootiest pronunciation. I planned never to take it off. I was to sleep in it, in the most sumptuous bed I planned to never leave. After the prior late-night rush, bedtime on that second evening was a performance, a lovely ritual that I could get used to.

"Down feathers," Atsuko told me, and I luxuriated, a word never before imagined, as she helped me up the step into the bed and drew the curtains, cocooning me inside following the most strange and magical day of a girl's life. And glory of glories, as for my almost-husband, I nearly felt — what was that? Could it be? A wisp of a hint of a ghost of fondness for the strange bird, for all he had brought unto me?

"This is the top sheet," continued Atsuko. "You lay under that and then the comforter on top of that, and then this," she placed yet another layer on top of me.

"Is that," I swallowed, "velvet?"

Atsuko nodded. I had been so tired last night I'm not sure I did it all correctly.

"I am a queen, and you may bow to my great good fortune." And then I pealed off into laughter which strangely caused my eyes to water. I hiccupped. Atsuko stroked my hair off my forehead.

"Goodnight, Miss." She pulled the covers closer and tucked me in as if I were a precious baby that must not take a chill. I let her. I loved it. But she had one more gift. "The master says you must be so overwhelmed he wishes you to sleep in peace this evening." I had thought for sure it was high time to pay the piper.

I slammed my eyelids closed and faked a slight snore in case that was not true.

"Must be what heaven feels like." I yawned. It was only partly an act. I was dreadfully tired after the whirlwind of changes my life had taken.

Snuggled with the warmth of the fire and the velvet that I nuzzled against my cheek, I slept like Mr. Meade's ancient hound dog, Hector, when he hogged the hearth space, secure in the knowledge that for once, I smelled much nicer.

The next morning, my wedding day, Atsuko tapped on the door and entered to help me dress. She caught my look at something that had been puzzling me. "It's to summon help. If you need anything — coffee, tea, water, hot water, help dressing. It rings downstairs, and Mrs. Farfuddle or one of her maids will answer."

Who could believe that? I went and tugged on it, not hearing anything — tug tug tug.

"Just once will suffice," she advised.

"We shall see," I said, practicing my grande dame role. As Atsuko helped with my dress and sat me down before the looking glass to arrange my hair, I had nearly forgotten my imperious yanks on the velvet rope. A tap at my door announced the arrival of one of the maids. "Ma'am. How may I be of service?" My mouth gaped. I couldn't think of one iota of service I desired. Not wishing to appear foolish, I ordered — ordered — her to bring me a rasher of bacon! She curtsied and disappeared only to reappear a short time later while Atsuko continued her challenge with my toilette. She had my hair piled high atop my head. "Ow," I jerked from Atsuko's sadistic fingers and pins of torture.

Even though she wouldn't let me move my head, my own fingers reached out for some bacon. I chose the crispiest pieces and left a few of the limp, flabby ones on the plate. "Have some," I grandly told Atsuko. I felt quite virtuous, as I had known no one who would ever share their bacon. She lowered her lovely brown eyes in a refusal. Or maybe it was disapproval. No matter. I was riding this high horse, and it was certainly no time to get off.

I was born for this life. Maybe my mother truly was some kind of lady or princess. Kidnapped against her will and ravished by a fallen nobleman who, in my little girl fantasies, was always a well-intentioned rogue of a pirate.

Atsuko bade me put the bacon aside and washed my greasy fingertips. "How do you do that?" I griped at her.

She inclined her head; her smooth dark hair was so perfect it looked like enamel.

"You know. You make no sound; your face is perfect, symmetrical, no rolling eyes, no heaving breath, no sigh, no slip, no hiss of the tongue. And yet I hear you, my fine lady, loud and clear. You think I'm a pig. And ignorant. Probably a slut. Most certainly not worthy of marrying your patron, Lord Fluffernutter."

She dried my hands with a linen cloth. "Ha!" I saw it. "You winced. Just like this." I exaggerated my face into a horrified mask. Her laugh was a crystal chime. Which, as of yesterday, I never even knew there existed such things.

She helped me into my wedding costume. She cinched my waist so tight I felt I had been kicked by a horse and couldn't catch my breath. "Mind you, I've been eating for two these past months," I rasped out. Wasting precious air on complaints. The whole blue silk rigmarole could have outfitted the sails on The Looking Glass. It was shot through with threads of silver. "God's arsehole, it weighs more than I." I knew I would bear scars from the pinching pins and whatnot securing my armor in place, but then Atsuko spun me around.

As I stood before the looking-glass in my sumptuous bedroom, the magic velvet rope reflected over my right shoulder; I shut my gullet. "Gorgeous," I whispered, even as my head shook no, in disbelief. "I am fucking lovely." I caressed the undersides of my tits which were pointing this side of far north. "You could stand me barefoot on hot coals, and knowing I looked like this, you would never hear another complaint from my lips." I made the solemn vow. "What's that?" I asked Atsuko. I felt sure I heard her say she'd believe that when she saw hogs fly.

She led me downstairs, which was a good thing as my legs were a quivering mass. Who knew beauty was so heavy? As for jitters, I had nary a one. The household, my betrothed's odd collection, was gathered below. I reached the second-to-last step and stood proudly, seeking my lord's eyes. His hand was at his heart, and the whole lot of them broke into cheers. I modestly cast down my eyes and almost spoiled the moment by tripping, my fancy slippers had a heel, not quite sure yet of their purpose, but my darling caught my arm.

"This is my beloved, in whom I am well pleased."

Why did that send chills up my spine? Perhaps because in the Bible, that pronouncement didn't exactly end well for someone, now did it? I wasn't Catholic, nor did my fiancé or any of his gang seem to be, but other than munching on stale bread and pretending it was bones or gabbling away on a rosary studded with stones that I always thought were sins, I hadn't much experience as to how Catholics acted. I once found a broken, castaway rosary that was missing the main event, the man himself, splayed on a cross. It was a chain of hard little rat-turd beads, and I remember thinking, Jesus, how many sins can one sinner sin? I got through eleven easy enough; lying, profanity, joy in another's misery, shouting, gluttony, despair, doubt, cheating, stealing, self-pleasuring (which as far as sin goes is a bit dubious in my book, but what would I know?), and fornication. In any event, I never really figured out what all those beads were for. Those Catholics were numbskulls if they were trying to get the flock to add up beads of sin, or more unbelievable yet, expiate them by praying them away. Ha ha. Such a deal. I'll fuck my neighbor's husband, and boop, finger a little holy bead, sprinkle with Latin — *veni, vidi, vici* — *miserere*, sorry about that — and we're square, right, God?

Lack of sanctity didn't stop us from heading to the chapel to perform our vows before man, God, the constabulary, a drunken priest (sometimes they are axioms because they're true), a few horses, and townspeople promised a coin to attend and fill the pews. When my lord walked me down the aisle, and all eyes were clocking me — my gown, my hair, my footsteps — I felt giddy that for one second this was for real.

"I do, I did, I will, I shall." What a good wife I will be. Meet Mrs. Lord Elliot Pfeiffer-Mondragon. That I shall continue to stumble over the spelling for as long as I live, I've no doubt, but my signature, as I held the quill, was a sight to behold. My husband leaned so close as I made to sign, I could hear the air whistle in his nose. Lovely.

Even if they hadn't been paid, I believe the townspeople, my townspeople now, rejoiced with me. I fully expected to be their Lady Bountiful and attend to their needs. I could see myself with a lovely white basket I had espied in the back room off the kitchen, filled with lavender and tulips. Oh, how they would greet me with cheers. The fact that no more than three days had passed from my hellish existence was not lost on me, though I was prepared to forget it all. Had I seen an elegant lady of the parish trouncing by the saloon with a fanciful gay basket filled with flowers to distribute to the less fortunate, I would have spit in her path. I used to jeer at those sanctimonious church ladies bearing not much more than holy words. "We'd prefer a leg of lamb or coin, you thick drudge." I used to curse in their path. "Take your prayers and shove them up your..." Fortunately or not, Mrs. Meade usually managed to pull me out of the way.

Nevertheless, I was convinced I would be different. The crowds would greet me with cheers. I vowed to have a care. I would be the perfect helpmeet to my husband, who was full of his grand plot to farm and raise better crops. My baskets would contain copious amounts of vegetables, and far and wide, all would marvel at my generosity, especially as I'm not fond of anything green. I would smile and lift their spirits. In fact, I would fashion little lavender sachets for the women; they would quite welcome those gifts, I suspect. I would Encourage them in their En-deavors. And you better believe those words belong in capital letters. Their brats better not be sick, though. A snotty nose was enough to call forth my breakfast, no matter what time of day it was. The wracking cough of Mrs. Catarrh interrupted my goodwill daydreams.

"You've done it." Pause for coughs. Deep rattly inhale. "You'll do. Especially once the babe's here." Oh God, she came in for a kiss. I turned my cheek as she aimed for my mouth.

We bid the commoners adieu. Dear God, how I loved that. "Run along, little peons, and take your oozing blight, poor garments, and worries back to where they belong." I didn't say that out loud, of course, for I was a lady. It's no one's business how quickly my good fortune spun my back on their plight. I wanted them out of sight so I could put them out of mind. Let them eat my wedding cake. Mrs. Farfuddle had not outdone herself, as it was a slanted, tiered thing, vaguely recognizable as a cake. I wasted no prayer that it tasted better than it looked.

Our merry party returned to Mondragon Manor.

There, I drank more than the fiddler's bitch, who at that point was nodding off, respectful like, in the corner, while her husband continued to saw away at the strings. The music was lovely, the potted gardenia that Elliot had worked magic to make bloom in that heathen season blessed the air with a scent of heaven, and the food, always sumptuous to me, was both burnt and raw at the same time, a marvel that I consumed all the same. Mrs. Farfuddle was glowering at what I could only presume was everyone's appetites. I linked arms with her big ball of obesity and tried to spin a jig around the dance floor, but she shook me off.

And the party. My soused-up little heart gave private thanks to the occupants of that manor, for Lord knows I'd never tell them how I could see my way to begin to care for them. They all insisted on a dance with me, and each gave me a gift, a new tidbit about Elliot.

"He's a keeper, lass," Gordy said. "I've known him longer than all this lot put together. He rescued me from a life of slavery." He spun me around, my eyes agog. "Literally," he continued when we met back together. "He bought me with a huge bag of gold coins, more than I was worth, mind you, and asked if I'd like to join him on his adventure. I help keep him out of trouble, you see?"

RayRay cut in then. "You are a sight, my dear Brandy. What a fine girl. Your eyes could steal a soldier from his sword," he executed an intricate dance step and made me look elegant in doing so, "and a sailor from the sea," he continued without missing a breath.

I gasped, and he apologized. "Sorry, Brandy. That was thoughtless. I've heard about your black-hearted sailor. But surely, you see what a life you will have with Elliot. My family disowned me, never mind the reason, and Elliot found me. I was living behind a tavern, trying to decide the easiest way to end it all."

"Don't believe a word this vagabond says," my husband said, cutting in on our dance. He moved so surely, he taught me the steps without my notice.

"How did you come to know RayRay then?"

"RayRay saved me," he said. "Let's just say I fell upon ruffians at an unsavory drink house and was in fear for my life. RayRay came out swinging with a wooden bat, cracked a few heads, and managed to get us both out the door." He fell silent to help me with the steps. "I was a complete stranger, but he got me out of there, where a party of four or more meaty ruffians was bearing down upon me, and he led us down a secret alley into a private door. I have never been more frightened in my life."

I stopped dancing to hear his words better. "What about Atsuko and Mrs. Catarrh?"

My groom encouraged me back into the rhythm of the step. "Gordy freed Atsuko, who had been kidnapped and forced into the sex trade." My mouth gaped. "Of which we need not make mention, dear heart." I shook my head no.

"And Mrs. Catarrh." He cleared his throat to pay the good woman homage, I expect. I laughed. "Keep your humor, my dear, for things are never as they seem. Some of the finest families you see know naught but trials and tribulations, travails." He had a bitter bark to his laugh. "Though most do everything in their power to hide their dirty secrets." I tilted my head up to see his face.

"Mrs. Catarrh. She was one of the most famous courtesans in the land."

"Never," I said.

He nodded. "A wealthy, besotted fool, a nobleman, went so far as to make her his wife. They were happy together for more than twenty years. When he passed, his scurrilous sons, who had no time or thought for their father when he was alive, took it upon themselves to steal the fortune he had rightly bequeathed to her. She had no recourse and was evicted from not only her home but her town. She was near to death with pneumonia when RayRay and I were on the run and hid in the abandoned hovel she was living in."

I vowed to be kinder to her. (Oh, keep reading, it doesn't last.)

The dance ended, and my husband bowed to me. He held my hand up to his mouth and placed a kiss.

"Promise me, Elliot, that won't happen to me?"

"Dear girl. I promise. You are home. You are the answer to all our prayers." I wanted to believe him. "And now to bed, wife."

Oof. I only hoped I had had enough to drink. I grabbed one more cup of wine to be sure. He took it out of my hands, a glint in his eye. "Not to fear, Brandy. Tomorrow begins your real education." He kissed me on the forehead and sent me off with Atsuko.

And thus ended the best wedding day a girl could hope for. Off the hook again. I linked arms with Atsuko and made her sing along with me all the way up the stairs to my room, to blessed solitude and an empty bed that was softer than a swan-shaped cloud drifting in the sky.

Chapter 8

"Curse the light and close those drapes. And your mouth while you're at it!" I whisper-shouted at Atsuko the following morning, totally reverting to my plebeian accent.

Clunking boots entered my room and stilled at the foot of my bed. I pried an eyelid open to clock my groom in full lord and master regalia. "Rise and shine," came my husband's very, very loud voice.

"You clap your hands once more like that," I warned him, "and you'll be missing a complete set of ten." He peeled the covers off me.

"Up, up, up. I told you. We haven't much time. We have three days to kit you out as the mother of the future of the Pfeiffer-Mondragon line. And three days to polish you into a delicious enough morsel for my mother to swallow."

My head ached, and I groaned.

"No need for goosebumps, my dear," Elliot said, his arm flung around my shoulder. "Imagine the worst devil in Dante's Inferno, one who eats children as an appetizer. That's my dear mum. She's a fire-breathing dragon of nobility who believes both that she is doing God a favor simply by her presence on this earth, while also being steeped in resentment that His Holiness has yet to uphold his part of the bargain by rewarding her as she believes is her just due.

"Now, Elliot, she's your mother." Mrs. Catarrh.

I squeezed open one eye. "Fuck. What's she doing here?"

"Profanity, you little cum-bucket," said Mrs. Catarrh.

Elliot held up his hand to cease the fire. "We need to begin your training. Not to worry. You're a fine girl. My family will be happy to welcome you into the fold. My mother is simply Satan's foot soldier."

Atsuko laughed, which sounded like the hum of a nun's song.

"That's a little harsh," Mrs. Catarrh said. "She's simply congenitally unhappy, dear."

"Just wait," RayRay said. "You'll see the termagant for yourself."

"Who has left me terminally terrorized," Elliot said. "My older brother died in the war, leaving little ol' me to carry on."

"What about your father?"

"Michel de Pfeiffer-Mondragon clings to the past like a teething baby to a rag soaked in Scotch. His claim to fame is his fine lineage. So fine his ancestors ran like rats off a sinking ship during the French Revolution." Elliot smiled. "He would be the most horrid human being you will ever have the misfortune to meet if not for the fact that spot is already taken. Have you met my mother? You will see for yourself in three days."

Mrs. Catarrh coughed. Without covering her mouth, and clapped her hands. "I will instruct you on how to sit, stand, fawn, and indulge in sycophantic warfare. Remember, the less you say and the less you do will go far. I think you have just enough brains in your head to play the idiot, no?"

"I'm your woman," I said with bravado, making my new family laugh.

After breakfast, they left me alone with Mrs. Catarrh in the library. Now, I'm sure we've all heard tales of books balanced on a gentlewoman's head to ensure the gliding grace of her walk. And, of course, the sweet tale of the princess, the lass who was so sensitive she bruised atop many mattresses lofted above one small pea. If I had expected a soft landing and genteel instruction, I was soon disappointed. For Mrs. Catarrh, I soon learned her aim seemed to be an arrest: for murder. Hers or mine remained to be seen.

"Get off me," I shrieked when I could stand it no longer. "You godforsaken crone. Witch! Witch!" I held up my fist, thumb enshrined in a feeble attempt to ward her off.

Elliot came running. "What's the ruckus?"

"She stuck a hot poker down the back of my dress," I said, throwing it to the ground.

Mrs. Catarrh coughed out a yawn. "It wasn't hot."

"Then, declaring a book wasn't heavy enough for a stubborn mule like me, she tried to kill me. Look. Look."

Elliot took in the chipped, marble chess board on the rug that weighed as much as a dead donkey and the averted eyes of the old lady.

"It's not like I made her use the pieces," she said. "That would have been a disaster." She held two carved chess pieces in her knobby old hands.

"Mrs. Catarrh," he said. "Hush, wife," to me. "Let's be reasonable. Brandy is not much more than a child."

Mrs. Catarrh rumbled phlegm from her throat like it was a buttery toffee and sucked on it.

"Jesus. Spit that out, woman," I said. "Elliot, your mother has nothing on this evil viper. I know how to walk and talk; I know how to sit and stand. By watching Gordy and this old hag here eat, I know better than to chew with my gob open, spitting and spraying food here and there."

Mrs. Catarrh cackled. Literally.

"Elliot, please. I beseech you. I can act the genteel lady."

"If by lady you mean trollop, and by genteel you mean pulling your skirts well above your head as you lay on your back and introduce yourself by the soles of your feet, then yes, my good mistress, you are a lady." The old bag of pus and bones executed a stiff curtsy.

"Elliot." I wailed out his name. Frustrated beyond belief, I saw him wavering in favor of that crusty corpse. She caught me staring at her and slid her fingers in her mouth, stretching her smile wide on either side, showing me exactly what she will look like in the grave.

"I am your wife. How can you let anyone treat me like this?" He considered. I straightened my shoulders slowly. I pretended that the fucking marble chess set, complete with its utterly tasteless leering dragon pieces, were on board atop my head, and the poker shoved up my arse. "I am Lady Pfeiffer-Mondragon, of Mondragon Manor. The future mother of your heir." I issued a deep curtsy, my right big toe aimed at the skull of the future corpse of Catarrh.

Elliot quirked his eyebrow. And with that, I sailed out of the library, confident enough lessons were learned. I heard Mrs. Catarrh cough and take credit. "I told you I could do it, Ellie, my boy. She'll do. Yes, she'll do."

I clenched my fists and stomped my foot, then lifted my skirts and ran upstairs.

Chapter 9

Two more days passed. Lessons were learned. Tempers were lost.

The morning of Elliot's parents' arrival, I stretched in my gauzy soft linen shift in my soft down bed surrounded by the tapestries that enclosed my private little dream world, a fort of sumptuous fabric. My stomach rumbled, impatient for Atsuko.

"Dear Heart," I heard the tap on the door. I sat up, and instead of Atsuko, it was my husband. He was such a gentleman, for all his talk about babes and heirs, he never once tried to impose himself upon me. Not once. It was almost enough to send a quake up a lass's confidence. Endless looks in the looking glass convinced me otherwise. I grew fonder of the odd duck by the day. Truth be told, though, I did wonder when he might finally invite me into his room.

"Brandy. Rise and shine. Today is the day."

"Yes, I'm up. I am well aware of what day it is."

"I'm here to help you get ready."

I sat and dangled my legs over the side of the bed.

"Atsuko." He clapped his hands, and in came Atsuko, not bearing my cup of coffee, but a topaz-colored satin dress with so much fabric she could have pitched it as a tent. Elliot took my hand to help me out of bed, and she laid the dress atop the mattress.

"For once, you are speechless." Elliot was that proud of himself.

"I had it made, and they just delivered it this morning. Atsuko, get her in her shimmy." As I threw back my shoulders, shook my hair, and wiggled sensuously, my fine gentlemen never once watched me; he was that considerate. Instead, he fussed with the stomacher, which, damn me, looked like it had actual pearls sewn into it. What a lark! Who would ever think to do that? I had so much to learn. I wagged my finger at him. "What's all that then? Pearls before swine?" I cast a conspiratorial glance at Atsuko, pleased with my joke.

"Yes. Exactly," Elliot said. "Now, let's get this on you." He towered over me and guided the garment over my head while Atsuko pulled and pushed it down. Two grown adults dressing one gypsy as if I were a helpless newborn babe. "No peeking," he cautioned.

He spun me around, pulled out a chair, and pushed me toward it while Atsuko fussed with the flounces to guide me to the seat. Elliot stared at me, then held his hand out to the side, palm up. Atsuko slapped my brush into it.

"What do you think you are doing?"

"You are a living doll, and my parents are going to be so very happy to make your acquaintance, Mrs. Pfeiffer-Mondragon."

"Ow. That hurts. You are a madman."

"Hush. Be still. Beauty is pain."

"As I've not had the education you've had, I should like notation as to which philosopher actually said that."

"You are a most curious female," he said.

He held out his left hand, and Atsuko supplied pins. He pulled, pushed, twisted, and braided my hair.

"What are you doing back there?" I asked, "Tying a noose for me to hang myself?"

"Au contraire, my love."

"I need breakfast."

"I think not," he said. "Not today."

At long last, he finished his ministrations, which were far from tender. My head throbbed. Never one to shy away from a complaint, "My head throbs. My stomach growls. I feel faint."

"And you've never looked better." He pinched my cheeks, hard, before I jerked away. "Ta da." He took my hand and led me before the looking glass.

"Hail Mary full of fucking grace." For once, my vocabulary shorted me. "Blessed am I amongst women." I twirled around. "And I shan't pray for you sinners now or at the hour of your death, amen."

"Blessed be the fruit of thy womb," Elliot said. I actually caught him doing that spastic thing that I'd seen people in church do, flapping their hands hither and yon. I tugged on both of my earlobes and made it look like that caused my tongue to stick out.

"Ah, of course. The final touch." He dug into his pocket and pulled out topaz earbobs. That dangled. He screwed them onto my earlobes, and I swiveled my head no, no, no. Ah. You're mistaken. I wasn't against the jewels; in fact, nothing in my poor, shriven life has ever felt so uplifting. I couldn't stop. One, staring at myself, and two, shaking my head to make the earrings jingle.

"I am never taking these off."

Dear Lord. I would like to say there is not enough time to recount the visit of Elliot's parents, but it was remarkably short. They arrived for a grand feast. In which I played no part. Except to look the part of a fine lady of the manor.

His mother, "Please call me Lady P," made me laugh and want to pee. Lady Piss of the Upstarts, perched high upon her throne of the bony crone. If you've ever wondered about the origins of hoity-toity, look no further. His father, Michel Oh-just-plug-your-nose-and-honk-out-whatever-sounds-you-like, since that's what the rest of his names mangled together became, kissed my hand, clocked my tits, and then bussed me again, right on the mouth.

The four of us arranged ourselves at the great table in the dining hall. I had just started to spit out, "Where are Gordy and Atsuko?" when I saw the look on Elliot's face. Lady P sniffed it out as well.

"Elliot, whatever is wrong? Are you having a seizure? Sit up. Stop that." She took the butt end of her knife and whacked his knuckle. She turned to me, seated at the other end of the table.

"My," pause, "son, is known far and wide for his," pause, "collection of strange and bizarre unfortunates. Surely, your position as his wife is to curtail his unseemly attachment to those odd creatures, who are little more than servants. Do tell me they don't dine with you?" She flared her nostrils so magnificently I imitated her.

"What was my darling Elliot like as a child?" I warbled in a tone that was such a parody of her I thought for sure I'd be caught out.

She sniffed. "He used to bring me flowers."

"How lovely."

"Not really. I had to let the gardener beat him. He was told not to interfere with those rose blooms. He sheered a patch clean off. It took two seasons for them to return."

I turned to Elliot. "Ah. That makes sense. You love your plants and gardening and farming."

"And grubbing in the dirt like a peasant, when we have people for that." She was so dismissive of him it made my heart hurt.

"Maman, where do you think food comes from?"

I passed her a plate of greens for which Atsuko had taken time to help me make a malmsey dressing with oil and mustard seed. Lady P's mouth looked like the bridge a troll resides under, yet she took a plentiful enough portion. The cow.

I was eager to defend him. "Mondragon has such beautiful grounds. Elliot is experimenting with fruit trees and vegetables for as far as the eye can see." I ignored Elliot shaking his head. In that moment, I was so proud of him.

"He was given every opportunity. He waited much too long to marry. He ran away from university. He refused the military. We have to act like we're happy he's holed up here in Mondragon Manor and tell our acquaintances he is involved in land management and investing lest they think he's dabbling in farming." She shuddered. "They whisper like I can't hear them that they think he's in trade." Her voice lowered.

Papa stopped chewing long enough to chime in. "Never had a shine on his brother, mind you. Now there was a man's man. Rode like a centaur, fought like a tiger, and as for the ladies..." he wiped his mouth with his napkin then smacked his lips.

Elliot rubbed his finger on the tablecloth. "Yes, well, the only thing he wasn't good at was staying alive." Elliot didn't tell me; Atsuko did. His glorious brother seemed a bit of a sot, fond of the drink, who galloped off during a battle one night. Unable to keep his seat on his horse, he slid off, and his own weapon discharged, killing him. It was either that or the horse that caved in his skull.

"You dare?" His mother said. Oh, Elliot, you've done it now, I thought. Papa and Mama both rose up in defense of their dead firstborn. Granted, he wasn't there to defend himself, but why should the dead be able to just scotch it when it comes to misdeeds and miseries? Gordy had told me Elliot had been tormented by his sibling, who used to call him Smelliot, among other things.

"And you," Lady P turned to me. Note how she couldn't even bring herself to say my name. "What of your family? Siblings? Scandals?"

My Lord, that woman would have been a welcome interrogator during the Spanish Inquisition. I could hardly enjoy my repast even though I hadn't eaten in a very long time. Every minute was a torturous grinding of questions seeking answers I didn't have.

Her nasally affected voice was so disturbing that I was tempted to hand her my handkerchief. The thought made me smile. Alas, it was a serious question about my poor, deceased parents. "You are glad your parents are dead?"

Elliot had concocted a story of how I was the poor daughter of a vicar who had been killed along with my mother in service to needy orphans, blah, blah. "Of course not, forgive me, my lady." I sighed. Simpered. Maybe laid it on a little thick since I heard Elliot clear his throat. "They were such lovely people. Good, kind, caring for their fellow man." All the things I must have truly wished them to be but knew they never were. "My mother was so beautiful and had such a lovely singing voice. She used to brush my hair when I was a girl and whisper magical dreams in my ear as she tucked me in at night." How did a spill of water land on my cheek?

"Well. We can't imagine why Elliot didn't allow for the marriage banns and at least wait for us to witness your marriage." She stared hard at me and twisted her mouth.

"Are you feeling quite well, Lady P? Is it gas pains? I thought the cabbage and potatoes a little potent tonight myself." I was beginning to know Elliot well enough to realize I had said something a little off, but I didn't know him well enough to know what. He appeared to hide his laugh in yet another gulp of wine.

"Gordy," he hollered, raising his glass. Gordy shuffled back in again, humbly pouring more wine in both Elliot's and his father's glass. "Good for the goose," I said, perhaps a little too loudly, raising my own glass.

And then I realized the good Lady P wasn't writhing with gas pains; she was actually smiling at me. "We never thought Elliot would get married. Or, beget an heir. Or knew how. Or would want to. His idea of what goes where apparently requires a compass, astrolabe, and a stable of sturdy young men."

"Mother!"

"Wife!" Both Elliot and his father exclaimed at the same time. But since mother and wife had also dipped into the flowing wine, she may have spoken more freely than perhaps she might. She held her glass up in a toast to me. "I have no idea from what gutter Elliot unearthed you. You are a liar, uneducated, and it's plain to see you haven't a drop of blue blood in your completely fabricated lineage."

Her mouth twisted, and she held up a finger.

"And if I were a betting woman, you have no idea who your parents were." She inclined her head, inviting me to agree. I took a sip of my wine. She was right.

She continued; glass raised high. "Elliot probably scraped you off some tavern floor. In fact, the way you handle your drink, I'd venture to say you serviced sailors in a port, and when I say 'serviced,' I'll leave that definition to you."

We both drank to that. Touché. I whispered. Touché is French for fuck you; you're right, and I hate it.

"And I've a toast for you," I said. "You wonder at the haste of our nuptials?" Elliot shook his head again. I imitated him just for the sheer joy of feeling the ear bobs tap tap tap the sides of my cheeks. What did he think? I was going to trot out the old bog, "There once was a woman from Gloucester"? (Ye never heard it? You know, how she lost her... No matter.) I raised my glass.

"We knew destiny was to blame." My eyes sparkled down the table toward my husband. How had this kind man come from the likes of these two badgers? "And as for our banns," I kissed the silver ring with a blue gem set in a star that Elliot had given me. "The priest blessed this engagement ring." I held my goblet and bade them drink. "And my wedding ring," I showed them the heavy gold band with a nearly obscene-looking ruby that I wore on my index finger, which should prove a fearsome weapon in any sortie I may find myself in, "which I believe came from your own dear Maman." Again, we sipped. "Which leads us to the third ring of a successful marriage, as you and Lord Mondragon obviously share." They joined my raised glass. "To suffering." I glugged the rest of my wine before I noticed no one joined me.

Old man Michel finally got it and barked out a rusty laugh. "Hear, hear," he drank and called for more. My new mama stared him down until silence reigned supreme. Elliot's shoulders were slumped, and he looked like he thought they were going to toss him out alongside his bride.

The missus regrouped. "The best thing that can be said about you is that you have child-bearing hips." Her eyes were slits of cruelty. My heart rattled. Here it comes, I thought. She was going to denounce me. I'd be out on my wide arse faster than you could say, "What causes the furrows in your brow — in which one could sow an entire corn crop — and makes you so desperately unhappy?" and there was nothing her husband or son could do about it. No one could defy this one. What would Sir Stone do? If I was going out, rather on a gale than the pale, he always said. I gathered my favorite curses, sat poker-up-my-arse straight, and collected my newly-genteel self. The bitch beat me to it. She stood for her finale.

"And for all that I say, cheers," she said, standing stiffly. "Welcome to this god-forsaken family. May your brats be healthy, hearty, and hale. And male." She threw her wine straight back her throat.

"Welcome to the family," said Elliot's father. Elliot, his mouth agape, quickly recovered and drank along.

"Thank you, Mother." Elliot was trying to signal me something with those eyebrows of his; what, I knew not. I was spoiling to set that fine madam straight and let her have it. I even shimmied in my chair, preparing my defense.

An admiral I once blew taught me that sometimes, when listing on a leaky barge, retreat is the best strategy. Somehow, I think Sir Stone would agree. And honestly, I had to admire her capitulation in the face of what I imagine was unimaginable disappointment, the old cow. This time, I thought, this time only, discretion was perhaps the better part of valor.

When I had my son, I would be sure to allow him the kisses I never had as a girl. Should he occasion to bring me a flower, I would swoon with happiness. For the time being, I held my tongue, bowed my head, and wished them good night. I will deny to the bitter end if they claim to have heard good riddance. Elliot held up a warning finger at me. One of these days, I just may have to bite that digit.

Chapter 10

Hmm. Apparently, my three days' training was not good enough. Who knew being trained to sit around in a stupor while others brought you food and drink was so difficult? I wasn't insulted, just a little chafed that I didn't perform as well as I had anticipated. No matter. Mrs. Catarrh tried to warn me. I owed that old bag an apology. Never having had a mother, let alone grandmother, I could see there was a lot to learn from those old harridans.

Once the old geezers were safely put to bed, Elliot returned with Atsuko, Gordy, and RayRay. "That went well," I said. I hid my smile at the shouts of laughter from Elliot and his real family.

The next morning, while I slept in, Elliot's parents arose early and departed. I declare that a golden rule for all future visitations.

The days passed with us all settling into our new routine. Elliot is a man among men, a courtlier gentleman there never was. While I made several come-hither overtures, I was fully prepared to honor my side of the bargain; he would pat my hand, compliment my hair or dress, and say, "All in good time, sweetheart. Let us get to know each other truly and well." I sighed and couldn't decide if I was insulted that Elliot had yet to fall for my charms or if I was simply relieved. Relief it was, then.

I was happier than I ever dreamed possible. Elliot set me about reading books, and we had spirited discussions at dinner. I even ventured into the kitchen to wrangle a dish or two away from Mrs. Farfuddle; I wanted to contribute in some way to that family. I took some of the vegetables Elliot would bring and fashioned them into a cassoulet. Even though it took several tries, I don't think they were telling tales when they said they enjoyed it. Elliot even asked for seconds. (Mrs. Farfuddle took grievous affront. She would hiss at me and draw her skirts sharply away from mine when I dared enter the realm of her kitchen.)

As I'd fantasized, I did take baskets of herbs and vegetables to graciously visit the tenants on the lands, and I like to think I did the great name of Pfeiffer-Mondragon proud. But listen to me now and mark my words later; I will never be known as Lady P. I'm worthy of all those extra syllables, Fs, and the hyphen!

While I enjoyed the fawning and lickspittle of the families on Elliot's farms (and truth be told, it was a relief to dispose of the extra vegetables, which I did not care for; they could have every radish ever plucked), the brats could be a bit much, crying and trying to clamber up into my lap. Of course, the whiniest ones were always dripping horrors out of their snotboxes. What fresh hell I faced when one of the urchins wiped his suppurating face up and down the length of my sleeve. The detritus glistened; though it truly did, that's too sanitized a word for the horror slimed on my second-best visiting dress, the one shaded a pale green of new celery, in a swishy satin fabric. Nasal expulsions on satin? I quite gag at the mere thought. It has put me off that color green, and suffice it to say, I will eat celery nevermore. While I fancy myself a great actress, well-suited to playing the role of mistress of the manor, you'd have to get up early in the morning to pull a fast one on the wives of those serfs. They knew upon which side their bread was buttered and that I not only held the creamy crock of butter but the knife as well.

The mother of the flea-bitten lad who had expelled the string of mucus had to turn and hide her smile as I practiced, "Shush, shush. There, there," and pretended it was of no great importance. She came to my side with a cloth and wiped the young offender's grisly visage before turning the cloth over to sop up my ruined sleeve.

"Sorry, ma'am," she said. "Just a part of life. His coughs always take him down for a week or two, so we thank you for the willow bark and peppermint." She was perhaps my age but already had four children as far as I could count, milling around the cottage. She had a glint in her eye that made me think that we could have been friends in another life. But in my other life, she wouldn't have deigned to toss me a crust of bread.

My favorite hour of the day was helping Elliot with his herbs and plants. I had a fair enough hand, and he allowed me to draw pictures of seeds and sprouts in his notebook. Leaves and stems. Flowers and roots. And now I will dazzle you with my etching of a pistil and stamen, those naughty parts that did insist I add a cock-like doodle with a pair of bollocks to the stamen, and atop the pistil, a curled wig with a blossoming bosom. I believe Elliot has yet to discover my handiwork.

My head spun at the speed with which I embraced the role of Lady of the Manor. Perhaps it was just in me trying to find my place that I may have acquired a few bad habits. Started by Mrs. Catarrh and enhanced by Lady P's recent visit, my tongue grew sharper. Funny thing, the more of a bad thing you do, the easier it becomes to repeat. The first time I shouted at Elliot, I felt a pang. But he can be so wooden-headed and irritate me so. Some mornings he would sneeze, three times in a row, with such velocity that I could feel the spray. It got so I refused to bless him and then told him he and his affliction would perhaps be more comfortable with the hogs.

To my great shame, I was short with Atsuko, who merely gave no response, which made me even angrier. I would volley insults at Mrs. Farfuddle, which didn't matter as she took no notice, and the chambermaid I abused with each imperious tug on the velvet rope in my room. I began to channel the peculiarities of Lady P, and for good measure, some of those from Mrs. Catarrh.

"Bread!" I would shout. "Why did you forget the cheese?" "Coffee!" "Where is the cream?" And so on. Please and thank you belonged to the peasants, and they were welcome to them. For you see, I was special.

I relished my position as a grande dame. No one was more surprised than I how quickly I shed my gutter past and forgot my, ahem, humble beginnings and flea-infested middles. And no one dared say a damn thing to rebuke me. Elliot would just as soon take his twitching eyebrows and be off. Atsuko spoke volumes with the daunting stillness of her face. "I know what you are thinking," I screamed at her. RayRay laughed and danced out of my way, and Gordy just looked sad. That hurt. And fueled my fire even more.

We enjoyed a digestif after dinner one evening, brandy for me, of course, especially seeing's how it was some fancy import from France that Elliot loved to serve in my honor. Atsuko had returned from some errand to join us when I pondered, or perhaps pontificated, that she should curtsy before me. (She didn't, in case you are wondering.) There may have been some gasps.

Elliot carefully placed his crystal goblet on the table. He dabbed at the corners of his mouth with his napkin, refolded it, and placed it next to the goblet. I felt a tremble. What was happening?

"Enough," he said. He pushed back his chair.

"What? You have to stand up to literally stand up to me?" I taunted him. "You don't think I'm good enough to be respected by your," even I paused for a moment there, "servants."

They were all there, gathered around. Mrs. Catarrh, RayRay, Gordy, and Atsuko. Technically, they were his servants. They were nothing to him, certainly not his family, as he liked to infer. I may or may not have said something of the sort out loud.

"Brandy. You're a fine girl. You are a delight, you are quick-witted, you have adapted to this lifestyle, you've caught on fast. Before long, you'll quite pass for a member of the nobility." He held up his hand to stop whatever outburst I was furiously trying to spin to head him off at the pass. Fair play, I knew I was due a tongue-lashing but damned if I was going to sit there and allow him to embarrass me. Who did he think he was? I know what you are thinking, that I behaved like an ingrate. But you don't know what I was thinking. Any irrational vitriol that may occur in a young woman's life from time to time is solely her privilege. Have a care and beware. I gave him a fearsome scowl. The poor blighter found some nerve to continue.

"And you are my wife, a good wife, and soon to be the mother of my child."

There it was. "Mr. High and Mighty. You are certainly intent on putting the cock before the horse, so to speak."

He was impervious to my insult and carried on in that scary monotone. Not even his eyebrow was atwitch. "You are very clever and have insinuated yourself into a life of luxury quite well. Too well, I'm wondering?"

I stood also. "How dare you!" I threw my napkin to the floor.

"Pick that up."

"Make me."

To my very great surprise, he grabbed me around the waist and turned me upside down, nearly mashing my face to the carpet and the napkin. "Now, Brandy. Pick it up."

I kicked and bucked to no avail, until I had no choice. Elliot righted me, and I threw the napkin on the table.

"Just because you have married into the good name of Pfeiffer-Mondragon," he said calmly while I snorted, "does not mean you can do and say what you want. There are consequences, manners, decorum, and expectations. You can't act the fishwife. It is simply not done. And I don't care for it."

My temples pounded, and I can't recall everything I shouted. It's none of your business anyway. "You dare, sir, to name and shame me in front of everyone?" I wagged my finger in his face, shrieking so loud Elliot suggested I quiet down lest I disturb his mother, who was some hundred miles away.

"I am your wife! You cannot demean me and infer I am no better than a gutter-snipe."

He quirked his eyebrow. "If the little bitty shoe fits," he said. "Now. Please apologize to all of our friends here, and then you may go off to bed."

"I won't. You can't make me." Notice, I couldn't bear to look anyone in the eye.

"Apologize."

"Never."

"Brandy. What is wrong, dear heart?"

"Just because you throw an endearment at me in an argument doesn't magically set things right."

He held up his hands, his infernal lace sleeves dripping. "What is wrong with you? Tell me, let me help. If I don't know what it is, I can't help you. This behavior of yours isn't right or just, and you know it. We all love you. Search your soul; you feel affection at the very least for us, too."

Then he had to go and ruin it. "Now be a big girl, and say you are sorry."

"I am not a child."

"Then quit acting like one." He grabbed my wrist.

"You're hurting me."

"You deserve a spanking. Apologize."

I was that mortified and didn't know what to do with it. I wrenched my wrist from him and ran from the room before they could see my tears. "I hate you all."

Chapter 11

Tears soaked my pillow, yet I resisted pulling the velvet rope for a new pillowcase as I was torn between never wanting to see them and wondering what they were saying about me. Misery. The next morning, after abusing my poor chamber pot, I pulled the velvet rope, which remains my favorite thing in my new life. Atsuko entered, and damn her if she didn't execute the minutest curtsy. As I was not quite sure if she had done so, I restrained a shrewish retort and stayed the hand that itched to slap her. I ignored her and the great cloud of my ill behavior from the prior evening. I asked her for a mug of hot chocolate, and if cook wanted to be generous with a little schnapps, well, who was I to demur? "And don't forget hot water for my bath, and would it be too much to think this barn had a hot brick to help soothe my troubles?"

She nodded and asked, "Anything else?"

"Rags."

She left me to my agony, and while my bath didn't help, the hot chocolate might have.

I heard them talking about me, the thick plonks. Right up the fireplace flue, their muzzle-headed, feeble-minded thoughts floated.

I remained in my peignoir because I felt like it and planned to stay in bed all day. I returned to my heavenly cloud of dead baby duck feathers (which caused me not one moment's guilt, they were that soft) because I could and had nothing better to do. I groaned and rolled over and hugged my middle tight.

"Is it the babe, do you think?" I heard one of the mugginses ask from below.

Another voice came through; Gordy, I think. "I do not know. You saw what happened last night. She's been fractious and moody and snitched three pickles for breakfast yesterday morning."

"Ah," said bollocks-for-brains, my husband, "the cravings." I could picture him nodding in his know-it-all way. "I've heard all about them."

His cronies murmured their apparent agreement.

"And after that great scene last night," Elliot said. "My friends, you do know she is just not herself. It is the baby, and breeding women are difficult. You know she adores you all. She told me so."

"She hollered at Atsuko this morning and sent her for willow bark. She screamed something fierce, she did," Gordy said.

"Her titties are looking quite well," said RayRay. The silence that ensued made me think the gang looked at him as if he had shat himself. He hurried on. "And I saw her holding her baby belly. Maybe it's the gripes," he rushed past the state of my bosom. "She did eat a lot of the mutton stew yesterday."

Ah, there was a horse they could ride. "And a second helping of suet pudding with half a carafe of wine. To say nothing of the brandy."

Jesus, those chin-wagging sloths. They need to keep their eyes on their own plates.

"I heard her tell Atsuko it was her monthly."

"Monthly what?" Wondered the great philosopher, Elliot.

"You know, ladies. They take all kinds of ideas and churn up their bile. It takes a lot to keep them happy." Oh, Gordy, *Et tu,* Brute? (Oh, come now. Some years back, a Roman was in the pub with a nose like a spud who called to mind Sir Stone, who waxed poetic.)

Where the dickens was Mrs. Catarrh? She'd have set those mongrels straight right away. Of course, she liked to sleep in even later than I.

I wondered if our queen had to put up with nonsense like this from her courtiers. Our queen is a different story, though, as I don't know many who quite consider her a woman of wiles. I saw her once, her carriage tearing through our burg at as fast a clop possible — fair play to her — and a more dissatisfied, collapsed lump of pudding I've yet to see. One thing was clear, she never met a pastry she didn't like.

I slurped the last bit of my chocolate from my cup. For once, Mrs. Farfuddle hadn't been stingy with the schnapps, though come to think of it, I probably had Atsuko to thank for that. I pulled my sheet up over my face to just under my eyes and pretended I was a queen, and everyone would have to be beguiled by me.

"I've heard tell that some of them bay at the moon during a monthly." Was I still under discussion down there? I strained in vain to hear more, hoping for a morsel like, "Brandy is so beautiful, genteel, charming, intelligent."

"And parade in a circle in the forest in nothing but their pelt."

"I heard they bleed. From down there."

Oddly enough, that tidbit was perceived as the lone fallacy, caused those three men to erupt, and Gordy was shouted down. "You've gone too far, my good man," said my not-so-good husband. "That is my wife, and to say that she," I heard him cough, which was probably a gag, coming from him, "bleeds, from there? Preposterous."

"But I think it stops at night and only happens during the day," Gordy tried to sell it.

"Well," said RayRay. "I also heard they bleed."

Gordy picked up the tale. "And when they bleed, they can't have a baby."

I could feel my husband's rage. "Out of my sight, Gordy." But they were all thick as thieves, and Elliot softened his tone. "Cards later?" I could hear the clang of utensils as they finished breakfast.

"A wise man meanders a woman's peaks and valleys with care." That from Gordy.

RayRay, I think it was, laughed at that as if it was a lewd thought.

"Dear God, RayRay, not those peaks and valleys," Elliot said. "You know, a female's, er, kindnesses and, and..." oh, how he searched, "her bizarrenesses."

Come now, is that even a word? I couldn't take any more and stormed down the stairs, not even bothering with my wrapper, as I was now hot as with a fever. Still in my peignoir, as beautiful a name as it sounds, I flew, like a witch, if you must know, down the last few steps into the dining room.

"You cretinous imbeciles. Have you never known a woman before? Were you lot not begotten by poor, long-suffering mothers? Any sisters in the bunch? We are living, breathing, complicated creatures."

I paused to draw a breath, just in time to hear RayRay mumble, "You can say that again, though fire-breathing creatures more like it." Gordy laughed, but my husband didn't dare.

"We have thoughts. We have feelings. We have ideas and intelligence, and information that you would be lucky to own. I will forget more than you will ever know." I threw myself down in a seat at the head of the table and reached for a rasher of salty, greasy goodness off of Gordy's plate. I took a bite, and those beggars didn't deserve to not see me flap my gums at them while I chewed. I waved the bacon at them. "Jesus, Mary, and Joseph. All women bleed from their cunny, every month, you clods. Sometimes, like a stuck pig. It's just what women have to do, don't ask me why, for I've no idea. Your good God above sees fit to give you smelly shits a magic wand to wave around hither and yon, and yet to us, the fairer sex, nothing but misery and mess. Another curse to add to our otherwise simply lovely existence. You great dimwitted gibbets! It's who we are, brave and resigned to our fate, and we deal with it every month. RayRay, I saw you cry when you tore your fingernail. Elliot, you still bellyache about the sore tooth you had last week." I finished chewing and held up my hands like claws and cawed at them like a crow.

They cast their fists over their thumbs to a man, if you care to call them that, to ward off the evil eye. RayRay was the only one bold enough to inquire. "But, milady, if one is," he swallowed, "bleeding…"

I hissed as he said the word just to have him on. "That's the 'Red Lady' to you, sir. Show some respect."

"I have heard," he closed his eyes, against my madness, I presume, before he clocked them open, his soft hazel eyes cloudy with confusion, the blighter. "I have heard," he repeated, "that when a woman bleeds during her monthly that she is not with child."

"Now, where would you have heard something like that, you beastie wombat? Not one of you has a wife by your side, and at the sight of you handling a bowl of soup, I'd swear you didn't even have a mother."

"Come now, Brandy," RayRay said. "You've met Elliot's mother. And you well know she lives in mortal fear of the estate passing out of their barren family and into the hands of Elliot's cousin, Earl Bootlicker Buttpicker." RayRay leaned back in his chair.

I laughed at that.

"It's not funny, Brandy. It's deadly serious," Elliot said. "My cousin loathes my mother only slightly less than myself, and if he gets his grubby hands on the family fortune, he will go out of his way to see to it that she, and all of us, will suffer."

He looked at me. "And that's why, my dear, our child is so important. I promise to love our baby, more than just for the inheritance. Though don't get me wrong. I'm pretty much penniless. My plans to modernize the farm need a little boost, just until I can get it going. I have several new inventions that I hope to have patented, as well as…well, I won't bore you."

I sighed, loudly.

My one-true lifted his finger. "Now, darling mine, please calm yourself. No need to be so agitated. We are all trying to help. Please be at peace; think of the babe."

There were so many things wrong with that pronouncement. Where to begin? Where to begin? I tapped my finger on my upper lip. Telling a woman on her course to calm down? My ire was magnificent. Beloved. Cherished. I nourished it like the kitty I used to set out cream for. "You think you've seen crazy?" I asked. I took a gulp of coffee and handed the cup to Gordy. "Hold my coffee." He held it with care, lest I snatch it from his hands and throw it.

"Think of the child," my dearest implored me. He flounced his hands with lacy cuffs in the air. Had they actually been caressing me, I would have screamed. Even louder.

Before I could hitch a ride on a carriage to the land of second thoughts, I pulled the trigger. "What child? You dolt."

His mouth gaped, and his shoulders shriveled.

"What child?" I poked the bear again.

RayRay picked at his fingernails and affected an innocent whistle. Gordy was obsessed with stirring sugar into his coffee.

"Are you saying you are not with child?" Elliot asked me.

I shook my head. "Jesus. How thick are you? The Red Lady rides again."

He still looked lost at sea.

I exhaled loudly and long enough to ruffle the heavy velvet drapes on the opposite side of the room.

"Not that it is any of your business, my lord, no. I am not. And if our wedding night is any soothsayer, it doesn't look like that state of affairs will change any time soon. I'm no medical expert, but it seems to me that a wife not only needs to be wedded, she needs to be bedded before there's a baby." I strode to Elliot's side and took his toast off his plate. "Fed and petted isn't going to cut muster." I chomped, crumbs spraying. "Though the victuals in this place are abundant."

I chewed another bite. "Oh, you are all feeble-minded dolts," I said, still sore at them all and their stupidity, and truth be told, embarrassed about my behavior from last night. "Sorry. Sorry. There." I clapped the toast crumbs off my hands and perched them at my waist. "Satisfied?" I asked Elliot.

"You are not with child?" My husband repeated.

"I am not with patience at this moment either, dear heart. I do, however, hope to be with a hot brick for my bed and maybe a little more brandy, sooner rather than later, if only Atsuko will hurry."

That man of mine covered his gob, began to cry, and ran from the room.

"Rich folks are tetched in the head." I headed for the stairs.

"Well. He may not be rich for much longer."

I turned. "What do you mean, Gordy?" Dear God, my stomach cramped even tighter. "What is it? What's wrong? Is Elliot quite alright? He looked like he was having angina pain."

"Your baby was the key to legitimizing his inheritance," Gordy said.

"He's not having angina," RayRay said.

"And I'm not having a baby," I said.

"Ergo, he's not having an inheritance."

Chapter 12

I ran so fast up to my room to outrun the horror and hid under the covers. Truth be told, I do some of my best thinking when my body is expelling its bloody humors. It's the execution of my plots that are better left to clear sailing.

The thought of losing my newfound riches paralyzed me. They would have to rip this nightgown off my cold dead body. The fact that that's just what would happen to me in the poor house was not lost upon my ruminations. My pillow. The velvet cord. Oh, how I wailed and kicked my feet. The house was strangely quiet, as if the occupants were all holding their breath. Their fate, too, was yoked under the guillotine.

Drama does take it out of a body. By the time I finally ceased my exertions, I dropped the caterwauling to a hiccup, and hoisted my fist to the fates. Suddenly, I sat up and blew my nose. I didn't know why everyone was so hot and bothered. There was but one simple solution.

The remedy was a baby. Should be easy enough. Everywhere I've ever looked seems like ragged little urchins grow on trees.

Atsuko returned with willow bark in a nice hot tea and a hot brick wrapped in a towel. After I took a nap, she helped me dress. I apologized to her sincerely.

"Atsuko."

She nodded her head.

And that's how ladies apologize.

A quiet knock at my door announced my husband. He bent his knee and attempted such an awkward apology I took pity on him. "My lord," I waived him to my favorite upholstered chair. (Upholstered, that's all it took to be a favorite of mine.) I minded my words, but more importantly, my volume. "Please, do not despair."

"I need an heir by midnight of my thirtieth birthday," he explained morosely. "Or everything, the rights and legacies, the land, more than one hundred acres, this estate," he explained, "will be reassigned to my cousin, one Lord Churlish Clarence Pfeiffer-Mondragon." His nostrils flared. We may be newly married, but I already feared that expression. "Clarence is married. And has three sons."

"But we have time," I reminded him. "When will you turn 30?" Truth be told, he looked at that point in time like he was not even old enough to shave off any whiskers.

He ducked his head. "I had my twenty-ninth birthday last month. That morning I saw you, I was just returning from a belated celebration with friends. And that's how it all happened. I heard… I thought… you seemed." He buried his head in his hands.

"I know. You thought I was carrying a child. And why wouldn't you? I acted as if I was pregnant and knew the gossips would bandy that morsel about. It was part of my plan. I almost believed it myself."

He looked up. "To catch your sailor?"

I nodded. "Elliot. I knew you needed an heir, but I thought I'd be pregnant before you realized I wasn't."

He sighed and came and sat next to me on the bed and squeezed my hand. "I'm sorry," he said. Only someone who had had a broken heart could be that vulnerable. We shared a smile.

"You know," I said, squeezing his hand back. "There's a very simple solution." His eyes leaped. Perhaps the word 'simple' didn't apply to only the solution. I squeezed his hand harder. "Come on, Elliot, you can do it."

He sighed. "Brandy. You're a fine girl."

"And what a good wife I will be."

I shooed him away; no sense trying anything since the Red Lady was visiting. I appeared at supper two days later, only to find my beloved had hied himself off to the city to try yet again to find a loophole in his inheritance. Either it was a little bitty loop-hole or, my bigger fear, he was going to drum up a son some other way, toss me aside and marry some widow or some such. Time to up my game.

I held court at the dining table, and we gossiped like geese.

"You need to get pregnant," RayRay said.

"Or else," Gordy added.

"Or else what?" The nerve of these gobheads.

"We lose it all. Me, you, RayRay, Atsuko, Mrs. Catarrh. Out on the streets. With nothing. You've seen his parents. They never forgive; they never forget. Though they'd like to forget him. But with an heir, a son, all would be forgiven, don't you see?"

"I see more than you know."

"We thought you were pregnant. The whole town thought you were pregnant."

"As did my sailor," I said glumly.

We ate, and I learned more of this crew's stories. Atsuko and Gordy were an item, though his inconvenient wife on the Continent made it impossible for them to marry.

"More wine, Mrs. Catarrh?" Gordy was pouring. At the sound of her name, she raised her glass and coughed. "I almost married an Indian; he was Muslim, too. He worked on the plantation where my father had a business exporting tea to Britain. Well, I tried to run away with him, but the elephant was damned stubborn and went the wrong way." She sighed. "He was so handsome. So exotic. My lover, not the elephant. Needless to say, my parents bundled me back home before I could get into trouble." She coughed again. "I guess I showed them."

We toasted ourselves and each other as our stories became more exaggerated, yarns even greater than those the sailors had told in the tavern. (Whom I didn't miss at all.) "Fetch another round," I ordered.

"So, what is the plan?" Gordy asked, topping off my glass. "With you and himself."

"That's a little personal, don't you think?" I took another sip of some very fine wine, enjoying myself. Lord, they'd seen me at my absolute worst monthly, and they all waited for my answer as if I were one of them.

"When a man and a woman marry," I cocked my head and twirled my hand.

"Go on," RayRay said, with relish, resting his chin in his hand.

"Are you sure you're old enough to hear this, RayRay?"

He and Gordy shot a quick look at each other.

"Are you courting anyone?"

"Haven't found the right girl yet."

"You are a very handsome git," I told him. "And your clothes are much nicer than mine."

"Thank you," he said.

"Perhaps if you'd only stop whistling, you'd have better luck enchanting a mate."

He gave a short 'whoo' of a whistle. "Cut straight to the heart, Brandy. But do tell us more about your grand plan to save the sorry lot of us."

"What part of fucking doesn't your poor pea brain understand?"

After a shocked silence, in which this miss was just starting to wonder if she had gone too far, my new brothers and sisters laughed. Mrs. Catarrh laughed so hard she began to cough. They seemed to trust I had this radical strategy well in hand and were all too glad to leave me to it.

As Atsuko got up to clear the plates, I stood to help her. She shook her head slightly.

"I don't know how grand households are run, my dear Atsuko," I said, imitating the imperious tones of my mother-in-law, "though I suspect not such as this. That said, I find I quite like the family my dear husband has accumulated, and if I choose to help, I will do quite as I please."

Gordy and RayRay clinked their tankards and cheered. "Hear, hear."

I looked over my shoulder. "Surely you do know who I am? You can't think that Lady Pfeiffer-Mondragon will actually plunge these milky white hands into hot water to scrub up after your gluttony? We'll carry the plates through. Cook has gone to bed. You can wash them." That shut them up.

Atsuko and I bid Mrs. Catarrh goodnight and shared a wee tot of brandy, a fancy sweet drink I have become fond of, especially when consumed in small but heavy crystal glasses. I could swill old tub water out of such an ornate vessel, and I fear I am so shallow it would still taste as sweet.

Chapter 13

Nearly three days passed before my husband returned with nary an explanation. To celebrate his homecoming, I had even ventured into the kitchen with herbs Atsuko had given me to try to add a little flavor to the chicken Mrs. Farfuddle had murdered, twice. First, when she wrung its neck and then again when she roasted it to a burnt crisp. I made a batch of biscuits, so heavy on the butter and cream they tasted better than they looked. No matter, the palates of those scavengers were fortunately not picky. Gordy and RayRay had wine and brandy at the ready, and I had never looked so fine.

We all did our best to lighten the mood. My misery had passed; the Red Lady had galloped on to return to fight another day. And I was fond of Elliot; how could I not be? He was earnest and kind and scrubbed up well. He was passionate about his farming methods, cared for his tenants, and was lovely to his friends. It had been a while since I'd lain with my sailor, so I wasn't averse to a game of 'hide the sausage.' (Of course, I knew better than to call it that.)

"Why do you look like you're about to be executed, husband?" I teased and tossed my hair, which Atsuko had left long and hanging down my back. I fluttered my eyes at him, and he passed me his handkerchief.

"Do you have a lash caught?" He asked.

I drank more, but not as much as Elliot, though I laughed louder. His friends, mine too, now, I thought, rallied to keep the conversation going. He said nothing more than that his solicitor is a doddering old fool. Elliot barely participated in what I recall as scintillating conversation. "Did you know Atsuko is kin to an emperor?"

"I know I've told you lot before," Gordy said, "but Atsuko is more royal than our very own queen." I had been fascinated and begged her to recount it. As a woman of few words, and those blasted few delivered so quietly, with what Gordy teased was her 'zen' voice, I had no idea what her real story was. Something about being forced into an unwanted marriage and her intuition guiding her to refuse. She said nothing much about the consequences, which was where I'm sure the real story lay. Give me drama over zen any day of the week. It was dashed hard work forcing smiles and charm through an entire evening. My cheeks ached.

Throughout, Elliot grew morose yet seemed reluctant to end the evening. "One more," he called out, raising his glass.

I contained myself well enough during the lively dinner, though I was itching to duel. Several drinks later, Elliot was proposing a game of chess with his lads.

"Forgive us, friends," I said sweetly, rising from my chair. They all rose with respect, dear Lord, how I love that. "But this bride has been pining for her groom. Darling, I'm sure our guests will understand."

I took his sticky glass and set it down on the table. "Let's go to my room, and you can have whatever you want."

"Eek." He actually said eek as though he had seen a mouse. My groom visibly paled. Drank the rest of his wine, grabbed Gordy's, and drank that too. I held out my hand as royally as could be and bade him escort me upstairs.

"Good evening, friends," I said. "Until the morning." They were strangely subdued, not looking at Elliot and unsure where to focus.

"Good luck," RayRay said. My ears strained for morsels of gossip, for by then, I had been intrigued by what I could learn through listening at doors. True, most of it stung as it had been very uncomplimentary of me, but I was addicted to the secrets. I turned my attention to the task at hand as we reached my bedroom.

I pulled Elliot into my room. Atsuko had the fire burning, a carafe of brandy on my side table, and my bed covers pulled down and plumped up enticingly. Atsuko had been teaching me about the Japanese art of wabi-sabi, an imperfect beauty. She sometimes called me Wabi-sabi under her breath. Friends, I have a nickname! And in that moment, I felt exactly like an imperfect beauty. I knew I looked well, the lights were low, and Elliot's alcohol content was high. I could not understand my nerves. I softly closed the door, relishing the friendly look on my beloved's face, belying my true intent.

I don't mean to build suspense, and if it seems as though I am toying with you, perhaps I am in an effort to understand what happened next. I went to the bed, but Elliot sat in the chair.

"And just where do you think you have been, my high and mighty?"

"Attending to business." He quirked an eyebrow. "Dearest."

"Don't dearest me."

"I have been trying to unravel this hash we are in."

"Hash? Is that what you call it? You stand to lose everything. Your money. Mondragon Manor. Your farms. Your plants and seeds. Everything."

"Because you lied to me."

"I did no such thing. It's not my fault you're stupid and saw what you wanted to see."

"Shush. Let me think." He pressed his fingers to his temple.

I put a fond smile on my face. Pretending can help color reality.

He looked at me. "What's wrong?"

I'd better pretend harder. I counted backwards toward my last monthly. The time was ripe. I clambered upon my dearly beloved's lap.

"Blech," he said, and pushed me off. I tumbled at his feet.

"Oh, so it's that way, is it?"

I reached up to caress him.

His heels dug in the floor and pushed back himself and the entire chair.

"God, no. Stop. Please."

Undeterred, I spun around and asked him to undo the buttons of my dress. He stood up and was gentle and quite adept. "This is a new silk shantung," he told me, "imported from France. The color is marvelous with your complexion." He tossed my hair to the side. "I love the texture," he said. I could feel his fingers against the fabric as he unbuttoned the dress. He helped me step out of it and hung it in the armoire while I quickly shed my petticoats. As much as I loved my peignoir, there was something naughty about him seeing me in my chemise, with its lace and ribbons. The gauzy material was nearly transparent and cinched in at my waist.

He reached out and tied one of the ribbons that had come undone. I felt the heat from his hand as he touched my shoulder. He jumped as if he burned himself.

"Elliot," I said. I held his sweaty hand. "Relax. Don't be nervous. We're married. It's fine. I think you will find it is going to be even more than fine." I licked my lips, and he blanched.

"Brandy. I feel like we need to know one another better. We can't just rush into this. I respect you."

Dear Christ. If I had to make a wager, I'd win five shillings against the odds that he'd ever been with a woman before.

"Respect this, sir." I ran my hands over my chemise. I was trying to jimmy up some excitement for the deed, but no matter. My hands gliding over the soft material was very sensuous, and I could have made love to myself. (Haha, who are we kidding? I did that just the night before.)

"Elliot, we'll get pregnant. Let's just do this. We are running out of time." Judging by the look on his face, that was the exact wrong thing to say.

"Don't rush me!"

I changed tactics. I slowly climbed on my bed and arranged myself. I bent my knee and pointed my toe. I kept my silk stockings on for two reasons. Firstly, I own silk stockings. And secondly, my husband was so prickly, I knew not his thoughts on feet. While mine get the job done, they are a bit wide and peasanty, if you must know. I can and have stood on one foot and balanced a piglet atop my head. Poor people don't have much in the way of entertainment.

I slid my hand up my leg. Jesus, what's he waiting for, a hand-engraved invitation? Dear Sir, your wife requests the pleasure of your cock for an intimate *pas de deux* in her boudoir.

I arched my back. It's not like I had much else to do. "Come on, Elliot." I patted the bed beside me. The whirlwind of the last month caught up with me. From losing my sailor to adjusting to this new life, it was all very overwhelming. I topped that off with one more little glass of brandy and toasted myself. "To Brandy," I said. I felt gratitude toward Elliot—and you know what they say about gratitude. No? Me neither, but I'm sure it's something about fuck you and thank you, being different sides of the same coin. But my husband, despite my lush offerings, sat there like a lunk. I twiddled my hair and made those suggestive humming noises, and if you have to ask, then you're a lily-livered virgin, too.

He looked scared as a runny-nosed brat who lost his mother at the fair.

"Elliot? If you are nervous, I can help you. I know how this goes." He burst into such a vehement denial I tried to calm him down. "Shush, shush. There, there." I scratched my head and then tossed my hair over my left shoulder so it fell in front of me. I knew it looked fetching as I caught a glimpse in the mirror. "Fine." Some gents liked it when you took a more active role. I had eaten so much at dinner; I had hoped that wouldn't be the case. I rolled to my knees and faced Elliot. It was time to handle the situation delicately. I couldn't feel the ocean fall or rise or see its raging glory. I needed to stop drinking so much.

But what in the good Lord's name was wrong with my husband? I have never had to work so hard for the attentions, let alone affections, of any man. My pride was quite injured.

"Are you ill?" I asked him. "You're sweating."

"No, no." He stood up and began pacing.

I hopped off the bed and stood on tiptoe, preparing to kiss him. Hm. We never did kiss. Except for at our wedding. Even then, he had missed my mouth. Then he pretended all solicitousness at the newness of everything and gave me time to get to know him. I was beginning to wonder.

I lowered my fine eyes and flicked my hair. I whispered what I wanted to do to him. Then what I wanted him to do to me. He covered his mouth with his hand. Which was wearing four big shiny rings.

"What is wrong with you?" I asked him as he backed away from me and sat on my bed. Good. At least I got him on the bed.

I made a motion to join him, and he screamed and jumped up.

"Elliot. Are you quite all right? What is it?"

"Spider. I saw a spider."

I caught the little bugger sneaking under my pillow and reached in to grab it. "It's good luck. At last. An omen." In front of my quivering husband's face, I squished it between my finger and thumb and tossed it in the fireplace.

"Now, come on. Dear heart. We're married. It's legal."

Elliot was backing away from me, sidling toward the other side of the bed. "I just think we should get to know each other better."

"Aw. Ain't that sweet. But, no worries. I know men. Trust me. You are not hurting my sensibilities."

"Isn't that sweet?" I wasn't sure if he was correcting me or being sarcastic.

"Come on. Let's just fuck. What's the big deal?"

"Um. Er. You remember. My one true love?"

"Men don't have 'one true loves.' They have the one in front of them. Or under them."

I will attempt to gloss over some of the skirmishes that ensued. But know that I once saw a pig wrestler attain more satisfaction.

Elliot was nearly buried beneath the pillows. There was such a thing as being too much of a gentleman. I sat astride him. I jiggled my prized pair right in front of his nose, an enticement that had caused more than one lad to fire his cannon before he was even able to lower the drawbridge to cross the moat. "Don't be shy, sweetheart," I said. I lovingly held my breasts in my hands, and if my forefingers dared to caress the very ends into tightened little blossoms, I cannot say. "Did you drink too much? Are you not feeling well, sir?"

He swallowed so loudly I wouldn't have been surprised if he coughed out a hairball. "What is it? Shall I speak naughty?" Maybe he was overwhelmed by my beauty — poor sod.

I took pity and aimed to please. "Oh God, my cunny is simply dripping with desire for you and your cock, good sir," I said in my new posh accent.

He cringed.

Hmm, maybe I did sound a tad like his mother.

I tried the dirty words that the vicar had taught me, but Elliot covered his ears and begged me to stop. I played innocent shy maiden; that always earned me more tips. He grimaced and shook his head.

Time to pull out the big guns. My sailor had been enthralled. I never met a toff I couldn't get off. Game on. With the fire glowing behind me, I wriggled my soft, see-through chemise over the sides of my shoulders. (Sorry, I'll stop bragging about it one day, but it is a wonderful diaphanous material, perfect for seduction.) I shimmied, sending it a little lower. Lower. I cupped my breasts as a gift worthy of a king, and they are. They are magnificent, everyone says so, and I love them very much. Fuller than a peach, perfectly round with the pertest nipples in the land. My sweet fruit loved nothing more than being sucked and licked and kissed and nipped. The rendezvous was starting. I shivered and felt a genuine wave of fondness for this man.

My sailor had once brought me peaches from Spain. Just thinking of those peaches caused me to shift my legs. And my nipples, eh, what can I say? My husband should write an ode about them. They are so sensitive. Small, round, and tinted the color of the softest pink of the first bloom of a rosebud in May, one besotted Romeo had proclaimed.

This was going to happen, and I was wholly armed for battle. Except for my dear husband's soldier who appeared unfit for duty. I could see I would have to take the lead on this. I squeezed my breasts. "Feast your eyes, my darling." I thought for a moment and wondered how best to please him. He was more of a literal sort. "And if eyes are the window to the soul," I said to him, "these orbs are the passage to my hole." Suffice it to say, poetry didn't do the trick either.

He actually groaned with disgust. I thought for a moment he was going to vomit. "Cover yourself," he said and shielded his eyes.

Mortified and embarrassed more than I can ever recall, I let out a screech. "Are you shittin' me? My tits do nothing for you?" I climbed off the wretch. My eyebrows launched up my forehead, setting sail for Japan for all I knew. "What is happening? What is wrong with you?"

He ran out of my bedroom. All is lost.

Chapter 14

Breakfast the next morning was a subdued affair. No one would meet anyone else's eyes, to say nothing of mine, and believe me, I tried. They all looked away as if they had witnessed my ignominious defeat of the night before. There was no secret in this mausoleum. I cared not. I had no shame as it was all on me. I was not going to be tossed back into that pox-ridden hellhole of a harbor. It is not better to have loved and lost, as the puking poets would have us believe, for I have a genuine love for my bed pillow with its embroidered linen case and my velvet rope. I'd be damned if I was going to lose them.

"Elliot, a word?" The lot scrambled like fleas deserting a dead dog. I pulled him aside. "We're trying again tonight, my good sir. So, load up on your finest rum or what-have-you. I'll do all the work. You just need to lay there." What a strange turn of events.

Sober. Drunk. All for naught. I tried my mouth. Who doesn't like a good tongue lashing? Sorry gents, any trollop worth her stripes takes no joy in licking the pickle. Ask any miss, I dare you. She'd rather suck a rotting haddock and swallow its salty spew. A gold coin on that bet. (True confession, it was only a shilling that I won, but that's not the point.) Well, I've done it enough. Most times, it is absolutely a time-saver and easier than going through all the bother of a bloke trying to lift my skirts. For Elliot's sake, I even kept my peignoir on. Oh, allow me to allay your suspense: that made things worse. I raised the hem of my gown over my head in a white flag of surrender.

My husband was so skittish I knew I'd never get him to give me the what-for. I got creative and slid his, oh dear god, I hate the word flaccid, but needs must, prick between my breasts and gave it a go thataway. I thought he would faint. And not in a good way.

He ran out of my bedroom again. Forever, as far as I could tell. All is truly lost.

Chapter 15

"All is lost," I announced at breakfast. Through some magic, they had already known. A solemn group, nothing is sacred in this household of miscreants. My husband hung his head in shame. "We are penniless! What is to become of all of us? Any of us?" I pounded the table, rattling the coffee cups.

Elliot's voice answered in a shrill. "To make a go on the farm, we just need more time to be self-sufficient." Elliot had done nothing but bemoan the lack of time for him to bring his revolutionary farming ideas to the literal table.

"Time we do not have!" I reminded the county.

He slunk out without a word and left the table without drinking his coffee. I moved down, slid into his seat, and gulped at it. "Any ideas?" They all looked in a different direction. "Come now. You know what's going on, and you know what's at stake. We need a baby. In my belly. Don't much care how it gets there at this point, no?"

"What are you looking at me for?" RayRay said.

As I had no intent behind my frown that RayRay just happened to be in the way of, I did not reply.

"Look. Look, I couldn't," he stumbled over himself. His ears turned red. "I mean, I never. I mean, I am honored that you would think of me. But. Brandy. You're the sister I never had."

"And RayRay, you're the brother I never wanted."

At that, Atsuko looked at Gordy. Gordy looked at RayRay. RayRay started at the coughing entrance of Mrs. Catarrh.

The old lady shuffled to the other end of the table. As she caught her breath, she said, "Desperate times call for desperados." She coughed. "We need Beau."

Two days hence, my husband's very dear, very handsome friend, aptly named Beau, short for Charles Beaumont, showed up on the doorstep.

Mrs. Catarrh almost knocked me over in her joy to greet him. Funny how the old whore could move apace when she wished. She elbowed me out of the way. "Miss Saucy Tits here is wedded, not bedded. You're here for one reason: we need to be aided and abetted." I tilted my head. Not bad for an old puss.

Was I to be chuffed that they expected me to open my legs to the first beetle-headed Johnny-down-the-pike? "Oh, here's one, filled with seed and apparently working parts; try this one, see if this doesn't do the trick." What kind of strumpet did they take me for? I have standards. Men may think all cats are gray at night, but women aren't like that. When the candles flicker, our imagination runs away to the moon — our fingertips tingle, our nose sniffs out clues like a hound on the trail, and oh, how hard we listen. A quick inhale, a low growl, a hum that sounds as if it hurts. If I was giving up my treasure for the cause (and I was), I wanted to maximize our odds of success. I hadn't even been consulted. Granted, there was no one at Mondragon Manor to do the trick. Pity Atsuko didn't have something to offer; our child would have been beautiful.

Back to Beau. At first glance, I thought he was a swaggering, idle-headed horny toad. I instantly decided he'd do, but still, a girl likes to be asked to dance.

Somehow, Beau deduced that, right quick. He had a charm — no, not the chivalry kind — rather, an actual magic spell that set about to mesmerize me.

He was gracious, and I was giddy. My confidence had been a wounded cur, coiled up in the corner, forgotten by the sun, molded into a mushroom of defeat. Elliot was more handsome than Beau and possessed all the right parts. Elliot had wavy dark hair and a shiny smile; he was not a bad-looking gent in any way. He dressed better even than the queen, I expect, and he was clean. But between you and me, I don't know what the difference is that makes one man handsome and the next beguiling. As in, I'll be letting this guy under my skirts. Meet Beau.

Honestly, if an artist were to paint their portraits, Elliot would fare that much better. Beau had a crooked smile, pox scars on his left cheek, and such a great beak of a nose, a small child could no doubt shelter under it in a storm. But there was something about Beau. He had that *je ne sais quoi* which I believe is French for *mais oui*, I'd like to fuck you.

As I would soon discover, Beau's eyes were nothing to write a poem about either. Two normal-sized orbs, neither blue nor brown, they appeared to get the job done. Until he spoke and smiled that crooked smile. Then his eyes sparkled as if they were connected directly to his cock.

Beau and Elliot had been friends since they were boys. Elliot had once been getting walloped by bullies, and Beau, one of the popular boys by dint of his claim to have 'done it' with the village milkmaid at the age of eleven, saved Elliot's day. For his part, Elliot, who had a surprising streak of justice, I was coming to find he had the soul of a Catholic priest, in most things, that is, made Beau laugh and helped him with his lessons.

Wherever Beau had been banished remains a mystery. Atsuko, in her oblique manner, as if she had any other, hinted that both families decreed the two gents had spent too much time together and needed to grow up and set upon their own paths. As it did not affect me one way or the other, I concentrated on the very pleasant task of being pleasing to Beau.

Beau complimented me on my eyes, my light step, my cheery disposition, my attempts at speaking properly. He laughed at my mistakes, corrected me with an ease I did not despise, and most importantly, he lasciviously eyed my tits. Thank God. I was desperate, and he provided a turquoise balm of anticipatory delight. Nothing was overtly stated, but we entered an unholy alliance, and I was truly smitten. Is there anything more intoxicating than the dance of seduction? The maiden takes one step forward, the gentleman bows, she retreats, he follows, reverse everything — such a delicious drama.

Everyone in the house seemed to be holding their breath, myself included, because, believe you me, something was going to happen. The anticipation was almost manic in its display. Short tempers were triggered over such trivialities as burnt toast. Yet, kindness was on display as well as all realized our fortunes were tied together by a most tenuous, taut cord, frayed with anxiety braided with anticipation.

Chapter 16

I spent my mornings reading to Mrs. Catarrh and learning how to become a lady. As I wasn't up scrubbing and serving the great stink of townspeople from morning till night, I had time on my hands to spare. I did help Elliot with his plant projects, and I quite liked that — his ideas were contagious. But I had the run of the house. *Mi casa es su casa*, Elliot had told me when he had given me a great ring of keys early on.

I had tipped off a quick curtsy in thanks. "What's yours is mine, and what's mine is mine." It wasn't as amusing as Elliot made it out to be. Too bad his cock wasn't part of *mi casa*.

One morning after I ditched the old bag of bones, I set out on another foray. The sound of keys jingle-jangling at my waist brought great joy. I had jiggled every door, drawer, shelf, armoire, pockets, papers, and books in that dragon of a manor with the pride of ownership. I, who only a short time ago, didn't even own a ribbon for my hair. My searches eased the regret with which I had nearly tossed my silver chain from my sailor into the drink, with the belief it had to have been an evil charm. Consider this, when did my luck change? When I tore it from my neck. Put that in your pipe and smoke it. I was now set free, ready to begin a whole new life, and let me assure you, I was not miserable. The tarnished, broken chain lay rolled in a tangle in a handkerchief and as forgotten as my sailor, in a bottom drawer in my room.

Outside my bedroom door down a side hallway in the opposite direction from Elliot's chambers, I had made a delicious discovery. Tell me you wouldn't have checked out every nook and cranny of this place. I found a closet for holding linens — a grandiose space in and of itself, to be sure. I had plenty of opportunities to explore freely, so don't dare label me a snoop.

Keep your judgments to yourself. I may have light-fingered a few household goods for safekeeping. An ornate gold clock that was heavier than a pail of water, a ring I had twigged off Elliot, a golden thing with a dark green gemstone, and a jewelry box, with get this, jewels on the outside. Good Lord, I am a magpie. Elliot had also gifted me a purse with my very own gold coins, so I was able to diversify. I see how this life works. I am prepared for the worst.

Sir Stone had despaired of that side of me. "Of course, I'm a greedy-guts," I had once tried to explain to him. "I've got to be now, haven't I?" Though in those days, my loot was usually food — a hunk of cheese, or an apple, an occasional coin I managed to part from a drunken sot.

I secreted many items away in my lair, under my bed. A bejeweled letter opener, it was a sharp bugger, but the handle was so beautiful. Rubies, emeralds, and diamonds were embedded in the filigreed silver handle. I went into rooms not much used and gathered up the dross. One man's trash is a poor, hard-working suspicious girl's treasure.

I picked up an ornate book here, an enameled snuffbox there. A chest hidden in a closet of a dusty closed-up room that looked like it hadn't been used in a king's age. I was worried my sneeze would give me away. No one held me liable for my time, how I spent it, or how I abused it.

One morning I nosed around in the linen closet — I say that with a snooty quivering queen's voice — because it was beyond my ken that rich folks actually have a room to put their cloths, towels, bedclothes, and the like in it. Once upon a time, I would have killed to sleep in that linen closet. I had my arm stretched all the way back, buried under a great tablecloth when my fingers wiggled to the edge of the shelf at the wall. I was startled when I heard a step coming up the stairs down the hall. While I wasn't doing anything wrong, who's to say I wasn't con-templating it? I bumped my head at a place right near the inside door jamb on the right side. I heard a strange click as I rubbed my head.

Whoever was on the stairs went away without notice. I pushed the linen closet door closed with me still inside, plenty of room for me to twirl full circle if I'd a mind, but I wanted to explore that click I had heard. It was now full dark, but my nimble fingers found a crack that I was sure hadn't been there before. I opened the closet door to shed a little light, then closed it again to facilitate my purpose. I wrenched my fingers deeper, and the panel, taller than I, three shelves deep, weighted with tablecloths and napkins, opened out. I felt again the side of the door jamb where I had bumped my head, and my fingers came upon a block of wood, just smaller than my hand. I moved it up and down; it felt as if there were a spring or some sort of device that triggered the latch of the panel. I held my breath and tried to peer into the opening. It was dark as Hades.

I ran for a candle but was waylaid by Atsuko. She brushed a cobweb out of my hair. I'm sure I looked as guilty as sin. Mrs. Catarrh gave me the evil eye and beckoned me back for more lessons. Curses. I needed to explore that passageway.

The shriven prune wasted the rest of the morning as I stubbornly flubbed my lessons. And then it was time for lunch. And then Elliot requested my help in his lab; he wanted me to sort herbs. I sighed as if I were greatly put-upon, ah, the problems of the elite, yet truth be told, I was gaining a new respect for my new husband. It wasn't until the next morning, loaded with candles, I set sail.

What if the secret passageway led to a curse? I nervously rubbed my hands up and down my arms. I couldn't wait to see what I would find.

I practiced the latch many times to ensure I wouldn't be entombed in the place. Just my luck, I'd unearth a treasure trove of gold and jewels, and in the mysterious ways of the universe, just as I caught my heart's desire, I'd die, starved to death, sucking the grime off a gold coin, my skeleton bedecked with necklaces, my fleshless, bony fingers sporting rings. A hundred years from now, another nosy miss would discover me and wonder at my fate. Would she think me a great lady who suffered grave danger, forced to escape some evil mother-in-law? Or worse, a poor serving maid enticed by the family fortune? My own true story, one that I previously hadn't been half-arsed to see through to my own ending, would never be known. I never knew my parents, though I was pretty sure my mother had not really been a tragic princess. I had no family, no friends, a rag-tag education of the kind I'm sure church-faring folks would take against. That I could spout a smattering of philosophy, as in, 'slow and steady wins the race,' while expertly polishing a gentleman's prick didn't seem the right sort of history. Just as well if my story never was known.

I stuffed a tablecloth on the ground to keep the panel door propped open. There was a regular sliding door latch on the other side of the panel that I also manipulated. It worked as if it had just been used yesterday. I thought about leaving a note behind in case I what, encountered a pirate? I was too impatient to leave my hidey-hole and vowed I would just explore a short way. With an extra candle tucked in my left pocket and a hunk of cheese in my right, I set sail.

Aside from the cobwebs, the walls were plain plaster. The floor was wood planks, and I made sure to keep my step light. I couldn't figure if the direction had changed until I came to two openings. That day, I took the one on the left. You'll find out soon enough where the other one leads.

The passage that veered to the left had stairs leading down. I reached a plateau that seemed to be on the ground floor. There was a door that opened into a small dark room. It contained a bed covered with moth-eaten linens and what looked like an indent left behind from a ghost with a distinctive behind. I wished I had not thought upon the word 'ghost.' Along with the bed, the stuffy room contained only a chair and an empty bookcase — and enough dust that could have formed another piece of furniture, say a dining room table that could seat twenty. I sneezed. It was very small quarters, though, larger than my own room at the inn had been. If I was on the lam, I could see how I could bide securely here for a good long while. No one would ever be able to find me.

Upon grilling Elliot about Mondragon Manor's history, he never once alluded to a secret passageway. How could he not unless he himself did not know? For trust me, it was the single most interesting aspect of this melancholy manor. He had babbled about his French ancestors, Catholic the lot of them, so I put two Hail Marys together with two Glory Bes and came up with an image of one papist padre plunked down this passage to pray in peace — out of sight of any pesky

Protestants. Good one, I thought. I'd want to share those bon mots with Beau but realized the power I had, being the only one who knew about this hidey-hole.

Respect. Sir Stone had always advised me to have a backup plan to pivot to when life inevitably disappointed me. Perchance I'd used up my quota of words with the letter P in them that day. No matter, there was one more of those left, as I was soon to discover.

So much for a hidden treasure. Yet, I wasn't that disappointed. I left the dark little room and shut the door, and continued right on the trail as it meandered along a sloping ramp downward. I held my candle high and followed the passage across what seemed a distance the length of a field. It felt very damp and even darker than it had by the little room. The ground leveled out until I reached four steps topped by a panel. I climbed them and searched for a door handle or latch. There it was, higher than my forehead. I reached up and pulled it and tugged gently at the panel. It creaked a reproach at being used after what must have been years. I stilled, for heaven alone knew what awaited on the other side. Pirates? I shivered and peered one eye through the slit at the door. No pirate. Just my husband. Elliot. Hard at work in the barn at his workbench. He had stilled and raised his head at the creak. I held my breath. He recommenced his task at hand, extracting seeds from some kind of flower as near as I could tell. I stepped back and latched the panel. I smiled in the dark, proud of my husband and the man I was just beginning to understand.

My candle grew short. I held it in front of me with one hand, hiked my skirts with the other, and ran on tiptoe headlong into the darkness. I counted in my head to try to figure the distance, but I was going very fast, as fast as one can in a dark, unfamiliar secret passageway. I highly doubt I gained the length back into the linen closet in 100 seconds. It's impossible to count slower than the pace one sets. We'll call it five minutes to the time I tripped over the tablecloth. I picked it up, folded it, and slid it back on the shelf. I latched the panel and quietly opened the closet door to peer out. I would have hated to have been discovered after all that.

I went back to my room to freshen up — one of my favorite things about becoming a lady — soap and water, whenever I wanted. I brushed out my hair, plaited a simple braid, wound it up and around my head, and secured it with a tortoiseshell comb.

My cheeks were flushed with the day's adventure. Too bad I couldn't tell anyone. And just because there was no treasure in my secret hiding place didn't mean I couldn't hide my own. I kept in practice in case I should ever be called upon to pilfer for survival. I moved my collection from under the bed into my hidey-hole storage space. Every few days or so, I would lift a small treasure and secure it on the shelf in the small room off the secret passageway. No one noticed a thing. Sir Stone would be proud of me, I thought. But I needed to be ready for when things went tits-up.

Chapter 17

I headed outdoors, looking for my paramour. Remember that final word with a P I had hinted at earlier? That's a good one but not quite it. Beau made me a better person, and while I'm the first to admit that it wouldn't take much to improve upon the likes of me, his attention polished up the best parts of me.

He would pull out my chair for me. Then press my hand. Then kiss my hand. He happened upon me in the garden, where I paraded with my basket to and fro, in front of Elliot's barn. Officially I was collecting daffodils, the first blooms of that chilly Springtime and some herbs to take to the tenants. Unofficially, I was hoping to bump into Beau for a few private words.

"My dear girl." My heart quickened. "Why are you marching to and fro? I fear you will wear a hole in your shoe."

Which allowed me recourse to stop and lift my skirt, daintily, of course, to hold out my ankle. "No, my lord. I am gathering flowers for the baskets of produce we are sharing with the tenants." I was also chewing a mint leaf for fresh breath, and it was too late to spit it out. I coughed like Mrs. Catarrh as I tried to swallow it.

"Silly child." He came and adjusted my shawl up a little higher on my shoulders. "It is still cool out here; you will catch a chill."

As I had on a light cream-colored dress of thin silk, and I was indeed chilled, my bosom was pointing out the obvious. "Took you long enough to come and make sure I was warm."

He noticed. "Ah. You are a heartbreaker, little Brandy." He tweaked my nose and left me with a smile on my face that lingered. I grilled Atsuko for details on Beau that evening as she helped me dress for dinner.

"They are the yin and yang," she said. "The master and Sir Beau. Completely contrary forces that complement each other." She paused as if to search for what to say next. "Brandy, no matter what happens, they are good men." She patted my hair, and we went down to dinner.

How I wished to tell Beau about the passageway. Secrets are no fun when no one suspects anything. The hints I dropped fell on deaf ears and salted ground. "Eh?" Old lady Catarrh cupped her hand at her ear. "No ghosts here, though there should be."

"Quite a bloody history, if the locals are to be believed," Gordy said.

Mrs. Catarrh continued. "Murdered priests, philandering padres, an unfaithful wife who took her own life; you know, the usual family secrets. And as for fighting," she jerked her head toward Elliot, "you can bet your last coin his parents had forays that made Waterloo look tame." Elliot merely twitched an eyebrow.

RayRay made an infernal tuneless whistle. "RayRay, noise is only fun when you're the one making it. Please be quiet." He stuck his tongue out at me, which at least prevented further whistling.

Elliot joined in. "And as for buried treasure, my dear, I fear you've been talking to Gordy." He shook his head at Gordy. "Kindly stop filling my wife's head with stories, my good man."

"No. Gordy's stories are the best," I said. Atsuko sent a soft smile his way and agreed with me.

"Have you told Brandy the story of how you almost found a buried treasure?" Atsuko asked.

I clasped my hands together. I loved nothing more than pirate tales.

Gordy began, "Well, we were that close. Not far from here but far enough, there are the most beautiful islands. Isla Azores." He rolled his Rs. "Isla Azores is an itty-bitty chain of islands, off the coast of Portugal, due west, would be south, southwest from England, wouldn't it?" He clocked my reaction.

"You've gone east on my last nerve, Gordy. Enough with the directionals, or I'll shove my slipper north up...."

"Brandy." From Elliot. He motioned Gordy to continue.

"No shortage of rumors of buried treasure for the lucky sot that'll have the first notion of how to find it." He took a drink and settled into his chair.

"Pirates used to hide out there, in and out of coves and caves. There was a bunch of them. Uncharted. It's God's country, green valleys, flowers like you've never seen before," he cupped his hands as if he were holding a large duck." Now, who was telling tales? "And the waterfalls. Everywhere you turn. Turquoise lakes, rainbows, a veritable paradise. In fact, the pirates used to call it 'Is Az' for short, like it is as beautiful as paradise. Not many folks know about it."

My eyes were wide. "What about the buried treasure?"

"Aye," he said, just like a pirate. "Those islands are tricky. A captain's got to know what he's doing. Good place to slip away if someone's after you, but treacherous, you see? Some of the fiercest storms brew up on those rocky coasts. So, pirates would loot cargo ships sailing to England or Spain or France, filled with bounty headed for kings and queens. Seas would get rough, naval ships would be hot on their tail, or plain bad luck made them moor their vessels wherever they could harbor on one of the islands. The pirates, of course, the smart ones, knew the waterways and had their favorite spots. Oftentimes they had to jettison their prize and bury it for another day."

"Why wouldn't they come back for it?" I asked.

"Brandy. What kind of guarantees do you think one gets in this life? Death and taxes. This pirate was captured, that one shat himself to death, those two killed each other. Who knows?" He held up his hands. "Fate is in the last place you look for it because when it finds you, you can stop looking."

I had nearly stopped breathing. "What about your treasure?"

"Ah, well, we were shipwrecked off one of those islands years ago. We set to making repairs, but it was taking a good long time. One of the men, you'd trust him as far as you could throw him, was talking wild, about knowing where a treasure was buried. We had time on our hands, and we set off to find it."

"Did you?"

He shook his head and held up his fingers in a pinch. "That close, though. Shifty said he had memorized a map from his brother-in-law's cousin's uncle's second wife's dad. You know," he twirled his hand. "Ten paces toward the setting sun. Head due west until the cock crows." I leaned forward. "The trickiest part of any pirate's map, though," Gordy said, drawing out suspense, "is making sure you start in the right spot."

I clasped my hands together. "Turn due north," he continued, "until you have to relieve yourself, look for the bird beak rock pointing the way." He took a sip of wine. "Then dig up the whole island, and maybe you'll find a nugget or two."

Sir Stone would have loved this tale. We all laughed. Gordy did, too. "They were the vaguest directions, and we never did find out if Shifty was making it all up as he went along or not."

"Did you dig anything up?" Elliot asked.

Gordy nodded. "We did. We found a skull, which sent us buzzing, thinking that some nefarious deed had occurred on the site. We dug and dug and dreamed about what we would do with our riches. And then our ship was repaired, enough that is so we could sail her, and we limped home to Spain."

"What would you have done with your treasure?" I asked him.

"Brandy. The good news is, most folks, like all of us here, will never have a king's ransom of treasure."

"What's the bad news, then, Gordy?" RayRay asked.

"Let me finish the good news. It's good news to make the most of the life you have now without pining for some magical hocus-pocus of riches that will take away all your problems. That's the good news. Be grateful for the problems you do have."

Gordy, of course, is full of horseshit.

"The bad news is," he said, "that it's a tricky proposition to understand, and most folks don't realize it until it's too late. The real treasure is to be found sitting right next to you." He stared across the table at Atsuko. And reached over to pat my hand.

Elliot raised his glass in a toast to Gordy, and we all followed suit. I was about to wipe my hand across my mouth, but catching that old shrew Catarrh ready to pounce, I dabbed with my napkin.

"Well then, I have good and bad news," I said. "As I expect I'm grateful for all my problems, which are all sitting around this table."

"Well done, Brandy," Elliot said. "Sadly, and alas, there are no treasures here at Mondragon Manor, either. Merely debts upon debts. That's why I've been working so hard to get some good years of crops in. We've rotated fields, much to the chagrin of our tenants, but by and by, if we get some healthy produce for market this Spring, I've promised them bonuses like have never been seen."

"Is that wise?" Beau asked.

Elliot playfully tapped Beau's shoulder. "I know you are the financial and legal counsel of this operation, friend. But it is imperative to have their buy-in." He paused to make sure he had Beau's attention. "They are good men who want what we all do—food and a future for their family. The loyalty of those farmers to their land and their own families cannot be dismissed. They are the soldiers on the front line of our farming revolution."

"If only money weren't so tight," Beau said. "If only your land weren't entailed, and you could sell off a few acres."

"If wishes were horses, beggars would ride," I added to the conversation.

Beau wasn't married and, according to Gordy, had left a trail of broken hearts across the countryside. "I've nothing to contribute to the coffers here either, I'm afraid. I'm the youngest son of seven, so not much of a catch," Beau told me.

"Well, that and the scandals that seem to follow wherever you go," Elliot reminded him. They shared a secretive look.

"What is it? Do tell, now." But they refused. Don't you love a man of mystery?

Beau raised his glass to toast Elliot. "Ellie keeps me on the straight and narrow."

Elliot raised his own glass. "And Beau is the best piece of my puzzle."

Peculiar.

Chapter 18

The next morning both Elliot and Beau roused me from my bed. "Come on, lazy bones," Elliot called out. "We're going riding. Come with us, we will teach you how. And make a picnic of it."

I went out to the stable with them, happy to be sandwiched on either arm between Elliot and Beau. But then I put my foot down. Literally, atop Elliot's fine shoe, the pointed one with a jewel in its buckle.

"Kit out the carriage, or I'm not going. If God intended me to clamber atop that beast, he wouldn't have made me so pretty."

I loved making them laugh. "La-di-dah, Princess," Beau teased me.

"At your service," Elliot bowed, and we all had a good chuckle.

The strange relationship, our threesome, if you will, wasn't strange at all. Elliot was such a kind friend. Husband, I mean husband. And Beau. Well. I have a secret. We are in love. True love. Forever and ever. I had never felt like this before. You may not know this, but I have been accused of having a hair-trigger temper. The barkeep once told me Irritator was my middle name and Instigator my surname. Sir Stone advised me never to believe that, and I knew that he too doubted that tub of lard could have been my sire. Nevertheless, for the first time in my life, I was possessed of the most joyous of all feelings. I was carefree. Love and lust and romantic daydreams of our sure-to-be idyllic future flooded my brain. I sang and danced and could barely focus my eyes or attention on anything but Beau.

What had I done before I met Beau? Where he was when he wasn't with me was all I could ponder. I could only imagine what he was thinking, doing, saying. And when we were together, no one else existed. Call it a fairytale. Call it madness. Call it whatever you like, but do not doubt the power of *infatuation*, which I believe is French for a situation of obese bliss. I would have given my life for Beau.

Love is the opposite of life, nay not death, you idiot — the opposite of the mundane drudgery of the maintenance of living. Innocent unnoticed tasks like washing my face took on new import and made me thrill at the look I would see in his eyes as he gazed upon me.

I was filled with energy and darted to and fro in the kitchen, escaping Mrs. Farfuddle to lovingly season the food for my beau. For the first time in my life, I had a purpose. His name was Beau, and to show you how impudent I was in considering some sparkling future, I had dared to foment the sole reason I was born was to know Beau. Sigh. One day I shall read these twee sentiments and only hope not to gag.

They packed me off in the carriage and climbed in, fussing about my skirts taking up too much room, and we set off. Food, wine, and delicious wit. We went to an embankment up a gently rolling hill filled with soft grassy slopes and Queen Anne's Lace flowers. Elliot set out a blanket and the basket, and Beau picked the flowers and wove them into a fairy crown he set upon my head. "Queen Brandy's Lace has a much better sound, don't you think?" I nearly swooned with happiness at his wink.

"Serve me up some cake first, don't you think, love?"

"Get it yourself," I said and pushed the basket toward Beau with my foot.

They took turns serving me. Beau threw grapes at Elliot and me to catch in our mouths. Need I remind anyone I proved to be quite adept. Lewd comments were made to attest to my prowess, which served as a balm to my sordid past. I had never had the time nor occasion, nor selection for that matter, to indulge in friendship. I highly recommend it.

They encouraged my outlandish comments. "Do you think there are any ladies who like to fuck as much as a man?"

They corrected my grammar. "Do you think there are any ladies for whom fornication is as enjoyable as it is for the male?" Beau said.

Then Elliot corrected him. "I'd use the term copulation."

"Beast with two backs," Beau said.

"Jiggery-pokery," Elliot said.

"Pickle-me-tickle-me," I said. We three burst into merry laughter.

"Well?" I said once we had calmed. "I want to know the answer." The laughter that ensued was not in proportion to my question but made all the more enjoyable because of it.

Their genuine curiosity in me was headier than the brandy Elliot kept in his cabinet. Keep your coins and jewels, that 'nothing' of a day was a treasure.

Elliot made me put my sunbonnet back on, and I bid adieu to my wilted crown of flowers.

We arrived home in jolly spirits, just before sunset. Elliot's yawn kicked off my own, and we decided to forgo the evening meal. I pulled my beloved velvet tassel for bathwater. Then again for a lavender compress because I felt a headache coming on. And then again because I needed a bit of bread and cheese from the kitchen. At my third summons, Beau arrived at my doorstep. Complete with brandy and two glasses. Finally. I wasn't used to courtship of any kind, but I had begun to worry this was taking too blasted long. We were supposed to be on a mission.

"Fancy a nightcap?" I had my robe on, but my hair was still tangled. Beau seated me before the fire and brushed my hair. We spoke of nothing and every-thing, and upon my yawn, he truckled me into bed and tucked me in chaste as a nun. He leaned in as if he would kiss me but whispered, "Sweet dreams."

The next night, Elliot tried to teach me to play chess. After I finally conceded that he could check his mate up his own arse, I suggested they teach me cards instead. We all played a game of vingt-et-un, and I signaled to Atsuko to be my teammate. We took them for five pounds. "You forget," I said, "I worked laying whiskey down since I could walk. Watching those sots play cards was my favorite drama."

Beau escorted me to my room that night. We gossiped about Atsuko and Gordy and RayRay and even Mrs. Catarrh. He played with my fingers before giv-ing my hand a final squeeze to escort me to my bed. I held my breath. He dropped a kiss at my shoulder, the part that just starts thinking about becoming my neck. I shivered.

The third night, Gordy made sure the wine flowed. He kept my glass more filled than my plate. I didn't mind. Beau had even brought me a sprig of Lily of the Valley that I knew Elliot had picked, but no matter.

Nearly two months had passed since I paid a fare-thee-not-well to the arse-end of my good-for-nothing sailor. For those of you keeping score, let's just say the music box was well-wound and ready to twirl. Such a short time ago, I had dared dream of a future with my sailor. And out of those ashes of despair, I found myself ensconced at Mondragon Manor with a family I had never dreamed possible. I pinched myself. Beau lifted his glass in a private toast to me. I merely nodded, as a lady would.

That night, he brought me two pails of heated water for my bath. He did not leave. He bathed me clean with fine French soap and washed my hair with such strong fingers I never wanted him to stop. He settled my gown gently over my head. The heat and dampness from my eager flesh made the soft gown cling to my curves. He ravished my breasts so, that I, well… Why don't you mind your own business?

"Oh, darling girl, you are a delight."

"I've slept with worse for less."

"Is that true?"

He punished me with his touch until I was forced to admit, "You've caught me out. You're not the ugliest bloke I've ever lain with." How we laughed. Not that I would ever tell him, I clean forgot I was on a mission because Beau was the best kisser I have ever kissed.

Hold your horses; I'm closing the curtains of my bed. What happened next is for me to know and you to find out.

Though my fertile time of the month was close, close enough, I whispered that we probably needed several more times to make sure. I breathed in his scent, not as sweet as Elliot's; Beau was horse saddle and tobacco. Even my sailor, whom

I had loved with all my heart, never made me feel that which I'm sure good women shouldn't be made to feel. It was that wicked. It was that wonderful.

I was smitten. Well and truly. I should have had a care that smitten must be some form of a complicated French verb, warning of the dire consequences of the good Lord who seems to spend inordinate amounts of time smiting beggars and sinners alike. I refused to believe that folderol and brazenly nestled into the curve of Beau's arm, which tightened against me.

Beau smacked my derriere in the morning to wake me. "Thank you for your charms, lovely mistress."

I widened my eyes at him. "Am I your mistress now?"

His sparkling eyes fluttered, but he laughed it off. "Always, my lady. You can't know how I feel about you," he paused, "and your husband. He is my dearest friend, and now, you have become such also."

I couldn't resist asking for more. "Wouldn't you ever want to run away, you and me? Have our own little house, with a garden?" A true romance, with a real marriage, was what I wanted him to yearn for. There may have been several faceless children and a stray puppy for some reason in my daydream, with a benevolent Sir Stone looking over us all.

He quirked an eyebrow at me. "And live on what, you goose?" He leaned over me menacingly and raised his hand. "If you say 'love,' so help me, I will tickle you senseless."

I stretched my arms overhead and snuggled in for a much-needed rest, afraid to break the spell after that magical night. My body was well-used, and I wanted to sing. I could count on one hand the times I've ever felt an urge toward song. Let it be noted, I would not be the first to say I can carry a serving tray far better than any tune. I settled for a self-satisfied hum, and words to the wise; one doesn't have to be a water witch to know this: hear me now and listen to me later; smug smiles will be smitten from your face before the clock strikes midnight.

I put off using the chamber pot as long as I could to keep Beau inside me.

Chapter 19

If a lady isn't supposed to kiss and tell, she probably shouldn't count the wondrous romps over the past four nights, either. Try to guess. Fine. Eleven. Beau tried to say it was fourteen, but I'll tell you the same as I told him. "Nice try. Eleven for me."

Dinner a few nights later was nearly as entertaining as the escapades of our bed sport. Not really, fool. But truly, one cannot live on love alone, though Beau and I gave it a good go. All of our emotions ran giddily with expectation. No one mentioned the illicit hopes and dreams; no one had to. Everyone knew the score.

Beau teased Elliot and me, and Elliot and I teased Beau back. I taught them a sailor's song, and our whole table, even Mrs. Catarrh, joined in. I only remember the chorus, but it was quite catchy:

In the salty spray of the sea, fetch me my cup of rum,

In the salty spray of the sea, drink to my gal and her bum,

In the salty spray of the sea, catch the salty spray of my cum.

Beau sang loudest and made us all rise and place our hands on the shoulders of the one in front of us. We danced and sang and kicked our way through the dining room into the parlor.

Beau always brought out the best in my husband, and that night, he was exceptional. We all laughed and flirted with each other, and the hazy glow of love surrounded by these folks, who felt like family, suffused my cheeks with a natural blush. That, and the thought of the night to come.

"You should retire early, my darling," my husband encouraged me after dinner. I slugged my second or perhaps third brandy — God, I love brandy — and protested. "I'm not tired," but a yawn slipped out.

"Yes, indeed. You must rest, sweet Brandy of ours," Beau said. We shared what I thought was a meaningful look. I took myself off, sashaying up the stairs as provocatively as I could. Even as I tripped, I played it off and rolled to heave my bosom.

"All right over there?" Elliot shouted. As no one fussed or came to my aid or even noticed the pretty picture I made, I sulked all the way to my room. I dressed for bed, brushed my hair, brushed it again, and tried provocative poses. Bent knee. Finger in my cunny. (Looking back now, I am filled with self-loathing.)

Not tired enough to fall asleep and await my lover's sweet kisses, but tired enough to be cranky from waiting, I tossed on my bed. I missed Beau and how he made me feel. I was fretful he wanted to play with Elliot and the others instead. After last night, I couldn't imagine why he would want to be anywhere other than in my arms. I couldn't get comfortable and hoped he would return to me soon. I heard footsteps and sat up in anticipation, but they passed right by my door. I threw back my covers. I heard Beau's light laugh as they stopped at what I imagined was Elliot's door. He must have invited Beau in for another nightcap. Ha. I would surprise them.

I took a candle and slipped on my velvet slippers. Beau's room was quite a way down the hall, just past my husband's own suite. But the joke was on them, for I had a surprise. Do you remember me mentioning the path not taken in the secret passageway, off to the right? I had gone back and explored that the very next day and christened it 'the journey of right turns.'

I didn't need to glance in the mirror to know I looked fetching. Candlelight favors the glints in my unbound hair, and please, hush, I won't go on about my peignoir anymore. (Though it is one of my favorite things.) I slipped out my door and headed down the hall in the opposite direction to Elliot's room. I lit out for my beloved linen closet and disappeared inside. My bare feet in soft velvet slippers were light upon the floorboards as I made my way assuredly to the passageway on the right. I went a little way and made a short turn to the right, followed by two more turns at similar intervals. The final right turn led to two odd little steps. I climbed them and slid the small wooden bar to open the panel. I blew out my candle because, of course, I didn't want to catch my husband's clothes aflame. I stepped into the floor of his armoire, using my feet to scoot his boots aside. Oh, this was going to be so much fun. I could hear their voices. What are those rascals up to? Heaven only knows. I pinched my lips and quieted my breath to steal a spy on them.

"Ah, Brandy is something else."

I hugged myself in the dark. How delicious.

"Should I be jealous?"

"Ellie, you have the damnedest way of collecting the world's misfits to your coterie. I consider myself fortunate that my character is one you'd choose to bring together in your idyll."

"Some idyll. A mountain of debts. A crumbling manor. A family who hates me. Experiments that I know will work if only I had more time and money. Neither of which I have. Unless this crazy plan to get Brandy with child actually works."

Beau must have soothed him because I heard nothing but the rubbing of fabric. Come on, gents, more about Brandy, please. I keened my ears.

"Beau. You must know, I couldn't do any of this without you."

A Beau I hadn't known existed replied, "I'm the biggest misfit of all. I've done nothing with my life."

"Beau, you have one of the finest minds I know. You could have been a solicitor if you hadn't dropped out of university."

"There were about a hundred pounds of reasons I had to do that. Besides, I didn't fit in."

"And you could sell butter to a cow. What a help you shall be on our farm."

I heard rustling.

"Nothing but a useless life."

"You've made mine better."

Ah, I took that as my cue. I was going to make Beau an offer he couldn't refuse and thank my husband for being so understanding about the course of true love. I had no idea how it would all work out; I was just lovestruck and knew it would. I'd help Elliot have his heir, and Beau and I would be together. That's all that mattered.

I tossed my hair, pulled at the décolletage of my gown. I levered the clasp in the armoire and popped out.

My scream was not louder than Elliot's. You see, they were in a state of undress. Elliot's shirt was unbuttoned and pulled from his trousers. Beau's lovely legs and arse were on full display. They were kissing. As Beau had kissed me just the night before. The looks on their faces. No, not with shock as I gave them the surprise of their life. They had looked at each other the way that I feared I looked at Beau. With my heart. With devotion.

My nose detected a musky odor, but my eyes refused to believe the tableau. My silly, innocent child of a husband had been kissing and fondling Beau. My Beau and Elliot had been in raptures.

Beau wouldn't meet my eye but had to play droll. "Excuse me, my lady." He pulled on his britches. "I'll escort you to your room."

"You've done quite enough." I ran from the room through the right door, not the armoire, before my tears threatened to drown us all. I disappeared and ran to my room as if I was pursued by the devil himself. Who knows? I am sure I was. I cried so much I was too weak to fetch a towel and blew my nose into my pillow.

I hid under my covers and fell asleep at some time after the clock chimed three. Would I have welcomed Beau if he returned to me, slick with my husband's seed on him? A quandary I needed not face as it never came to pass.

Was it even possible? Men? In love with each other? I replayed my interactions with Elliot and decided yes. He was in love with Beau. I had, of course, missed all the signs. Because I had never even considered the possibility. And Beau! That two-timing accursed. My venom dissipated as my heart shattered into pieces. He had not lied to me. He lay with me, but he did not lie. It was my traitorous heart that had fallen for the cad. My mind whirled. I had never heard of such a thing.

While I contemplated and wondered how, exactly, it all worked, I wanted to declaim my fair sense of justice. I considered how it would be if I loved someone of my own sex. There are gentlewomen in my past whom I had admired, of course — the pink dress of this one, the sprigged parasol of that one. One ma'am did have a lovely bosom, I remembered thinking, though she had nothing on my own. I imagined what it would be like if I kissed her and her breasts and played with them the way I enjoyed caresses on mine. I could imagine a pleasant sensation, as the women I had seen were clean and pretty with a light scent of soap and perfume. Their hands had been soft and fluttering. I thought I might like the attention, but when push came to shove, I ached for the manly arms of a sweat-scented hairy chest, the scruff of a beard against my neck, the rough play of big, clever hands at my waist, and below. Then I cried with despair.

I had nightmares as my brain tried to decipher what it was that I had seen. I couldn't decide who I hated more, Beau or Elliot.

The following day, after he slid a note under my door, I heard nothing more from Elliot. Or from the love of my life, Beau, not a word. Seems Elliot spoke for Beau, too.

My dearest Brandy, the note said. *You are loved, my girl, more than you can know. I am sore of heart in the certainty that you will never forgive me for the fraud I perpetrated upon your young person. It is the great burden and shame of my life and one I've no choice but to carry. And conceal. My only hope is that one day you can find the glimmer of affection I am sure you once felt for me and believe that I never meant you harm or heartache.*

Fondly,

Your husband,

Elliot

I kept to my room for three days before I could bear it no longer. I asked Atsuko to help me dress and do my hair. I was magnificent. She wisely kept her council, unlike Mrs. Catarrh, who had tried to batten down my door several times and demanded to know what was going on.

When I finally deigned to appear for breakfast that morning, everyone stilled. I was ravenous. I sat in my place and gobbled a sizable repast and had my cup of coffee filled twice. I felt their eyes on me. They looked about to face a firing squad. I daintily dabbed at my mouth with my napkin, like the fine lady I had become. Ready, aim, fire.

"I know you all think you are so smart. High and mighty. How you must have laughed at me."

Beau dared interrupt. "Brandy."

I pounded my fist on the table. "Not one word."

"I thought we were all to be a family. Yet you keep this, this abomination, this secret, this craven facade from me. Perversion. You used me and let me think…" I paused. I will never tell them how I proclaimed my love to Beau. Jesus, I went beet red with shame just thinking about that. "How long has this been going on?"

After some seconds, realizing it wasn't a rhetorical rant, Elliot answered.

"Brandy. No one laughed at you. We all love you and are very happy you are part of our family. You can't know the shame I've had, growing up, knowing I was different. Always having to hide my feelings. Being ostracized by my own family without really understanding why."

"How does that even work?" I rolled my hand at him and Beau.

"Who can explain the intricacies of love?"

I snorted at that.

"No wonder you couldn't…" I stumbled, trying to find decent words to choose for how I had failed miserably at seducing Elliot. "Ah shite, you better not cry. You know there are no damn secrets in this house. I realize you could never be a husband to me. There. I've said it. It wasn't my fault after all."

Atsuko spoke up. "Brandy, no one is at fault. Inside your heart, you know this."

"And you couldn't have told me? Or you, Elliot? Beau? Of all people. Mrs. Catarrh? You seem to take joy in blathering about everything else under the sun? Seems no one thought to tell me, oh, miss, your husband only fucks men?"

"Enough, Brandy!" Now, Elliot grew a spine? "No need for that. We have all welcomed you and shown you nothing but loving kindness. You knew the score when you agreed to be my wife. I need an heir, and you needed a life. Not a bad exchange if you ask me."

"Lies! Lies! You should have told me." My eyes shifted to Beau.

"Why?" Elliot asked. "Would you have understood? Would you have been accepting? Would that have mattered a damn in your self-centered universe? Made you any kinder?"

"No, you goat fucker, it surely wouldn't have." I grabbed bread and sausages and piled my plate high, and stood, prepared to storm off.

"Wait." I gave pause at Elliot's command. "It is no secret my family hates me, as you fully witnessed. They always believed me to be different and weak." He swallowed. "Womanish." He stood up and faced me across the room. "I left them as soon as I was able. I wanted to start my own family, be around people I could care about and who cared about me. I met them, the bruised and battered, the humble and vulnerable, and found the miracle of this group you see here. I believe in providence and the fact that the good Lord provides. I love you as a kind-hearted sassy sister. A brat with good intentions, and no matter what happens, I will always take care of you." He put his hands on his hips. "And by the by, are you with child yet?"

I sailed my plate full of food down the entire length of the dining table, so on-target, he had to jump aside to deflect it.

"I hate you all!"

Chapter 20

Mrs. Farfuddle's ignorant serving wench, Alys, was so painfully stupid I took pity on her, even as I pumped her for details. She brought me food and answered my velvet rope demands. "What are they saying down there?"

She bobbed her head then recited. "The master says to give you time. Lord Beau is drunk and moaning that it is all his fault. Atsuko and Gordy are trying to pretend naught is wrong. RayRay makes jokes that no one laughs at." She blushed. The whole estate knew of her fondness for RayRay. Dear Lord. Should I share my new realization and tell her that dog won't hunt, either?

"And Mrs. Catarrh boxed my ears for spilling tea on her."

That sounds about right. Dear Lord, I was exhausted from my rage. Bored, too. I had rooms to pillage, flowers to pick, villagers to lord over, and damn me, I missed Elliot's workbench in the barn, where I helped sort sprouts, pluck weeds, and water the seedlings while he talked to me about his plans and plants.

You could never fault Elliot for not having empathy. He gave me space and readily gauged my appetite for solitude. That afternoon he invited me for an outing. I simmered with rage. How could they ever expect me to forgive them? Maybe one day I could forgive, but forget? Never. I will always be scarred from their crime, their lies, and my broken heart. It hurt to breathe. How could they even speak to me?

As I was finally bored enough, I could have cheerfully mucked out the stables; I graciously agreed to go on a walk with those two rogues. And if you believe I was gracious, you haven't been paying attention. Men-lovers. They ganged up to be as charming and agreeable as possible. They gabbed and chatted as if I were part of their conversation. I only answered in a short, terse, "fuck off," or "you wish" or "of course." Three handy phrases that got me through those dark days.

No one dared asked me my impressions and pretended as if nothing had changed. They were waiting me out. "You'll be old and gray by the time I cave," I had mumbled.

They took turns teasing and laughing. Telling stories. Truth be told, I bit my lip at times, trying not to smile. But, as the days passed, my great festering wounded pride, lust and love for Beau, and rage kept growing. At night, I hated that I still found myself listening for Beau. I would have scratched his eyes out had he tried to enter my room. Then I would be filled with loathing at myself because I knew I would not have done that.

I was churlish and sullen, Elliot and Beau worked hard to wear me down, and the rest waited for cues as to how they should act — when they should smile, what they should do. "Mindless sheep," I had cursed them.

It was to this uneasy household that Elliot's cousin appeared, unannounced.

At first, Cousin Clarence appeared dashing. He was taller than Elliot and broader of shoulder. And he knew how to pay a woman a compliment. His eyes glinted with approval as he kissed my hand. I lifted my chin and sparkled my own eyes back at him. I chose to ignore his portly presence as a sign of riches and breeding. Oh, you can only imagine what's to come.

Elliot ordered Mrs. Farfuddle "to kill the fatted calf," at which her own cow eyes practically rolled to the back of her empty head. "Calm yourself. It's just an expression. I simply meant, let us enjoy your finest savories as we have an unexpected, yet most welcomed, guest."

Had you never understood what it was to be "in a dither," you'd have wanted to have seen her flap her hands all the way back to the kitchen.

I looked forward to dinner because I was sick and tired of my black thoughts. I needed the balm of a handsome enough man to remark upon my face and hair, grace and form. I wanted to practice my fine lady skills and see how I fared.

Mrs. Farfuddle outdid herself. Later, I wondered if Elliot had put her up to it. The mutton was full of so much gristle I had to pry it out of my teeth, even though Lady Lessons clearly states, never, ever removed chewed victuals from one's mouth, no matter what. That I've swallowed worse was not lost upon me, but I could not have cared less. Fortunately, Cousin Clarence did not see my performance, though Elliot toasted me. I answered with as dirty a look I could muster.

Cousin Clarence, however, ate with gusto, drank with great thirst, and shouted his opinion to all and sundry. His clothes, I noted, had been tailored to hide his girth. I caught him as he eyed me most appreciatively, and then he clocked Elliot.

Since he repeatedly informed me I was beautiful, I must admit it went to my head.

"Cousin Clarence, how does it happen you are here?"

He wiped his greasy mouth with his sleeve, ignoring the napkin at his place. "Well, dear Cousin Brandy, I wanted to meet the new bride and see what little Ellie here has been up to."

"Well, it's a pleasure finally meeting you."

"I also like to keep an eye on the family manor. Which most likely will be mine, sooner than later."

"What?"

"Surely Elliot and his minions," he spat the word, encompassing Gordy, Ray-Ray, Atsuko, and Mrs. Catarrh, "have told you by now. Mondragon Manor is all but mine. I don't have a doubt in my mind that Miss Fancy Britches here could never sire an heir." With that, he clapped a meaty hand on Elliot's back, and I could see he meant it to hurt.

"Why do you say that, Cousin?" I asked.

He laughed. "Look at him. Puny little whiny girl. Even as a child, he would run behind his mother's skirts until even she got tired of his sickening ways."

"Cousin Clarence," Elliot began. I held up my hand.

"Husband, let him finish."

"You're a looker," he said to me. "I'll give you that. Common, of course. Wonder where he found you?" He shrugged as if it was no matter. "I might be favorably disposed to keep you, if you catch my meaning." He wiggled his empty wine glass at Gordy. "I checked at the parish to make sure your marriage certificate is legitimate. It is." Then he laughed. "But not worth the paper it's written on. "Elliot. Married. To a woman. Ha. Ha. Ha."

I slid my face into repose and looked as if I couldn't wait to hear his next words.

"Nice enough tits, I supposed, but no sign of breeding as far as I can tell." He laughed again. "Elliot trying to rut with a woman. How was your wedding night, dear Cousin Brandy?"

I stood up very gracefully. "RayRay? Please go saddle Cousin Clarence's horse. He will not be staying under our roof. Riffraff is not welcome in our home." I went and stood by Elliot, who stood when I did. I linked my arm through his. He patted my hand but bore a worried smile.

"I'll have you know, Cousin," I said, "Elliot is twice the man you will ever hope to be. Your insults are noted for the tired phrasings of a fat, petulant bully. You will leave, and I thank you to take your filth with you. As well as my pity for your own lady." I looked down at his gut. "What must she abide to prop up that shelf?"

He sneered at me; yellow teeth glistened. The sight of a charred tidbit of meat that blackened nearly the entirety of one of his front teeth brought me immeasurable joy. "Elliot. Are you going to let this strumpet talk to me like that?" And to me. "Women should lay on the bed, quietly, like a blanket."

I waited for Elliot to defend me. Even a mere woman like myself knew that should have been the case. But his shoulders next to mine were slumped. He remained quiet. Cousin Clarence repeated his taunt. "Tell me. I'd pay good coin to hear tell the tale of your alleged consummation." He shook his head.

In my heavy dress of deep red velvet cut down to there, with a lace bodice, my dangling earrings bobbed at my cheeks, and with my hair dressed high on my head, I knew I could pass as landed gentry, born with a pedigree. If one didn't look deeply into my fine, jaded eyes. I was a good mimic, as I believe I've mentioned, and I'd had weeks to perfect my Lady Bountiful persona. Granted, there'd been a few breakdowns as the cretins surrounding the table, whom I was growing fond of, would jump to attest. Nevertheless, under the polished veneer of my face powder, I tapped into the survival mode from my tavern days. I leaned fully into Cousin Clarence's face as he sprawled in his chair and barked out a shout.

"It's none of your business, you swag-bellied gout-ridden gaffer. You may have been cock-of-the-walk at one time, but how long has it been since you've actually managed to cop eyes on your own poor little prick?" I tossed his glass of wine smack dab in his face. As expected, he jumped out of his seat, paving the way for the favorite maneuver of a slattern such as myself.

I grabbed hold of his family jewels and twisted. The gobble-head turned purple and, for once, was rendered speechless. One doesn't count panicked squawking and gawping as proper speech for an English lord, does one?

"Darling?" Elliot said.

I released the hostages and smiled, sweet as you can believe, at my husband. My heart felt near to bursting at the glint of tears in his beautiful eyes.

Clarence overturned his chair in his haste to exit and left without a fare-thee-well.

The fetid miasma that surrounded Cousin Clarence and his visit miraculously cleared. Perhaps the raising of glasses and toasts of "Brandy" helped erase the strain of the past several weeks and proved to be a balm to my aching insides. Hate is hard work. Quite wearying, actually.

Though we had yet to exchange a look, I decided to bury the hatchet. Oddly, not into the skull of my beloved as I had once desired.

"Beau," I called out. "You have a very good cock." He had the grace to look abashed.

"Now, see here, Brandy," Elliot started to protest.

"Dear God, not another apology or, heaven forbid, explanation. I am plumb tired of all this bowing and scraping and your hangdog looks." Elliot looked flustered; Beau looked defeated. This was not going as I planned.

"I am being serious. His tallywhacker. It worked, you thick heads. By hook or by crook. Or should I say by cuck or by cock."

It did take a minute before they finally did some impressive equations in their numb skulls. Beau leaped to his feet first, followed by my husband, and they smothered me with kisses. Toasts were tossed, and not a bleeding one of us could actually believe our good fortune. I had very sweet dreams that night, for the first time in a long time.

Chapter 21

The following morning, we all slunk into the dining room at a later hour than usual. Numbers were discussed. Not my strong suit. From the nine-hundred pounds owed on the house between mortgages and taxes to some nine-month time frame. Oh. I had better pay attention.

We gulped our coffee and counted on our fingers. Elliot's birthday was January 3rd. Surely there was time and then some. As it was the middle of April, I was confident all would be well. "I could very well deliver your heir exactly on your birthday, Elliot." He looked as green as I felt.

Mrs. Farfuddle, no doubt hearing the joyous news, bustled in with a heaping tray of burnt scones, runny eggs, and raw potatoes. She stopped at my side, and I reared from her for a split second, expecting some physical blow. "Now, you're eating for two, madam, and I will serve you first and best." She plunked her offering in front of me, her nail beds grimed with dirt, as usual. If I gagged now, she would never forgive me. I channeled the saliva gathering in my throat and hummed. I find humming has saved many a day. I reached for her wrist and squeezed it as if in gratitude but then launched her away.

If Sir Stone could see me now, I remember thinking. "Pride goeth before a fall," was what he most likely would have dinged me with, but perhaps he could have found a soft spot at my grown-up, married, breeding status. How I wished I could heed his advice and not mess things up.

I won't bore you with too many details, but alas, growing an heir is the most challenging maneuver. One never spoken about. My tits grew, but alack, so did my nipples. No longer soft and pink, they quickly became the size of teacup saucers and as rude a muddy brown as you would see beneath Elliot's boots. They ached. My back ached, my legs grew veins as knobby as tuber roots. I had headaches, dark thoughts, moody fits, and complained more than usual. I was restless yet tired.

Hungry yet bloated. Proud of Beau and Elliot, the two fathers-to-be, and their joy, yet repulsed at their kindness.

"Jesus, Elliot, you'd think you were the one who did the deed and spilled his seed."

Until words clunk out of your mouth and land in the air with a thud, can you begin to understand their power? Oh, I felt low after that. Especially since I said it at dinner in front of everyone, who, to a man, proceeded to ignore me. I've never had reason to say I'm sorry and had no plans to start now. There was enough stuff crammed in my head. Those blighters could get over it and treat me with the honor I deserved. Me, and that baby, were the ones saving their sorry hides.

My belly grew, and I waddled like a duck. No one dared laugh at me, and though I snapped at their concern, I reveled in being wrapped in cotton and put on a pedestal. I was saved the choicest morsels for dinner, my every craving accommodated.

I was petted and fed all the clotted cream I could lap up, a precocious kitten adored by all. And when the little lord frightened me out of my skin with his first vicious kicks, Mrs. Catarrh and Atsuko were able to ease my fears. Even Gordy and RayRay would join us all in my room at night, gathered around me in my nightgown for a touch and admiration of my mound. It made the day's pains easier to bear. I never looked at the calendar and scarcely realized what day it was.

I never gave a care for either the when the miraculous arrival would happen or, more to the point, the how. Old sourpuss Mrs. Catarrh hemmed and hawed and spewed dire warnings of the blessed event, but I shined her off.

Elliot still had me help him with his botany projects. I loved the earthy smell of the barn and the feel of the fertile earth under my fingers. When seedlings I had planted took hold and grew, I felt as proud as a newborn mother. "Look at these butter beans," I said.

He gravely explained each part to me and patted me on the back. "In a few days, they will be ripe and ready, and you can harvest them, and we will have them for dinner." I could hardly wait and felt very proprietary over my harvest. At a kick in my belly, I looked down. I must have sighed.

"Brandy. All will be well. You're a fine girl. What a good mother you will be. Look how you are with all these little plants. A baby will be the joy that makes this place a home."

I squeezed my hands together.

Elliot laughed. "Don't look shifty-eyed, Brandy. What I don't know about women and babies would fill all these books." He waved his hand over the books that littered the shelves and workbench. "But what I know about kindness," he touched his heart, "I am eager to share. This baby will be surrounded by people who love him." He passed his hand over my belly. "Think of it. Think of how many fairy godmothers and godfathers this child will have."

His finger tipped my chin up, forcing me to look at him. "We are all in this together, Brandy. No matter what happens." He paused. "No sass?" He mocked me.

"Thank you." I brushed my hands together. "I need to go water the pumpkins out back."

The villagers forgave my earlier airs and gathered round with the grisliest tales of year-long pregnancies, tortuous births, and bleeding like a stuck pig for hours on end. Their warnings went on for hours on end. As I'd stop listening after the part of some plug being expelled from my woman parts kicking off the festivities, I had no idea how long a birthing mother was expected to bleed like a stuck pig.

A few times a week, maybe more, maybe less, I continued scavenging around the manor. What of it? If things went aright (unlikely), it would continue to be my family home. There was none more familiar with the manor than I. But if things went south, which was far more than likely, my stash would be my saving grace and the only thing to keep my baby and me from the poor house.

Sir Stone always taught me to prepare for the worst but hope for the best. I rarely heeded his "hope" part of the axiom and believed it nothing more than a womanly sop. All hope had ever brought me was the inevitable jolting crash from the higher ledge I had dared set my sights upon.

One morning I took pains to shake off my entourage, "Jesus. I'm tired of you all watching me. What? Do you think the baby has tricks to perform already? Go away and mother hen someone else. Better yet, tell Mrs. Farfuddle to instruct Alys to bake some currant scones; I've quite a desire for them." Alys, who was prone to get things wrong (she still had a crush on RayRay), parroted the house gossip like a champion, and I grew quite fond of her. Even more so when I discovered she could bake like a pastry chef from France. (I'd had no idea how a pastry chef from France baked: it was Elliot who said that.)

Once they left me alone, I set out to explore a locked room off the servant quarters. It was down yet another side hallway, and if the dust visible under the threshold on the bare hall floor was any indication, it hadn't been visited since Jesus was a jester. The locked door gave me not a moment's hesitation. I had a skeleton key that gained me access to nearly every room in the manor. I approached, but the key didn't work. I tried several other keys I keep in my collection, since one never knows, to no avail.

I eyeballed the keyhole and found it blocked. How was the room locked from the inside? I ran for a piece of paper in my room, stored in the desk drawer. As I had no occasion, no family, or even home to write letters about how I was faring, many paper sheets were available. I had practiced penmanship via bleak poetry about my love for Beau. With hardly a pang, I tossed them into the fireplace. I still ached over the affair, but some days I managed to stop fantasizing that he would realize he couldn't live without me, and proclaim his love, and reclaim his spot in my bed. That was during the day. At night, shameful dreams, a byproduct of being with child, I suspect, left me aroused in more ways than one. Many were the nights when I needed a final soothing to sleep and thank God for the middle finger of my right hand. (She's a good girl, you'd like her.)

I grabbed a blank sheet of paper and my hatpin and hightailed it back to the locked room. Lord. I slid the paper under the door and popped the hatpin in the keyhole. The key dropped and was mine. All that bother for this? It was a small room. Moth-eaten curtains shuttering the windows. I pulled them wide and coughed at the dust like Mrs. Catarrh. At first glance, it looked like a drab bed-room. A poor metal-framed bed with sagging mattress. Dresser with drawers like crooked teeth, all empty. The faded mirror reflected my conniving reflection. Hmm, I thought. The image looked like a woman who had thought there ought to be more here than meets the eye.

Sir Stone always reminded me; appearances can be deceiving.

There was a dreadful faded tapestry on the far wall, a stag being put out of its misery during some war. I barely noticed — no armoire or secret door here. I still couldn't cob onto how the door was locked from the inside. I rifled the small desk, too. Completely empty. I was flummoxed and disappointed. Drat. I heard my name being called and didn't want to be caught here when they sent out the search party. It must be time for my daily nap that they forced me to take. As I usually spent it eating sweets, especially shortbread and jam with coffee, and reading a scandalous novel Beau had brought me, I quite enjoyed nap time.

As I tiptoed out past the desk by the window, my foot caught on a floorboard, and with my new load of growing cargo aboard, I tilted off balance and fell. Though some days I felt as portly as cousin Clarence with all my rotund greatness, I was appreciative that it cushioned the blow, and I easily rolled to one side. The baby kicked, and I was flushed with such a stab of anxiety I lost my breath. "Shush, shush. There, there." I massaged my stomach. Strange.

I checked the imperfect floorboard upon which I had tripped, which was just next to the desk and not normally a place a visitor would tread.

I had to lay on my side. The floorboard was nearer the desk and adjacent to the baseboard and seemed a little off. Shorter or perhaps darker in color? Who's to say? When it's right, it's right, and when it's wrong, it's wrong — Sir Stone, circa my old life.

Using the prong of a sharp key, I fitted it in the slightly loosened crevice and lifted the plank right up.

I was heartsick when I realized the hole contained nothing but the skeleton of a mouse. As I prefer dried-up bones to the rotting carcasses of voles I sometimes used to accidentally step on behind the tavern, I did not even bother to shriek. But then I thought, How did a mouse find its way there?

I pried all around and finally worked the board all the way up. Empty. Nothing else. Sweet Jesus. Then why had this damn room even been locked? And from the inside? Tomorrow. I would return to that room. The baby made my skin prickle, and I knew there was something there.

"Brandy!" The calls were getting closer; they must have heard my fall. I'd have to come back.

I hurried out of the room, locked the door from the outside as I had found it, but now I kept the key. I wiped my soiled hands on my dress and sped down the stairs toward my room.

"Where have you been?" Atsuko asked me. Her sharp eyes detected a smudge on my cheek and unraveled hair off to one side. "Did you fall? I heard a thump."

I shook my head. "No, a footstool overturned. That must be what you heard."

"Where were you?" Mrs. Catarrh asked. She couldn't see worth a damn, but she could smell when something was up.

"I like to explore Mondragon. It is such a beautiful house with such history. Did you know the portraits hanging by the west wing are Elliot's long-lost ancestors?" I giggled. "They give me the creeps. It's as if their eyes can actually see me and don't like what they see at all." As that was true, I was able to shiver. Convincingly, I hoped.

They ushered me into my room and were followed by Alys and my treats. My baby kicked and moved and caused the usual chaos, and the only things wounded were my pride and buttocks.

I had to wait three agonizing days to return to the locked room. No matter. I explored every inch and found nothing. Elliot knew better than to confront me, but those nosy busybodies told him every little thing I did. The whole household conspired to watch me, entertain me, feed me, walk with me and keep me under surveillance. Did I complain? Not one little bit.

Chapter 22

During the heat of the summer, we would have lovely picnics right in the yard of Mondragon. A pond in the background. Glasses of lemonade. I had never even known of such a thing and drank so much I earned sores in my mouth. It was worth it. One afternoon, as we supped in the cool shade of a towering tree over our table, rugs on the grass around us, we were all together. Elliot was reading some history, which I secretly loved, as it was more exciting than my scandalous novel, as entertaining as that was. Beau was interrupting with dramatic asides: "and then — Julius Caesar, this general, dictator of Rome, conqueror of half the known world, falls hook, line, and sinker for this sallow-faced, hook-nosed girl."

I sat forward. "What do you think she looked like? Cleopatra?" I loved that name. I said it several times for emphasis. He showed me the book that had a drawing of Julius Caesar.

Beau shrugged. "No one knows for sure, but there are tales of her beady-eyed, harsh looks." I'm sure it's a stain on my soul that makes me so pleased to hear that.

"Now, Beau," Elliot said. "History also points out that perhaps she wanted her image to be more aggressive, as she was the ruler of Egypt and wanted to be taken seriously."

"I quite think killing her two brothers, one of whom she was married to, and then also murdering her sister, could give one pause as to one's dead serious nature."

"But she was ugly?" I couldn't get over it.

"As sin, they say," Beau went on. "But, apparently quite divine in," he cleared his throat, "sexual congress. And ol' JC had a taste for the exotic. She was a far cry from any of his Roman mistresses, who were very fair. The only thing they had in common was their names, all ended in the letter A."

I laughed at that. "And she outsmarted all of the men?"

Beau nodded. "She always had a backup plan and was able to successfully pivot from each obstacle. All the way to the end." That Cleopatra sounded like my kind of woman. "This great general was simply infatuated with her. He tried to bring her to Rome, but they were having none of it. He even had a gilded statue of her made for some temple. Rumor has it she reciprocated with a statue of him, but no one knows what happened to that. It was millennia ago, anyway."

"Most scholars think Caesar's statue was likely stolen after his death and sunk on some ship, forever lost to humanity." Elliot smiled at me. "Give me those poor pumpkins."

With my eyes closed, I nodded. Alys's sister, Malys or Calys (for some reason, I had taken against her and never bothered to learn her name), had brought a footstool for my swollen feet, and Elliot slid off my slippers and massaged my feet in his lap. Alys had even sent out a fresh batch of strawberry scones for me.

"They're not all for you, Lady Pig," Beau said as he snatched two off of the platter.

"They most certainly are, "I said as I swiped at the purloined pastries. "They are for the lord and heir of this barn. He's a growing lad and needs everything we can give him. Don't you want a healthy baby?"

"Godson," Elliot said.

"Yes. Of course," I said. "You will be the godfather, won't you, Beau?" For once, the sarcasm was missing from Beau's eyes. It was a most bittersweet look that he chased away at once with an honest smile for Elliot and me.

'Twas a weird triangle, I'll grant you that. But, Lord, how we can adapt. I occasionally felt a twinge of regret and pang of pain, remembering my tender-hearted crush on Beau. Yet I only had to see him with Elliot, and the way they were together, to yearn not for Beau, but for my version of a beau, who would look at me like he looked at Elliot. And Elliot looked at him.

I have no intention of ever loving someone more than they love me. I would be the Cleopatra of any relationship. Survival of the fittest. Some bloke name of Chuckles Darwin had taught me that one time during a layover he had at our fine establishment when his carriage wheel broke an axle. (That wasn't really his name, but it was what I called him to try to cheer up his dour visage.)

So it was with some relief that Elliot, Beau, and I were forsworn friends bonded by the secret of a lifetime. We had settled into a friendship such as I had never known before, a teasing affair with affection not meant to cut and hurt. Took a little education on my part, that last bit. That there were consequences to my misbehavior had never occurred to me.

I would join in the repartee with the cleverest, meanest thing I could think on.

At first, with great patience, they would chastise me and guide me to perhaps a pithier way of saying some barb. If I didn't listen, they would flat-out ignore me. That, I could not bear. Gradually, I believe, I learned the finer points of friendship.

I heard the carriage first. I swear this baby had given me powers beyond belief. I could smell a spoiled glass of milk from three rooms away. I had forbidden Elliot and Beau from wearing any cologne. Old lady Mrs. Catarrh and her decaying, unwashed rotting sweat, for some odd reason, smelled of reassurance. Herbs were good. Cheese was bad. Dear God, woe be unto the head of Mrs. Farfuddle for daring to serve me clotted cream, which smelled of RayRay's unwashed feet. I could tolerate lavender, rosemary — the smell, not the taste, and, oddly, craved potatoes and pancakes.

"Who could that be?" I asked.

"Oh, no," I heard Elliot say. We stood and made our way to the entrance. With prescience, I bid goodbye to our afternoon idyll. Beau departed.

We approached to see Elliot's father exit the carriage. Bad. Followed by his mother. Very bad. Followed by Cousin Clarence, of all people. Fucking nightmare.

"Well, welcome all. To what do we owe the honor?"

"My boy, my boy," Elliot's father clapped him on the back as he eyed me. "Well done, yes. Well done."

Lady P, par excellence, stated it baldly. "We came to see this breeding miracle for ourselves."

"Mother. She's not a horse."

She galloped toward me and slid her hands over my belly. I was torn. I half recoiled but then thought better, and arched my back and proudly stuck out the little lord for her groping. Hot on her heels was Cousin Grabby-Hands.

I pointed at him. "Not a shot."

He shrugged, an "I tried."

Lady P carried on with my undercarriage discovery. "How are you feeling? Is he moving? What intervals? Are you sleeping? Has the doctor been retained? Have you morning sickness?" She peered at me. "You look..." She paused.

"Beautiful?" I supplied. "Fertile? Glowing? I'll settle for lovely."

"Well," she said. "You look well. When? When can we expect him?"

Elliot stepped in. "The doctor anticipates another three months. A Yuletide baby. Wouldn't that be lovely?"

"I don't care when he comes, just the fact that he is coming." She stepped even closer to me and squeezed my right breast. And I let her.

"You surely are not planning to play nursemaid to this child. Have you found a suitable wet nurse?"

As I had never even considered the feed or care of a squalling brat, I haughtily agreed with her. "Of course not. What do you take me for, a cow?"

Cousin Clarence coughed. The oaf.

"Well," he said. "Fair play. It appears you are about to secure the estate." He shook Elliot's hand quite fiercely, if Elliot's grimace was anything to go by.

"How long are you staying?"

"For the night," his father said. "I trust we are welcome?"

"Of course, of course." Elliot turned to me and gave me his arm. "Shall we, my dear? Let's go inform the staff of our visitors."

I hid my snort. The staff. They all knew the drill, though, and rose to the occasion. By the time we went inside, Atsuko, acting as housekeeper, had even donned an apron. She feigned ignorance that she couldn't speak English and was a font of overheard information.

RayRay, in an outlandish purple velvet livery, directed the coachman and horses to the stable. Gordy, in a black suit with gray waistcoat, was most transformed. His usual presence—short, stout, with his large gleaming dome, aspired to a pirate earring and a tattoo of a mermaid. In his formal attire, he scrubbed up well, though he acted exactly the same; quiet, reassuring, logical.

We put the interlopers in the East wing, far from all of us. I flashed Atsuko four fingers, which meant my room, 4:00 that afternoon. Elliot stopped by the kitchen with me to handle Mrs. Farfuddle, who wailed then pretended to faint.

I did her one better and grabbed at my belly, and moaned.

"Sorry, madame. Sorry. What shall I do?" she asked. "We've no extra bread baked, I've only a dozen or so eggs, and the only meat on hand is rashers for tomorrow's breakfast."

"Elliot? Are the runner beans harvested? And what about those mushrooms? Get Alys down here. We'll have her start baking bread and a pie crust. Beau told me about quiche, a French favorite of your mother's. I've thyme, basil, and the secret; nutmeg. Go, go." I clapped my hands at the paralyzed Mrs. Farfuddle. "Go out in the garden, refresh yourself." We really must let her dig in the dirt with Elliot. Alys would serve as cook quite well.

"Darling." Elliot took my hands. "You're the dearest friend. Thank you."

"Husband," I said, as I squeezed his hands back. "This family sticks together."

We rendezvoused in my room at four on the dot. Atsuko gave the update. "Lady P and your father can't quite believe their good fortune," she reported. "They are absolutely giddy with joy. Lady P says she's never seen a more handsome pregnant wench than you, Brandy. Lord P says he had no idea you had it in you, Elliot."

Elliot glanced at Beau. "That makes two of us." He paced with his hands behind his back. "They are counting their chickens before they are hatched," Elliot said. "But no matter. If all goes well, I shall be happy to pay them an allowance to stay far, far from here." He stopped. "And Cousin Clarence?"

"He gripes when there's none to hear him and breaks wind when there is." Atsuko's eyes sparkled. "I've started him well on his way. There is a full decanter of Scotch. Well, most likely far from full by now. He cursed your good name to the heavens. Kicked the chair, hurt his toe, said he'd bring his own doctor to validate any birth, and that a goddamn prancing prat could surely only manage to produce a girl."

I clapped my hands. "Focus. Let's get through this night — step by step. Elliot, stop biting your nails. It's a good thing they're here." I rubbed my belly. "They see the proof. You are married. We are having the heir. Let's get through dinner, and they'll be on their way in the morning, no?"

"I just have a bad feeling about the ill Clarence can get up to. You don't know him."

"I do know him. He's a sanctimonious bully. Who doesn't deserve this estate. And we're doing everything we can to prevent that." I turned to Gordy. "Gordy, got the goods?" He nodded with the solemnity of a great majordomo, which Beau used to call him when he rubbed his bald head until Gordy put a stop to it.

"I'll begin serving wine in the parlor in fifteen minutes. I have a whole case of the red put by for dinner. Brandy for after."

"Keep the drink flowing, and we'll delay dinner," I said. "It's the best way. Beau, I think you will be fine if you show up through the front door. Lead as many congratulatory toasts as you like."

"Challenge accepted."

"Hopefully, we can shuffle them off to bed by ten." Elliot rubbed his temples.

Atsuko helped me into one of my tightest gowns, a pale yellow gown, not exactly fitting for a cool September eve, which allowed for no mistake that I was carrying a baby. My breasts strained the fabric, and Atsuko suggested that I not wear the lace fichu collar. "Perfect." I shimmied my shoulders at my reflection. "This is for you, Cousin Clarence."

Atsuko left, and I tarried until I could no longer. Time to face the music. Unfortunately, I couldn't have timed it more imperfectly. I heard Cousin Clarence and his unctuous bonhomie echo down the hall. I waited as he met me, and I held out my arm and allowed him to escort me down the stairs. I smiled, aping Lady P as best I could. The man reeked. He was the unsteady one on this journey, I remember thinking. We had only taken half a dozen steps or so down when he bowed his head, oh so graciously, and stuck out his clodhopper foot and nearly tripped me. I wobbled but caught the banister in the nick of time. The false fuck at my side grabbed my elbow and was so solicitous I nearly questioned my own tale of the event. But no. His watery, red-veined eyes watched me ever so closely.

"Pray, take good care of yourself, ma'am."

"You can take your ma'am and cram your damn well wishes where your back meets your crack," I began. I caught myself. I was a lady, now. I held my head high and sniffed. Then wafted my hand under my nose as if I had smelled something bad. Which I had. I wasn't going to tattle, though, or tell Elliot or Beau. I fight my own battles. Besides, to what end? Cousin Clarence would merely deny it.

I heaved his arm off mine and continued down by myself, holding the rail securely.

My pulse galloped. I carefully guided my steps. At the landing, I chuckled, wished for a moment Lady P had caught me out at that, and wondered if she would be proud. No, that will never happen. I glanced back at the porcine prick, and the hatred I saw there gave me pause. Danger. I'd seen the daggers of hate before, of course, in the trash heap of humanity that lugged itself out and about to drown its sorrows back in the tavern at the port. Back then, I didn't have to be a Sally Seer to predict who would be dead before long. But now, this time, the lethal lance was pointed at me. Even the baby felt his foul intent. "Shush, shush. There, there." I rubbed my belly. The motion earned a sneer from Cousin Clarence. Was I deliberately taunting him? You know me. Perhaps.

The oaf brushed by me as he had a table of food to raid and a date with the liquor Gordy had put by. Cousin Clarence ate like the new threshing machine Elliot was developing and spewed crumbs to rival a pile of shavings sanded off a rough piece of wood.

The quiche met even Lady P's standards. That, and the wine, and dare I think her approaching grandchild made her nostalgic?

"Once your son is born," she said to Elliot as she dabbed her mouth with her napkin. I leaned forward, curious as to her words. Would she praise me? Notice my improvements? Thank me for my role in saving her son and her family's in-heritance? She continued, "Once the child comes," she dismissed me with a flick of her fingernails, "I trust we can expect a sizable stipend for our allowance?" The fat cow wanted new dresses.

Dinner was interminable. Dear Lord, how much can these people drink? Gordy flashed me his hand. Either they had drunk five bottles of wine, or there were only five left. No matter. I was tired. I was finished. I had performed admi-rably. I showed up with my fertile belly, and that's all that was expected of me. Lady P seemed to be at war with herself. She wanted to take me down a peg, but as I did not rise to her bait, I suspect it wasn't as satisfying. That, and she was torn with the idea that her son Elliot had finally done something of which they ap-proved: married and sired an heir.

I excused myself. The gentlemen rose, and all bid me good night. I was going upstairs, not down, and thought myself safe. I smelled him, his rancid sweat hot on my heels. He had the audacity to try to trip me earlier, make no mistake. How foolish I had been for not denouncing him. My breath quickened. "Elliot! Elliot!" I called with a quiver in my voice. He couldn't hear me. No one could hear me, and I didn't want to take a chance to confront Cousin Clarence, only to be laughed at. Was I seeing foolishness because all my brain cells had become clogged up at my midsection? He wouldn't dare harm me. Would he? I hastened up the stairs. There was no time to dive into the linen closet. I swung a sharp right corner and raced ahead. Unfortunately, my only option was that nearly empty room that I had found earlier, the one that had been locked from the inside.

I knew all of the rooms and all of their secrets, or so I thought. I opened the door and swiftly closed it. Too big to fit under the desk or hide beside the wobbly chest of drawers, which was my only other option. In an instant, I raced for the tapestry. The light was very dim, but what did I think I was going to do, blend into the scenery, bulging belly notwithstanding? As I swished behind its dusty drape, my hand swiped against the wall, and I felt a faint hairline crack outlined in the plaster. My hands patted and pawed at the wall. A portion knocked hollow. I slid a fingernail in the crack and felt a slight give. It was a panel. I heard his footsteps. He wasn't even bothering to be quiet. Fuck me.

I worked the piece to the right, the tapestry falling over my head. The opening was waist-high. Jesus. I turned to my right and heaved my hip up as best I could. I drew my legs up and over, letting my feet dangle into the dark opening. I shifted there, then pointed my toes to touch the floor below inside the space. I appeared to be on a ledge of some sort. There was very little room. I turned back around to face the opening, placed my hands flat on the panel, and slid it into place, hoping the tapestry hung undisturbed. The door to the room opened just as I lost my balance. I clamped my hands over my mouth as my unwieldy body, off-balance, tilted backward, off what was indeed nothing more than a ledge.

In the pitch dark, I was in free-fall down, down, down. Though it was over in seconds, it must have been a drop of over thirty feet. Come now. Surely you don't believe that. There are tragedies that call for some exaggeration. I flipped arse over heels and landed flat on my back on a scratchy velvet cushion of some sort. My baby felt as if he, too, had done a somersault. "Oh, baby." The scream I had swallowed churned up all sorts of bile. I had never been sick with this pregnancy, as I'd heard tell from every maven out there, bilious pukes for months on end. Still, at that moment, alone, in the pitch black, in the bottom of some unknown pit, I wanted to spew. I was dizzy, and all my tears had fled in fear. I sat there and tried to quiet my breath. I heard knocking and stomping from above and wondered if I had just sealed my doom. I listened to the stomps retreat and the door to the room above slam shut. I let out a huge breath. I would have said a prayer of thanks, but one, all I could think of was to thank Cousin Clarence for being so stupid, and two, I still had to get out of there.

I rubbed my belly, and the imp inside gave a couple of kicks of displeasure.

I stood up gingerly, got a bump on my noggin for my efforts, and used my hands to try to figure out which end was up and which way was out. I had fallen a distance not even as tall as I, yet it was fearsome. I scuffled around and tried to climb back up. I had no purchase on the plaster walls, and I would have had to be some sort of strongman to hoist myself back up to the ledge, right below the opening to the panel. I tried for a while, and all I got for my attempts were scraped knuckles and heartburn. (Lady Catarrh tried to tell me heartburn meant the baby had hair. I hoped she was right because I pitied babies without hair. How could a mother love one of those?) I tried the walls on all four sides of my catacomb. (Why did I think of that word?) I mean, I smoothed my hands up and around, feeling for an escape route.

Sir Stone believed there was always a path not considered. I liked to think perhaps he was urging me to never give up.

Nothing above me would gain my freedom. I scooted the velvet cushion off to the side and worked at the floorboard beneath me. I felt a little give in the top right corner and pushed myself back so I could slide it free if it was going to budge. It moved. I worked it back and forth until I could dangle my legs. I did not know what was below me. I took off a shoe and dropped it. I heard it hit the floor; it did not appear to be of a great distance. My stomach growled painfully. Watching Cousin Clarence at the table would ruin anyone's appetite. That, and the fact that once I learned I was having a baby chick of my own, the eggs that had been put to good use to produce a tempting quiche for our unwanted guests' dinner, quite simply lost their appeal. The baby kicked. I'd be damned if I starved in there.

I braced my hands behind me, and my fingertip nudged something. That's what I screamed at? I calmed myself and took my other shoe to poke at the object. I put my shoe back on and felt back in the corner. It was a metal box, the size of

Elliot's huge botany encyclopedia. Nearly as heavy, too. It was locked, and in the dark, in my predicament, I couldn't force the lid open. I tossed it down below, after my shoe. (I was filled with terror, not deplete of brains. There could be something good in there.)

I slid lower until I could no longer hold my weight, a great distance nearly the length of my pinkie, and I dropped. I landed on my feet, but my knees hit the ground and did not thank the extra weight I had just visited upon them. I was in a pitch-black hallway. I put on my shoe, picked up the box, and sidled along. My breath came in pants, and I tried not to picture someone eventually finding my bony skeleton, held together by nothing more than the sins for which I'd yet to atone. Perhaps I'd haunt whoever had the misfortune to disturb me.

Boohoo, I chided myself. Onward, Sir Stone would say.

My hand hit an indent on the wall. I knew exactly where I was. I hightailed it down the secret passage to my lair. (The personal pronoun was in great use by me, who has never owned a thing and once claimed a rock as her family.) My hand trailed along the wall until finally, the door appeared — hello, hello, hello. It was my secret sanctuary. I could and did recognize the latch in the dark. In that room, my personal respite, my heart slowed its beats, my breath lulled as if it was reciting a nursery rhyme. "Three blind mice, three blind mice." I hummed. I would have to learn better tunes for the baby.

Of course, I had candles and matches inside, water, a jug of brandy, and a tin of shortbread cookies. It would be nice to visit my treasures. They always soothed me. I lit the candelabra, took a slug of brandy, and eased myself on the bed. Baby seemed not too upset with me. I searched among my cache and came up with one seed pearl hatpin. I worked it into the latch of the box I had just carried with me on this treacherous sojourn, to no avail. I went for the jeweled letter opener-slash-dagger, fitted it in between the joint of the box, and popped up the lid.

There was a black crusted bag enclosed inside, dusty and molded. So help me, if there were human bones in there, like relics from some improper miss back in the day who buried her baby, I would scream bloody murder. I pulled it out.

Heavier than a bag of bones, that was a good sign. I opened the bag on the desk and tilted it to one side. Holy Mother of God! It was a pirate's booty. A king's ransom. And my backup plan. The treasure trove inside contained a pearl necklace with big creamy pearls the size of eyeballs. It's hard to be poetic when you are that excited. Perhaps I overestimate when there is not any need. I will amend my tale to say the pearls were the size of blueberries during an especially good season.

Gold bracelets, heavy gold chains with emeralds, rubies, and sapphires. A yellowed diamond necklace that gave me the heebie-jeebies, as if its owner had come to an untimely end. It was hideous, something a blind great-grandmother might wear on All Hallow's Eve to scare small children. It was heavy and must have been worth a fortune. I spread it out in front of me to try to catch the design. It minded me of a spider web of bones. I shivered. I will never understand rich folks. I shoved it aside and examined the rest of the items in the bag. Diamond earrings. Jewel-studded hair combs. Ornate, heavy designs from an era gone by. Gold coins! I scooped my hands in the riches before me and let them spill through my fingers. The entire cache weighed what I expected my baby would upon birth.

"Fuck you, Cousin Clarence, and the horse you rode in on."

Chapter 23

I carefully stowed the haul back in the moldering black bag, returned it to its box, and worked it underneath the shelf. I would have to find a better spot for it later. I admired the stash of items I had amassed on the shelves and enjoyed polishing and rearranging them. It was so dim, and I didn't have much time, but glory be, what a feeling!

"Where are you always disappearing to, wife?" Elliot asked me at lunch the following day after his parents and Cousin Clarence, those blighters, had left. I had slept in and pled "baby" so I didn't have to play hostess or wish them well and be far, far away upon their departure. I bid adieu from my window with a rude gesture to the dust of their carriage and couldn't wait to sneak back down to my hidey-hole. I needed another peek at my riches. I am not a reliable narrator — please, let me finish — not a reliable narrator when it comes to monetary value. Numbers make my arse itch. I sent up a prayer. I figured I'd beckon that Mother Mary wench, thinking she would see me as a sister in suffering, and when I needed to abscond with the loot, that would be enough to see me by.

It did my heart good to visit my assets that afternoon, and my time there was well spent. The stash was more magnificent than I had hoped. This was it. The ultimate backup plan. I was well and truly safe for the first time in my life — and for the rest of my life. No matter what happened, I had the means to make sure I would be well taken care of, and so would my child. He would want for nothing. You have to make your own luck in this world, Sir Stone would have told me.

I knew I would soon be missed upstairs, and I didn't want to risk Elliot asking more questions, so I hurriedly tidied up. I blew a kiss to my newfound fortune, spun around, and headed back up the passage and out the linen closet door. Prayer, check. Superstition, check. Secret door locked, check. I only had time to wash my face and pat down my hair. My dresses were getting tighter by the day, but since everyone loved the vision of me in my fecundity, no one seemed to mind. I was so relieved Elliot's hideous family was gone; I looked forward to relaxing with my friends at dinner.

Was I looking my best? Perhaps not.

"Come," Elliot said. He pulled out my chair. "We have a guest."

My eyes bugged out of my head. It was the one-armed man. From long ago. Who had pulled me from the drink. And not saved my life. What was that mongrel doing at Mondragon?

I chose the haughty don't-give-a-damn route. It had been dark at the time when Sir Stone and I had set about closing up shop, and I was completely doused with frigid bilge water, causing the worst chills of my life. I had never gotten a clean look, but it had been enough to recognize him again. It's hard to forget a one-armed man; I just hoped he wouldn't remember me.

"What happened to your arm?" I said by way of greeting.

"Brandy." Elliot was appalled.

"Sorry. What happened to your arm, sir?"

"It's quite alright," he answered. His voice was deep and reassuring, and I imagined it would be quite lovely to fall asleep with that vibrato humming in my ear. (Just where did that thought come from?) I tugged my ear lobe.

"I lost it in the war."

I waved my hand dismissively.

"He's a hero, Brandy," Elliot said. "And he's a carpenter. I've hired him to build a cradle for the child. He also is going to refurbish the kitchen shelves and do repairs on the manor, as it's falling down around our heads."

"You hired a one-armed carpenter?"

"He's very talented. You will be impressed, I promise you," he assured me. Turning to the man, he said, "Sorry, One, she's with child and prone to forgetting her manners."

"She is lovely, and congratulations on your blessings."

"Your name is One?"

"Yes," he said, pronouncing it a little differently with a trace of an accent. One de la Fuerte. Since I was in a room full of jesters sporting nicknames, I thought he'd fit right in, though even I was a little taken aback at the crudeness of his moniker.

"I was born in Spain, but my family moved here when I was a child. In their old age, my parents have returned to the warmth of their homeland. My father taught me how to build, and I love working with wood and creating beautiful things. Beautiful pieces deserve to find a beautiful place in chaos."

Why was I so against him? Because he had seen me at my worst? Oh, yes, I had seen the look he had given me. He knew full well who I was. I would avoid him. I'm sure it would be easy enough. My history was no one's business. It was my secret.

"Well, One, how does a carpenter with one arm hammer," I asked, stretching out my right hand, "Nail," I said, stretching out the left.

"God, Brandy. Vicious. You put my mother, Lady P, to shame."

While I seethed, One came to the rescue again. "She is merely asking what most of you question." He offered me a glance. "We all have flaws, my lady. Some so deep they can't be seen. And thus, we all have to find ways to manage, correct?"

Elliot laughed and cheered. He raised his glass, as did all the others, including myself. "To One, you will fit right in! Welcome to Mondragon!"

"Yes, welcome," I mumbled and quaffed my ale. Mrs. Catarrh said the malted barley made for a strong and healthy boy.

One excused himself and nodded his head at all around. I didn't even favor him with a look. I had a second or third glass of ale.

When we heard the front door slam and One was well and truly gone, Elliot started up.

"Brandy. Come. What's wrong?"

I shrugged. "Nothing."

"Next, she'll be saying she's 'fine,' with heaves and hos, and poor little Miss Put-Upon pouts," Mrs. Catarrh said.

"I'd rather not have this conversation."

"Brandy, please. I beg you," Elliot kept at me.

"I find the one-armed bloke off-putting. That's all."

"You don't even know him. Give him a chance. I find him quite reassuring, actually."

"You would," I said.

"What a brat," Beau said. "Tell us what is really going on. Are you ill? Or just ill-tempered?"

"What kind of carpenter can he possibly be? He only has one arm. I've never heard of that and don't believe it's possible."

"Whoever heard of a slattern playing great lady? A sow's ear, as it were, playing silk purse." Three guesses as to who spoke that. RayRay, the rat.

"Don't you start with me, RayRay. Let he who is without secrets cast the first stone."

Oh, how those pagans laughed.

"So there is a secret," RayRay said.

I crossed my arms and refused to say a word.

"Brandy. I know you well enough by now. There has to be more. Do you know the fellow?" Elliot asked.

"Pfft." I waved my hand.

"You do, don't you? How? How did you come to meet?"

"Turn all your bugger eyes on yourselves." The whole table continued to stare at me. Blink, blink.

"Out with it," RayRay said.

"He once witnessed a rather unfortunate, shameful…"

RayRay broke in. "When you sucked off that haddock?"

Oh God, why had I ever told that story? I rubbed my belly, hoping like hell the child didn't have ears yet.

"He saw you diddle a goat?" RayRay guessed.

I took a drink. "Feck right off, RayRay. I was in dire straits."

"And," Elliot said.

"Alright then. He may have saved me once."

"Saved you?" RayRay asked. "Were you being ravished?" His eyes were wide.

"Clop it, RayRay. Any hint of perversion, and there we find you." Everyone laughed. Even RayRay. "No. It was a misunderstanding. That's all."

"What was a misunderstanding? The fact that One saved you, or the fact that you needed saving?" Beau said.

"Blessed Jesu. He saved me. Happy? From, you know." I couldn't say it.

Everyone was leaning forward. Straining to unravel the mystery.

"It's a tale as old as time, you imbeciles."

"Prostitution." There went RayRay.

"No, arse. Not that old tale. The other one." Bickering commenced.

"You tried to kill your brother and steal his birthright?"

"A whale swallowed you?"

"Heathens. The lot of you."

Atsuko bowed her head and stared up at me with those eyes of hers. I narrowed my own eyes at her. "You could be the dumbest varmint in the land, yet you always look as if you have all the answers," I said. "What's your guess?"

"Hara-kiri."

"As I don't speak a lick of Japanish, I'll just say you're right." She usually did have all the answers.

"Brandy. Don't be embarrassed," Elliot said. "There's not a man-jack around this table who hasn't contemplated the same."

"Speak for yourself, lad," Lady Catarrh said.

"You were in the middle of it yourself, old woman, and had nearly completed the deed when we found you," RayRay said. "So, how'd you do it?" he asked. "Kitchen knife, I'd bet."

Gordy chimed in. "Nah, I bet it was the rat poison."

Elliot fingered his cravat. "Surely, not hanging?" he asked me.

I finally did what I should have done before things got so far. I grabbed my belly and ran from the table. "I hate you all."

Elliot called after me. "We are all living proof that things do get better if you allow."

"Then worse," Gordy said.

"Then better," Beau said. Then they all laughed.

"We'll just ask One," I heard RayRay say. Nothing is sacred.

Chapter 24

One had taken up residence in a small cottage set back a way from the manor. I would take my constitutional, as that miserable Mrs. Catarrh insisted. "You're looking like a beached whale; a walk will do you good. And blow the stink off you," she said. I often found my feet tramping in his direction.

He would wave his hand in greeting then carry on with his carving or hammering and nailing, as carpenters do. I don't know what I found so intriguing, the shavings of wood curling up and off a plank or the great indentations of art discovered beneath the surface. We rarely spoke. I loved the smell of fresh wood being cut, and One's quick, confident motions soothed me.

He sometimes joined us at dinner and proved to be a lovely buffer amid friends grown too close. After having heard the same stories too many times, I'll admit it was nice to hear a new voice. It wasn't I that asked the questions, but I admit that I listened carefully to his answers.

"Hello, Brandy," RayRay snapped his fingers under my nose. "Perhaps you're painting a portrait of One; you've been staring at him so hard."

"Shove off, RayRay. Perhaps you'd like to feel my pointy shoe shoved up your…"

"Brandy," Elliot said. "RayRay. Please, I beg you."

"Well, if Brandy could be kind for more than two hours in a row, I'd eat my feather."

"Oh, the one Mrs. Farfuddle left in the chicken?" Gordy pulled out a shriveled bit of gristle from his mouth.

"Just a bit of good fun," Beau said to the new member of our crew. "We squabble like a nice, normal family. Now you're in the thick of it, eh, One?"

One smiled and continued eating. "I'm grateful to join you all." He looked at me when he said the word *all*.

"Seriously, Brandy." RayRay wouldn't let it go. "You speak fine, most times these days, still have a bit of a lope to your stride — but that could be from the babe, what do I know — but your tongue could tear the stripe off a man. Ladies don't do that. Two hours. I bet you that you can't hold your tongue and be kind for two hours straight."

"Elliot." I turned to him for support. "Stop buttering that roll and look at me."

"Well, Brandy. You are doing very well in your lessons. However, it would not be amiss to add a touch, just a touch," he held up his lacy arm and pointed his finger, "of gentleness to your repertoire."

"Gentleness?" I banged my hand so hard on the table a piece of bread flopped out of Atsuko's mouth. "With you lot? I can hold my own, and you well know it. Yet you all insist on cutting me down every time I turn around. Brandy," I mimicked Mrs. Catarrh's creaking pipes, "do you really need that biscuit?"

"Well, to be fair, dear," Mrs. Catarrh said, "it's never really just the one biscuit now, is it?"

"I am having a baby!"

"Baby what?" RayRay said, his eyes dancing. "Here, Bossy, Bossy."

"Elliot." I turned to my husband for help.

RayRay wasn't finished. "Beg pardon, Lady Heifer-Mondragon."

I wanted to cry; I was that mortified.

As a significant amount of wine had been drunk, one by one, the laughter began to hiccup around the table, as catching as the plague. When I saw One cover his mouth to hide a smile, something inside me snapped.

"The lot of you can't be kind or gentle for an hour!" I pushed back from my chair and stomped my foot, but Elliot grabbed my arm. I shook him off. "Stop laughing."

I made to run from the room, but One stood in my way.

"You are right, Miss. We are all sorry. I see how much everyone feels their best selves here, a family in its own right. And like families, too much familiarity can be both a blessing and a curse. Though I am new here, I can see that RayRay adores you," he said. I could barely stand the burn of his brown eyes.

"RayRay adores the mirror." I looked back at the table. "Oh, hoot and holler away, you bunch of hypocrites." They obliged.

"Everyone adores you," One added. "This is their way of showing it." By then, Elliot and Beau came to me, each with an arm slung around me.

"It's true, you know," Beau said. He popped a kiss upon my head. "We love you, and you love us."

"Admit it," Elliot said.

"Not RayRay."

RayRay raced around the table. "Brandy, you're one of my favorite people in the world. Surely you know that. You give as good as you get."

"Better. I give better than I get."

"All hail, fair Brandy," he genuflected.

"Get up."

"Enough, you two."

"Declares the lord and master," I said.

"That's it. Brandy, you are my wife. And as such, everyone, everyone," he glared at RayRay, "will treat you with the respect due to your station."

I fear my smile must have been ugly, yet I was that proud of it. RayRay looked like a kicked puppy. I all but shimmied at him in my victory. Who was I but a dirty street urchin, literally scraped off the spit-infested floor of a wormy tavern, and the edict was proclaimed. Everyone had to be nice to me.

"And RayRay has to stop whistling." Elliot clocked his brow but acceded to my wishes.

Chapter 25

I flounced away, triumphant. Life is good. You do anticipate what happened, right? Those clever buggers did as they were told. "Yes, please. Of course, miss. I'm sorry, my lady." Though that little fecker, RayRay would whisper-whistle at me, some doom and gloom ditty that quite set my nerves aflame.

A few days later, after Elliot hollered at RayRay to desist, he began exaggerating his s-sounds, like a small child missing his front teeth. "Sss-certainly, misstresss. Sssshall I esscort you upsstairs?" Maddening.

I tried to break Atsuko and engage in a bit of tittle-tattle. "RayRay was surely taken down a peg or two, no?" Her fecking gorgeous face remained impassive as she helped me dress one morning.

Even Mrs. Catarrh, that battle-axe, had it in for me. She literally killed me with kindness. Of course, not literally, you buffoon, but her crusty tone quivered with etiquette. "Oh, but of course, your most high and mighty Lady Pfeiffer-Mondragon. We've saved the most savory meat pies for you and your heir-carrying self. Lord, you are feeding that babe so well; you are nearly unrecognizable with the layers of protection you provide for him." Seeing the look on my face, she continued. "Oh, there dear, you don't look like you've gained more than a stone since yesterday."

I ran, as fast as my corpulent legs could carry me, to seek out Elliot. "That old witch said she saved the best meat pies for me," I said.

"How kind," Elliot said, rather tersely, if you ask me.

"No. It's how she said it. She said I was nearly unrecognizable with all this blubber."

"Brandy. Did Mrs. Catarrh really say you are covered in blubber?"

"Not in so many words, no. She called it a layer of protection."

"Well, that sounds kind and positive."

"She said, she said," I stopped so I could swallow. Dear Lord, was I going to cry? Oh, well, use 'em if you got 'em, Sir Stone never once said, but I let the tears fall as they may. "She said I didn't look like I've gained more than a stone since yesterday."

If I expected the so-called father of this baby to crumble in the face of my agony, and I did, I was sore disappointed. "Well, what are you trying to say? She said you didn't look like that."

"You all are conspiring against me. You're twisting my words. And you know how they are. Your friends."

"How are they, Brandy? We are all ceding to your demands. Your wish is our command."

I dragged myself, this ever-fattening baby that managed to pad my very soul yet suck my energy at the same time, don't ask me how, and my reddened eyes out of the room and down to dinner. I only went because, fuck me, again, I was starving.

Elliot followed along and took his place next to me. Mrs. Farfuddle served me a heaping plate of oily potatoes, a fistful of green beans — that was literal — her grimy fingers gathered them up then released them onto my plate. The main course was chicken or fish; trust me, not a body there could have correctly chosen. I ate and kept sniffing.

"Do you have a cold, Mrs. Pfeiffer-Mondragon?" RayRay asked.

I shook my head. Being a fine lady wasn't all it was cracked up to be. Woe is me. A few days of being treated like a pariah had nearly broken me. I would never be able to worm my way out of it. Apologies are not in my repertoire, and as miserable as I felt, I wasn't about to start throwing them about. My head was bowed low over my plate.

The clank and scrape of cutlery against the plates and the tick of the clock nearly drove me mad. Finally, Beau broke the silence. "Seventy percent sure it's fish."

"What's the over-under on chicken?" Elliot asked us. My lip quivered with a smile that had been lost.

"It's either that ancient rooster roasted beyond recognition or pollock from the pillock," I said. I was eager to gain a laugh. If you ask me, that was quite clever, referring to our esteemed cook as a stupid pillock, unable to recognize pollock pulled from the Atlantic. But I only heard the sound of breaths being held. I peeped up to find Mrs. Farfuddle standing in the doorway from the kitchen, her hands twisted in her apron. She fled.

"Not very kind, Lady," Beau said. He pursed his lips.

"I didn't mean it." I pushed back in my chair. "I didn't mean to hurt her feelings. You all joke about her food. She wasn't supposed to hear that."

Gordy leaned over to look at me. "Dig deep, miss. Best find that apology you've been storing up and go make amends."

I went after Mrs. Farfuddle and said the words. "I am sorry. In fact, ma'am, you are the first one I've ever said that to." I squeezed her doughy, dirty hands. "I'm not myself," I said. "I'm with child, I'm emotional, I say things I don't mean. This is all new to me, as you well know. I am indebted to your kindness and your efforts in this kitchen to feed me." I couldn't very well lie now, could I? I'm sure she did take great efforts; it wasn't her fault they rarely reached the level of slop for the hogs. "Shush, shush. There, there," I pulled out. She nodded and told me she'd bring me the first piece of rhubarb pie for dessert. I thanked her because butter and sugar go a long way with a generous hand, and at least I'd have the upper hand when it came to recognizing what it was.

Alys waylaid me as I dragged my feet back to the dining room. She pulled me into the butler's pantry. "Miss, don't be too hard on Fanny."

"Who's Fanny?"

"Mrs. Farfuddle."

I assumed a stern look as the serious mistress of the manor before I locked on to the information that Mrs. Farfuddle and her ample behind sported the moniker of Fanny. "Yes. Quite. I've, uh, apologized for any misunderstanding. I didn't mean it, you know?"

"She's not a bad one."

Little Alys, pleading her case. "What's going on here?"

"She's not a cook, miss."

"Alert the constable."

"But they needed a cook, you see, when the master found her. She was in a bad state. Her husband had passed, she had no children. Her daughter died as a little one. She had nowhere to turn. Master Elliot is such a good man; he took her in, and she said, well, that she was a good cook. But she loves her plants and herbs and landscaping, but it's not a fit job for a woman, now is it? No one would take on a woman for that. Right? So she had to stretch the truth a little. Something we've all done, I expect."

"The kitchen garden? She did that?" Alys nodded. "I'm impressed." I had been, too. It had a plethora of herbs, anything one would need for medicines, poultices. I made an elderberry concoction just last week for Mrs. Catarrh's cough. If you must know, it didn't help much, but she did seem to enjoy the whiskey I put into it.

The layout of the garden was quite pleasing, something I hadn't realized before. It was a large square patch, bordered with an outline of low hedges. The groupings were well-thought-out; herbs here, cabbages there, with a thoughtful pattern of different flowers blooming throughout the seasons. I'd been here for nearly three seasons and never knew quite why, but I loved going into that garden. I would talk to Elliot. He could perhaps use her help, too.

I slunk back to the dining room and finished my plate. I'm sure it was the pollock.

Finally, RayRay spoke. "Brandy, Brandy, if you're able, get those elbows off the table. This is not a horse's stable."

I looked down the table at RayRay. This could go one of two ways. But I was so grateful tears appeared in my eyes, once again. (This baby was going to drown me.) I glanced at One and quickly looked away lest it be commented on. "RayRay, for what do you pray?" I knew my eyes sparkled. "With those great feet of clay, who'd ever come to take you away?"

Then I bet him a shilling he couldn't guess the dessert.

After dessert (and I had pocketed my shilling), Elliot rose and held my hand. "Let's play cards. Though, we should have a wager on who can be kind the longest."

"Starting now," I said. "And I will win. I accept your mealy-mouthed, lickspittle, arse-kissing apology, RayRay."

"Brandy," Elliot said. But I had succeeded in making them laugh with me.

"Come, my sweet sister," RayRay said. He took my hand from Elliot and escorted me into the next room.

We played cards and set up One as judge and juror over the night as to whom could be the kindest the longest.

"I beat Atsuko, I beat Atsuko," I said as I performed a shimmy dance. Atsuko had called Beau a bore but pretended everyone misheard her. Beau, who could be a bore, had been cheating at cards and sneered as One called Atsuko out. One then eliminated Beau for that, then, of course, me, for dancing.

"How is that unkind?"

"Sit down, Brandy," RayRay said. "Right here next to me on the loser lounge." RayRay had been the first one out.

"Since we are all out, it is almost as boring as the story Beau told recounting his time in the military," I said, swashbuckling with an imaginary sword.

"Who wants to sit around watching Elliot walk on eggshells around Gordy and Mrs. Catarrh, for Christ's sake?" RayRay asked.

We created our own fun, taunting from the sidelines, as RayRay commented on the play. "Mrs. Catarrh coughed twice, discarded once," he said. "Gordy thanked her, picked up a card, scratched his dome, and Elliot may have farted."

Mrs. Catarrh claimed she had been the one to break wind but wondered how RayRay could discern anything from his own dubious odor. That left Gordy and Elliot.

"I've watched your peas grow faster, and with more enjoyment," I called out to Elliot from my seat on the sofa. I yawned hugely, and my friends — I had my friends back — joined in. Upon noticing our declining jeers, One declared them both winners and suggested we take ourselves off to bed. As we left the parlor, they all stopped before me in a small genuflect and pressed my hand. No, they didn't, because, what? Do you think this is a fairytale?

Chapter 26

If life was a fairytale, that one-armed carpenter, whom I'd taken great strides to ignore and avoid, would create a magic cradle for the new little lord and heir and then disappear. Poof. Not before he bestowed a handful of wishes: long-life, true and loyal friends. Riches. I meant to say riches first. I rubbed my belly — poor little mite. I didn't mean to curse him with a long life; perhaps I should have wished for an imaginary gift of an interesting life. But true and loyal friends, yes. For the first time, I felt grown up and downright maternal. Despite the fact that my tits ached, my ass was nearly as wide as Mrs. Farfuddle's, and I had a constellation of blemishes on my chin. "Looks like the Big Dipper," RayRay had told me at lunch.

Since One had been at lunch with us, I felt double-blasted. I accused RayRay of stealing my best gloves, and he countered with the fact that they were too large for him.

"And why do you call him One?" he asked, jerking his head down the table toward the carpenter.

"Because. That's his name." I held up one finger. "One." I shook my head at his ignorance.

RayRay practically had a feather hanging out of his mouth, what with his look of a cat that swallowed the crow. "Don't talk to me like I'm a child, Brandy. We're about the same age. Besides," he started to laugh, "you're dead wrong."

Let it be known, my husband, plus my former lover, and my first and best female friend Atsuko, her lover and my father-figure, Gordy, and the worst pick of the draw of a grandmother, Mrs. Catarrh, howled until they cried. Perhaps what stung worse was the retreating blob of Mrs. Farfuddle and her shaking shoulders.

Beau wiped at his eyes and sighed. He held up a hand to try to squelch the mob. "So, this whole time, you've been calling the one-armed carpenter One?"

"That's his name. That's what you told me. That's what he answers to."

Beau sucked in his lips. "Brandy, my dear girl. His name is Juan. Juan. He's Spanish. It's like John. But Juan. Not One." There they all went again.

My face felt as if it had been shoved over a boiling pot of stew. My throat puckered as if I had swallowed a hot pepper from that blasted stew. The carpenter intervened. "Please. I always enjoy Lady Pfeiffer-Mondragon and what she has to say, and I felt honored to be singled out as One. To be honest, it made me feel part of your tribe here at Mondragon Manor. And I invite you all to call me as such." Though said with a smile, the last part had the bite of his carpenter's chisel as he carved out his wish.

I was that mortified. It was only a sharp pinch from Beau on the tender underside of my arm that still bears the bruise, I'm sure, that changed my reckless course. I swallowed the sting of the burning pepper with a burp of humility, as a lady does. "Forgive me; my misunderstanding."

This lot. Can't get anything by them. That's why I needed to be extra careful to not pay any mind to that dang-blasted carpenter. They all accepted him rather too quickly for my tastes. I'd been here for more than half a year by now, and they were just starting to accept me as one of their own. And let's face it, you can bet One was never in his altogether with both Elliot and Beau. Although... you never know with those two.

Chapter 27

Most days, after lessons, before my nap, in between my scavenger hunts, my feet seemed to find the path that meandered to One's cottage. (You do realize that will be his appellation until the end of time? Everyone now called him One.) In case anyone asked, I used the excuse, "Oh, I wonder how One is coming on with the cradle?" Then I would pat my belly to remind them what this was really all about. No one ever asked. Though they did cut their eyes at each other every time I explained.

We rarely spoke, One and I. He worked outside, in front of the door to his cottage. I found solace in watching his strong, sure moves, the curl of strips of wood as they fell, and the smell of the fresh dust from the cut boards. He had an iron screw with metal plates that bit into and held the boards for him as he worked. The cradle took shape. Once in a while, he would explain how he set his vision which was always over-turned by the wood itself. "I'm merely the interpreter of this board," he said, running his hand over its smooth plank, "but it's the boss of me. It tells me how it wants to be used." He held out his hand for mine and placed my fingers over a brown knothole on the plank. "What do you see?"

"A mistake."

"Close your eyes. Now feel it." He guided my hand over the spot. That roughened imperfection, the smell of the cut wood, the warmth from his arm, and the feel of his hand on mine all conspired to create a magical spell.

"It feels like a good place to start," I amended. I opened my eyes. Our faces were so close that someone spying out the window from up at the manor would get the wrong impression.

He nodded. I patted the board and walked away. I rebuked myself as I headed back up the path to the manor. Why did I pat that board like that? Like it was a good dog or something. One must think I'm such a dunce. Why, oh why, did I care so much what he thought of me?

I'm not saying I'm a creature of habit, but a few days later, I showed up, and One had a newly-made chair set out for me, out front beside his endeavors. As little lord baby was making his presence known more by the day, my bulky form was grateful as One helped me take a seat. The chair, merely a chair, formed from wood, odds and ends if you looked at the mismatched colors and pieces, was a delight.

"Did you make this chair?" I asked.

He nodded but continued to smooth the plank he was working, which rested atop a trestle.

"It's nothing but wood, but it's the most comfortable chair I've ever parked my fancy in." That earned a rare smile.

"I took into account your frame, and the wood helped decide what may suit you."

"You made this for me?" I stood up and took a good look at the thing. It wasn't merely a slab of wood for the seat, I noticed; it was a delicately carved piece of wood, gently indented with a large heart shape, though rounded at the point of the heart. The backrest, made of four slats, was curved as well, as if bracing the small of my back to provide repose for my weary burden. The whole thing was polished as soft as silver, and I loved it. The top piece was rounded and felt as good as a hug across my shoulders when I sat in it. He lifted an eyebrow at the top piece. I turned and peered closely. In the very center was an elaborate script carving that looked like a flower, but upon inspection turned out to be the letter B.

As in, be still my heart. "Thank you," I told him. Then I ran as fast as a duck back to the manor.

Chapter 28

Money was tight, but food and drink were plentiful, and I was as grateful as I'd ever been. When I wasn't complaining.

"I am the size of a pickle barrel," I announced one evening as we gathered before dinner. Hoping for denials, all I got was Mrs. Catarrh agreeing, "Perhaps it's because you've eaten all the pickles."

Atsuko had just returned from visiting with the tenants. I just didn't have the steam to plod on down with her that day.

"The farmers think he's crazy," Atsuko said. "They say he's making some of them plant peas to make the soil better."

Elliot came in. "And so it will," he said. "Thank you, Atsuko. Please feel free to spread that news."

"Now you've done it," I told her. We shared a smile.

"The wives are all for it, and they'll not have much trouble convincing their husbands to take your methods to heart," she said.

Elliot waved his hands. "The peas are a simple cover for the topsoil and will loosen the dirt, which makes for better drainage. The more prepared we are to receive our seeds, the better the outcomes. Oh, so much can go wrong. That's why it's my mission to control the things we can. Farming isn't for the nervous Nellies. Would an artist paint on a dry and dusty canvas? We will have stronger, hardier plants, mark my words."

I was that proud of Elliot, not counting on his inheritance to make his way in the world but hoping a portion could be used to set him on his way. He worked tirelessly, and we all had our roles in supporting him and our household.

Christmas was just around the corner. Guess where I went shopping? Go on. Guess. My little lair! By then, I had toured the attics and disused rooms of the entire place, gleaning treasures. I stored my cache in my secret room and visited it like a grande dame in a shopping emporium. By then, my hidey-hole was quite comfortable. I had candles in a brass candelabra on the desk, alongside a crystal cut hurricane lamp. I had dragged a deep red velvet upholstered lady's chair down the hall and through the passage, no mean feat, but it wasn't that heavy. My storage shelf was fair to bursting. For Elliot and Beau, I had found several uniforms hanging in a dusty armoire off some unused south wing of the house. I cut off the gold buttons, polished them for all they were worth, and wrapped them, eight to a set for each.

Atsuko provided me with plain muslin cloth for their wrapping, but it was Mrs. Farfuddle — I never will be able to call her Fanny — who helped me with decorative sprigs of dried flowers tied with twine. She had dried lavender stalks and tight little dried Burgundy rosebuds, and they were that special.

I had gifts for everyone. For Atsuko, I found a lovely mirror and brush set in a tarnished silver that I was able to polish. It was with a pang I let that go, but then I reasoned it must be a good gift then, right? I gave Gordy some sort of naval medal on a ribbon to pin to his jacket. It was quite ornate, and I have no care for its history, but he seemed quite impressed. I gave Alys a small cameo, and Mrs. Farfuddle a box of cut-glass vases I had unearthed in the attic. I felt it would be uncharitable of me to get her a good bar of soap, nail file, and pumice stone for those fingernails of hers.

Feeling it would be hurtful of me to give Mrs. Catarrh an old, rusted spittoon I had unearthed in the barn, I instead chose a small beaded bag. Oh, how I coveted the darling piece. It had jet beads that swung from the bottom seam, and once I repaired the torn drawstring, it was as fashionable as I'd like to think it must have been when Mrs. Catarrh was a young woman, seventy or so years ago.

RayRay was the hardest, but I found a bolt of fabric in another corner of the attic. It was a thick brocade, not moth-eaten. Once I lugged it down, in the light of day, I saw that it had gold threads among the blues and reds in a pleasing fleurde-lis pattern and had many possibilities. With RayRay, who knew? He'd either turn it into pants or recover a chair. Perhaps both.

It was the first time I had ever given anyone a gift, ever. Don't believe the nonsense that it is better to give than receive, but it is better to give than receive a clout in the head, I suppose. They were all gobsmacked.

"Brandy. Where did you get all this stuff?" Elliot asked.

"None of us has money, and you've never even been to a shop," Beau added.

"We thank you so much for your generosity," Atsuko said.

"That's more like it," I said. "You're welcome. Ask me no questions; I'll tell you no lies."

"Brandy."

"Fine. I explored the manor and found them. None of you knew about these things. Nobody was using them. No one will miss them. And look how much you all will enjoy them."

Elliot and Beau both hugged me and kissed me atop my head. "You are too much."

I even got One a gift, just because it seemed perfect for him. It was an old-timey watch that Gordy was able to clean and repair. He let me watch him and hold the magnifying glass for him as he used a teeny-tiny tool to move the works inside and repair the winder device.

"Don't ask Gordy for the time, Brandy," RayRay said, "he'll tell you how a watch is made."

"Says the pot calling the kettle black," Gordy responded, not even looking up.

"Ah," One said when I shyly gave him my present. "The gift of time. I will treasure it forever." The look we exchanged. I only hope no one noticed.

My favorite gift was the cradle he made. It was an heirloom piece, a word I had never cared to think on before. For my son. I knew in my bones it was a boy. Mrs. Catarrh agreed with me, for once. "The prow of her ship leaves no room for doubt," she would say to anyone who cared to listen.

Made of mahogany, the reddish-brown wood of the cradle gleamed in the candlelight. My fingers followed the intricate pattern of leaves and flowers woven in the headboard. I was tongue-tied for once and continued to examine the cradle.

"To think, our baby, and his baby, and his baby's baby will all begin their journey in this," Elliot said. "What a lovely legacy to dream on." He shook One's hand and then enveloped him in a hug. "It is magnificent, One. We thank you." I nodded in agreement and couldn't seem to stop rocking it. I'd never played with dolls nor gave a care to imagine being a mother. There were never enough hours in the day to pretend to be misty-eyed over a squalling brat that needed to be fed and cleaned and cared for. The solitary path had been my lot, so please understand my befuddlement as I considered that very soon, a small person that I would be responsible for would be lodged inside this cradle. I rocked it again and again.

"Darling, are you alright? Let's not wear out the rocker just yet," Elliot told me. He peered into my face. "Brandy, you're a fine girl. What a good mother you will be." Damn, the man does have insight. I smiled and asked One if he could bring the cradle to my room.

I led the way and entered my room. He placed it over by the window. "But not too near," he said, "we don't want the *pequeño* to feel a draft."

"Thank you," I said brilliantly. Dear God. I was practically a professional when I flirted with my sailor, never at a loss for words. I was often asked to hush. Mostly by Elliot, and Beau, too. Don't think I didn't know they called me Lady Chatterbox behind my back, and the only time there were silences, they were of my own device, to punish them. Not that they'd notice. Clods. For the life of me, I could not summon a coherent thought to say to One.

I woke every morning, puffed, bloated, and convinced that that day would be the day. Atsuko, Mrs. Catarrh, and Mrs. Farfuddle conspired to help matters along. From chewing on ginger root to cold baths of Epsom salts, where Mrs. Catarrh violently assaulted my nipples and tried to scrub them with a hairbrush, which she said would trigger labor, no old wives' tale was dismissed. Foul-tasting hot teas and hot peppers from the garden were all employed, to no avail. Mrs. Catarrh actually tried to make a bee sting me. Nothing seemed to budge the little lord. He seemed to have taken residence over my entire body.

Not that I had much modesty, but all bets are off when you are mare to the heir. The doctor confirmed Mrs. Catarrh's opinion that his head was down low and ready to go. They made me walk, jump, fed me, starved me. Beau and Elliot took turns massaging my mound, and endearingly enough, talking to it. While everyone tried to be adults in the room and claimed they only cared for my and the babe's health, you can imagine the pitched tent of anxiety as the days careened toward Elliot's birthday. You know, when all bets are off, and he loses the farm if he doesn't have his heir in arms.

The day before Elliot's big day, after a hot toddy and a noddy to a little more toddy, I bundled up in my cape and took myself on a jaunt. My eyes teared in the cold wind, though who was I kidding? A gusher was about to spurt out of my eyes inside that stuffy house with all those hangdog faces looking at me as if they wanted to just rip that baby out of me. Of course, I ended up at One's, who had seen me coming. He opened his door and welcomed me inside, just the tonic I needed. If what I needed was to cry and carry on and have a hissy fit of historic proportions.

He removed my cloak and sat me before as warm a fire as I've ever felt. I'd never been inside his cottage before. It was as sparse and polished and comfortable a space as I'd ever seen. There was something soothing about a place with all white walls and clean corners. He had my chair before the fire. Honey-colored smooth floorboards were covered with colorful rag rugs. There was a small table and chair in the kitchen. A white vase, filled with sprigs of wild thyme and rosemary, posed in the middle of the table and seemed just right.

He pressed a handkerchief in my hands and knelt before me. I snuggled into his embrace. "Shush, shush. There, there."

I blew snot for days out of my nose. One was still at my side. "Say it again," I told him.

I felt his smile at my neck. "Shush, shush. There, there."

I turned my head and kissed him as if I was glugging hot chocolate on a cold morning. I couldn't believe my body, so misshapen, stretched beyond belief, wretched beyond comfort, could still crave anything this way. I hadn't, you know, since Beau, but all I wanted was One's hands on me. Well, hand.

His kiss was enough to make me reconsider the existence of God and his so-called miracles. My tits tingled, and I had a hard time catching my breath. Something was definitely happening.

"I need to lay down," I whispered between kisses. He guided us to his room. It, too, was a simple room, with only a bed, a chair, and a washstand. And something else I didn't notice at first. One stretched down the length of the bed beside me. He held me close. "I'm sorry about all that crying and carrying on. But this baby needs to come, now. Or all will be lost."

My heart broke at the thought of Elliot losing Mondragon Manor and the others losing their home. I had nebulous thoughts about absconding with my treasures in the dark of night before they turned on me and kicked me out. I didn't know how I'd make a go with the baby, but that fat little bag of jewels would go a long way toward helping me manage.

One stroked my hair, and I mirrored his touch. His black hair curled around my fingers. I smoothed my mouth against the rough rasp of his jawline. When I would have reached down toward his buckskin breeches, he stayed my hand then kissed my fingers. I pushed his hand down and helped move my skirts aside. I was filled with desire, without a whit of shame. I deserved a good time, after all I had been through, and all I was trying my best to do was ignore what I was about to go through. A small part of my conniving mind rationalized that fucking One was a much better way to go about getting this baby out, far better than the foul mare-urine-soaked poultices, nipple-abrading shenanigans, and cod liver oil potions Mrs. Catarrh and Atsuko had been forcing on me. Beau had even put me on a horse two days ago. And I let him.

One drew his hand back and tilted my chin. "Brandy. All will be well."

"I know," I said, rocking to get his muscled thigh between my legs.

He straightened his legs and rubbed my back, the baby huge between us. I rubbed my bodice against his chest. If you thought his thighs were sturdy as tree trunks, you should have seen his chest. I rolled over on my back. I wasn't going to beg. This was worse than when Elliot had refused me.

Then three things happened. First, One cradled my face and told me things in that deep voice of his that I will never forget. It's really none of your business, but for the first time in my life, someone told me they loved me.

Second, I believed him. It must be true love, something my soul recognized because my belly tightened in delicious anticipation. I sighed with regret because he was too much of a gentleman to enjoy the one sure-fire way I knew of showing him how much I loved him.

You may want to sit down when you hear what happened next. I rolled onto my back and turned my head. I couldn't believe my eyes. I propped up on my elbows for a better look and saw what I had missed upon entering his room. I squawked and sat straight up, my hand to my throat.

One had carved an intricate wooden pedestal, some three feet tall, which resided in the corner next to the window, that he could see from his bed. Atop the pedestal: none other than Sir Stone.

Chapter 29

"Oh." I rolled myself off the bed and went to him. My long-lost Sir Stone. He was stern of brow, and his disapproving granite profile, as ever, bore the barest hint of a smile. I placed my hands around his ears. "You've no idea how I've missed you so," I whispered. "I'm in such a pickle."

He acknowledged my situation, his stoic visage betraying no shock at my protuberant midsection, puffy face, and gargantuan tits bordering on the grotesque. He reminded me that when the going gets tough, the tough get going. And then I was set upon by a steel band of rigid, unforgiving pain as a tortuous force locked up my torso in its vice-like grip.

I gasped, and One was at my side. He appeared bashful, as if not knowing how I was going to react to his rescue of Sir Stone. I'd deal with that arse-hole move of his for not telling me later when I wasn't gripped with the terror that set my body to shaking.

"It's happening, Brandy," One said. He picked me up with his one arm and carried me in a surefooted sprint up to the manor. In between the birthing pangs, I counted my blessings. One, One. Two, Sir Stone. Three, Elliot's heir was going to arrive and save the day.

Elliot and Beau bumped into each other in their haste to ride for the doctor. They finally decided to send RayRay, and then went off to hide in the library with libations. Mrs. Catarrh and Atsuko exchanged some waterwitch look which I found I didn't care for. One carried me up to my room and deposited me on the bed. The women made him leave. And I? I did not go gently into that good night; oh no, not I. A mere scream could not do justice to my bellows, which ricocheted around the manor. I could only hope those two rotten bastards cowering in the library could hear me loud and clear.

Atsuko helped strip me naked. I was burning up, slick with sweat and fear. I knew I would never survive. I wondered at what point I would breathe my last. Atsuko, all-knowing as ever, saw right through me and encouraged me, "Breathe, Brandy, breathe. You're a fine girl. What a good mother you will be."

"Rest in between," advised that old crone, Mrs. Catarrh.

"There is no in-between," I spat out. I managed to gasp in a quick breath and exhale, "you fucking old withered wombless witch."

At some point, Elliot and Beau, behind my closed door, sounded in tears. "Is she well? Brandy? We love you."

We all had heard the clock chime midnight some time ago. "Happy birthday, you prickless twat!" I had screamed.

And from Beau. "Oh, my poor honey. Don't scream so, darling. We are here; we are here for you."

"Burn in Hades, both of you!" I crescendoed on an anguished scream. Even I, who had once taken pride in the bellowing power of my lungs, began to scare myself. And tire.

Finally, Mrs. Catarrh slapped my face silly. "Girl. Pipe down. You've got hours to go. Best save your strength." I glowered at her as I held my stinging cheek, but truth be told, she did manage to cut through my panic. I labored long and hard throughout that night, well into January third, Elliot's birthday. After a while, I deleted the ignominious memories that I had hoped to share with other women of my heroism and bravery, covered as they were in blood and guts and shit and pain. I just wanted the baby out. Surely it couldn't be much longer, the young, innocent me had thought. What kind of divine creator decided it was a good idea to force a treasure chest through a keyhole?

To their credit, Mrs. Catarrh and Atsuko were by my side and if you think to have any modesty in this life, try landing on your all fours, buck naked, sweat and fear roiling off your hide, while you try to shit out a Sir Stone-sized albatross of agony. At that moment, I hated the baby, I hated Elliot, I hated Beau. Oddly enough, had I free hand to tip my imaginary hat, I would have doffed it to both Mrs. Catarrh and Atsuko.

"What time is it?" I asked them. "I know you heard me." They pretended to be busy, massaging my abdomen and lower parts. "Sure, why not," I told Atsuko, who was more intimate with me than I had ever been with myself. Then I heard the chimes of the clock.

"Fuck me. Eleven o'clock? At night? Jesus, Mary, and Joseph." I collapsed on my back, knees up to my ears. I heard Beau and Elliot again outside my door. They had to have been beside themselves with less than an hour to meet their progeny, and with him, the trust in the estate.

"Brandy. What's going on? Are you well, darling girl?"

"NO! GO AWAY!" I shouted.

"Do you need the doctor? He's below, awaiting to attend you."

"No!" Atsuko, Mrs. Catarrh, and I all yelled. We were in this together, and Mrs. Catarrh had never trusted the man.

I would have cried, but I just didn't have the juice for it. I wasn't going to make it. Maybe I could die before I let everyone down. I just hoped the baby would live. Perhaps they could still make it work. "Goodbye. I'm dying now." I smiled weakly at Atsuko.

"Nonsense," Mrs. Catarrh said.

Friends, I have plenty more unimaginable feats of atrocities, which I shall spare you. But heed my warning. Do not ever let yourself get with child. It's not worth it. There's plenty of lady folk who won't read this; let them have all the babies. When your man points his one-eyed snake in your direction, remember there is a multitude of other ways to pleasure him and yourself. I beseech you, do not let his seed inside the front door. I must have spoken this missive aloud as both Atsuko and Mrs. Catarrh laughed.

"Push," said Atsuko and Mrs. Catarrh together. I was beyond caring, beyond energy, beyond sanity. I gratefully reached for death's embrace with no regrets. I closed my eyes and bade myself make no sound. It was no use. The scream was torn from my very center. In case he was stone deaf, I held out my arms to make it easier for the grim reaper to find me. And as the old wives' tales had predicted, I bled like a stuck pig and finally expelled a lumpen shape that unraveled as I peered between my lashes.

Somehow, as the clock began its gong to twelve, the impossible was made life. I guess I did wrap the sentiment inside a little religious-sounding miracle there, but there you have it. It was a miracle. The baby was born.

Oh, the lusty wails that came from that one. The baby inherited my lungs. My pain set aside, not yet forgotten, I cried out. "Give me my baby. Now!"

Atsuko had wrapped the wee thing, still howling away, in a soft linen towel. Mrs. Catarrh appeared thunderstruck and had a dribble of drool as she smiled, showing one of the few teeth left remaining in her head. As if possessed, her gnarled, knobby hand stroked the infant's head. She took the baby from Atsuko and laid it on my chest.

"It's a miracle," I whispered. I tingled from my tits to way down low beneath my heart at this wondrous feeling. My throat, which was raw from screaming, now had a strange sense of strangulation. I squeezed that baby so tight, more squalls erupted. And I made a vow. Which is between mother and child.

I loosened the cloth and marveled at the infant skin. I rubbed the slickness of birth away to reveal the softest, most innocent, and beautiful baby of the land. My kisses rained everywhere. In return, the baby held my finger and stared at me with ultimate wisdom. I was gone. Captured. Of no import to this world any more.

Atsuko and Mrs. Catarrh were on either side of us. My bliss seeped to envelop them. "Thank you, good friends."

"Well done." Mrs. Catarrh stroked my brow and lingered on the baby's cheek. Atsuko's eyes were so bright. She nodded at me and pinched the infant's toes. I wanted to bite them.

Banging on the door threatened more cries from the baby. "Help me," I said. Atsuko took the baby, cleaned and swaddled it tightly. I would have to learn how she did that.

To their credit, the agonized men enquired about my well-being first. "Brandy. Is she well? Are you hurt? Darling girl, you are so fine."

"Come in, fathers." I cheered. "Meet your baby!" I couldn't be sure who held the tiny mite first, but Elliot and Beau held on to it for dear life together. And believe you me, there wasn't a dry eye in the room.

I beckoned them over. "We shall call the baby after your father, Elliot. Michel Elliot Pfeiffer-Mondragon."

Elliot dried his eye with the baby's foot that slid through the wrappings. He kissed the baby on the forehead and returned him to me. Beau sat on my bed, and they both thanked me. Elliot lifted my damp hair off my neck and twisted it atop my head. Beau held the baby's head which fit perfectly in his palm.

"You are amazing, Brandy. Thank you for this child," Elliot said.

"Thank you for being you," Beau added.

Elliot stood with a sigh of pleasure. "The doctor is waiting. I'll send him up so he can certify the child's birth. Michel. Little Michel. I can't believe it."

"And on your birthday," I teased.

"Nothing like cutting it close."

"I had plenty of time." I waved my hand languidly. The frantic buzz of my body had drummed down to a low-level hum.

"Rest, darling. I'll return with the doctor. He's in the library." He stood. I slid off his loving look and lifted an eyebrow toward Mrs. Catarrh.

"Nonsense, master. Stay here with your family and the babe. I'll fetch the doctor." She left and closed the door quietly.

Atsuko took baby Michel and dressed him in his diaper, gown and swaddled him again. The idyllic half hour we all shared is one that glowed with a happiness that shall never be matched. We took turns holding his royal highness and outlining plans.

Elliot couldn't wait to teach him about plants. Beau vowed he would be able to ride a pony before his first birthday.

"He has your eyes, Brandy. And my chin," Beau said.

"Hush. Let's see the ways he looks like his father," I said pointedly. "There, Elliot's nose, and let's see, ears, don't you think? He'll have his father's long fingers."

Oh, the little white lies we wove.

Mrs. Catarrh and Dr. Spach finally entered my room. The doctor was lucky he could find my bed, let alone the baby. Mrs. Catarrh had done her job well. He scrawled his signature on the certificate of birth, a very sloppy entry of one male child, "Michel Pfeiffer-Mondragon," he said in a sing-song voice. "Your parents will be delighted." He pinched the baby's nose and left.

Beau's eyes were shining. "His lashes are so long. He looks as pretty as a girl."

Mrs. Catarrh coughed. "That's as handsome and brawny a lad as I've ever seen."

Elliot tried to unwrap the swaddling. "Let me see my fine son in all his glory."

Atsuko intercepted him. "Please, Elliot. He's tired. We mustn't overtire the little lord. Or his mother," she shot me a look. I yawned, and while it wasn't contrived, I was reluctant to leave this bubble of happiness.

"Oh, yes, of course," Elliot said. Atsuko took Michel, and with one more dazed look, Elliot linked arms with Beau and left my room.

"Would you like to suckle the baby, Brandy?"

"Stick a red-faced bawling brat to hang off my tender, raw nipple and suck the very life juice out of me?" I gulped. "I can't wait," I said in a very quiet voice. Atsuko positioned the baby's lips to my breast.

"Cocked on like a fish, see?" said the old pro, Mrs. Catarrh. I wish I could relate the joy of an infant's trusting little soft tongue lapping up sustenance and nourishment at my breast. But I can't because it's a crock of shit. He slipped off-target, scrunched up his little face, and terrorized the lot of us.

"I've got another one for you, baby," I tried to hush the monster as they helped move him to my other side. He was having none of it. Alys's sister had just given birth a month before, and we called for her *tout de suite*, or rather for her sweet de tit.

Malys or Calys, I still didn't care enough about her to learn her name, arrived a short time later. I was already jealous of someone who would be feeding my baby that wasn't me. I planned to keep an eye on that one. Malice or Callous, indeed.

"Merely the heifer to the heir," I said, handing my baby over. That earned a sharp knuckle from Lady Catarrh to my skull.

"Hush."

Baby Michel jumped on her nipple like a bulldog on a pork chop. Of course, I couldn't be jealous. Oh, how the entire household already rallied around that little mite that weighed no more than a sack of sugar.

Atsuko settled them in a chair near the cradle. "You have a visitor," she told me.

My eyelids drooped, and I was desperate for sleep. "Fluff me up," I told her. She brushed my hair and tied it up on top of my head with a ribbon, and put a clean wrap on me. She bustled over to the door and escorted One inside. He made for my bedside, and the look in his eyes was a benediction.

"Congratulations then, my lady," he said. "A fine healthy son. Good wishes to you and your husband and the babe."

"Baby Michel, after Elliot's father," I said. I gestured toward the wet nurse. He turned and went over to the baby and passed his hand over Michel's head. Lucky baby. Malys or Calys held up the baby to him. One, too, fell under the infant's spell and held him snuggly in his arm.

"Well done, Brandy. He is beautiful, as is his mother."

I was turned inside out. Sore, exhausted, exalted.

"Very handsome."

"Thank you for helping me to the manor, sir," I told him. "And thank you for saving Sir Stone. That means the world to me."

Almost as much as the smile One gave me and the soft kiss he planted on my baby's cheek.

One gave the baby back to the nurse, came over to my bed, and stood next to Atsuko, an admirable chaperone. Mrs. Catarrh was busy hacking away on the other side of the bed, her eyes flashing hard on us.

"I'm grateful to be of service. And praise the Lord you and the baby are well."

I held out my hand as gracious folk do to their minions; not a spot of suspicion could be noted in either my behavior or One's. But Lord, when he took my hand, I only pray no one saw the spark I felt. He left, and the room felt empty.

"Gar, even with only the one hand, that's a good-looking bloke," Malys or Calys said.

"You're not paid to look or listen to anything, girl." Mrs. Catarrh went over to her. "You have one job, and that's to feed this baby. Baby is asleep. Now, you may leave. We have a room down the hall for you. Go get your things and have Alys show you."

Chapter 30

"Whatever did we do before baby Michel was born?" I wondered. Beau and Elliot were on either side of my bed, with Michel in between them. RayRay sat cross-legged at the end of the bed.

"He does put it all in perspective, my love," Elliot said. Then, in a baby voice, "All that worry, all that worry, oh, woe is me, what shall be? What shall be?" The baby hiccupped, and the three of them declared him the most brilliant baby of all time. "Seriously. How worried we all were. And, look here. Little Lord Baby Boo," he kissed the baby's feet, "comes along and saves the day. The inheritance has been transferred to my name. The manor is officially mine."

"Complete with an as yet unseen mountain of debts," Beau said. Michel was clinging to Beau's finger as Beau pretended it hurt terribly. "What a grip."

"You are the brains of this operation, Beau," Elliot told him. "We'll manage." Elliot received his inheritance, true, but it was very bad news of what was basically a deficit. Some of his crops were coming in, but as he said, it would take several years to break even, let alone start to earn a profit. He was giving away some of his discoveries — seedlings and fertilizers, while he waited for his patents. "The village farmers seem to be making good use of the implements and seeds, and most have followed my suggestions for crops this year."

"And Mrs. Farfuddle?" I asked.

Elliot smiled. "They don't know quite what to make of her, but you should see her in action. She stops at every farm over the course of a week and makes suggestions. And when the farmers or their wives dare get their dander up, she simply digs in, literally. She's on her hands and knees like the lowliest laborer, digging in the dirt. She'll use my short spade and create the perfect receptacle for the seeds, almost as if it's a holy ritual. Then, as she says, ice the cake. She'll take a fistful of fertilizer and gently mound it atop. Those plants won't do anything but grow if she has anything to do with it."

"They'll be too scared not to grow," Beau said. "And the farmers will be too scared not to succeed. There's been some grumbling, but overall, most seem a little excited by all the attention Elliot is providing them with. That, and they fair dote on him since he's become a father and true head of the manor." Beau kissed Michel's tiny hand.

"The sun rises and sets on this imp's head," I said.

"And you are the worst," RayRay said. Michel made a tiny peep, and RayRay scooped him up, flung him over his shoulder, and patted his bottom. While no one in that manor had anything approaching a lick of expertise on caring for an infant, Michel seemed no worse for wear, held like a sack of potatoes by this one, head bobbing dangerously over that one's arm.

"It's a wonder he ever sleeps — he's never allowed the opportunity."

"RayRay's right, Brandy. You're the mother ducklingest of us all," Elliot said. "You do too much. Let me give him his bath; you rest."

"Nonsense," I said.

Atsuko agreed. "He'll catch a chill, sir. We do just fine."

"But I want to help. I'm not going to be like my father." Elliot took a turn and cradled Michel in his lap. "I'm going to help Michel be the best he can be, whoever he wants to be."

Atsuko and I exchanged a glance. Mrs. Catarrh bustled in and declared it was time for his feeding. She took Michel and went down the hall in search of his nurse.

I shooed the gents out of my room and stole a glance in the mirror. Atsuko smiled at me. "Tell One how much Michel loves his cradle. He slept through the night again."

"I will." I paused. We're not a touchy-feely bunch here at Mondragon. But my emotions were all over the place. I squeezed her elbow, which was about as much of a hug as I was capable of. "Baby Michel is beautiful, isn't he?"

"He is a love," she said.

I looked down. Happiness doesn't sit right upon me. This time it was Atsuko who squeezed my arm. "We'll get through it, whatever happens," she said.

I went to the kitchen and pilfered some of Alys's shortbread and jam. Haven't you heard, she's the new cook? I put on my cloak and flitted down to One's cottage. We usually shared lunch there, though how many comestibles were actually consumed is an unknown. It's quite hard to kiss someone when crispy crumbs of shortbread cling to your mouth. I had even forsaken garlic to sweeten my kisses with One. I smoothed my hands down over my stomacher and felt in fine form. It was too soon following Michel's birth for more enjoyment. I fear you will never believe me, but that made our time together even more exciting. One would tell me stories in that sonorous baritone of his — relaxing, that's what RayRay called it; I just called it enrapturing. I had read that term out of a novel Beau had given me. Like a melody played on a violin, the vibration of One's voice hypnotized me. I apologize but have no control over it.

It was in this haze of contentment I dared set aside my burdensome thoughts. I accepted my good fortune as my just due. That was my first mistake. My second was a failure to plan for the inevitable. The gods rubbed their hands.

That very next morning, the household was in chaos. It was baby Michel's christening day. I descended the staircase holding him in my arms, dressed in the ivory satin long dress that Elliot and Elliot's father had been baptized in.

"What, ho, Papa," Beau, elegantly attired, as usual, played the role of doting uncle. He came in and clapped Elliot on the back. "Bless me, Father, for I have sinned," he said, with a wink at me.

"Stop it, both of you." I mimed the fly-swatting motion Catholics seemed to prefer, and Beau spoke a few words of Latin.

"I do not have the soul of a priest," Elliot said. "I don't act in the least holy, as you all very well know. Religion is an oppressor."

Together Beau and I parroted back at him, "And panacea for the masses."

Elliot came for the baby. "But needs must. Come here, my little man. So precious. Let's go enjoy your debut; everyone wants to meet you." He kissed Michel's cheek and smoothed the gown. He was that proud. "Everything set here?"

I nodded.

"My parents and Cousin Clarence are meeting us at the chapel. Then after the service, we'll all come back here to celebrate."

"Atsuko and I helped Alys with the food. Mrs. Farfuddle has all the tables set up in the back hall."

"The villagers are so excited," RayRay said as he entered. "Both for meeting this royal hiney," he said, patting Michel on his bottom, "and for the celebration up here. And I'll have you know I helped Mrs. Farfuddle. What she doesn't know about food she more than makes up for in plants. The old girl has been collecting cans and sprouting herbs in them. She's lined them all up on the tables, and she's going to allow the villagers to take them home with them after the party." He nodded his head. "I tied red ribbons, leftover from yuletide, around the cans. Very special. We used every tablecloth in the house."

"What?" I said, "Where'd you get them?" It just blurted out of me.

RayRay narrowed his eyes at me. "From the back outhouse, where do you think?" He scoffed. "From the linen closet; alright with you then, Madam?"

"Oh, yes, of course. I wasn't thinking. I didn't realize we had that many tablecloths." I had been so busy with the baby I hadn't had time to visit my hidey-hole lately.

Elliot clapped his hands. "Let's be off." We bundled up in capes and cloaks. Little Michel was so buried beneath a crocheted wool blanket he could have been a baby lamb had anyone wondered. The blanket was an offering from Mrs. Catarrh and her poor gnarled, arthritic hands. It looked like a spider web lost a bet with a fishing net. For some reason, it seemed to bring great comfort to Baby Michel.

The chapel was filled that cold January morning. Excited puffs of air vaporized out of the townspeople as they drew near. It took us nearly twenty minutes to walk through up to our front pew. We proudly unveiled the little master on our way and held him up to his admirers.

"Heard it was a rough time, my lady," said one of the farmer's wives.

"And aren't they all," I told her grandly, feeling part of a secret club. "But, so worth it in the end."

"Do you really believe that, Brandy?" Elliot whispered in my ear.

I showed him my crossed fingers. He pulled me close in a hug.

His father and mother rushed up to join us. Lady P examined Michel as I held him out for her inspection. She poked at his hand. "Look at those fingers," she said. I had never heard her quite so gentle. Even Lord P smoothed his beefy hand over Michel's beautiful hairless head. He nodded his own head several times and appeared unable to speak.

"He has the Pfeiffer-Mondragon chin, Michel, look," Lady P said to her husband.

He stroked his own chin. "That he does, that he does."

We continued our walk toward the altar. I can't suppose to give an honest description of the magic in that crowd in the chapel that morning. Everyone loved Elliot, of course; who wouldn't? Except for his own miserly family. He listened to his people, but more importantly, responded to their concerns. If they had a well that malfunctioned, he was right there, helping to dig. If a child was ill, he made sure the doctor was called immediately. They were a little slow to accept me, but if my feet were in their clogs, I would be the same. I did try to emulate Elliot, and I quite liked playing lady of the manor and sharing what bounty we had.

The folks there in the church that morning perhaps felt a little more secure, too, with the news that his inheritance had come in and that this baptism tied everything up nice and tight. With Michel's christening, the final papers were to be issued and recorded in the parish registry. Now that Elliot was secure as the legal landholder, they could rest easier and put their banner, so to speak, behind their man. Loyalty only goes so far. They needed a reason to be loyal, and Elliot gave them many.

"Quit fidgeting," I told Malys or Calys. She had fed Michel one more time in the carriage to make sure he was happy during the service.

We arrived up at the baptismal font, and the parish priest, Father Vicker, beamed. Elliot's parents, Lord and Lady P, dear Lord, what was wrong with them? Oh, they were smiling. Cousin Clarence joined us and had his badger's leer on. The priest started his greeting and gabbled away in Latin.

"And now, I invite Lord Michel and Lady Pfeiffer-Mondragon," he nodded at Elliot's parents, and, "Lord Elliot and Lady Pfeiffer-Mondragon," he beckoned Elliot and me, and the godparents, to gather round. Beau and Atsuko, One and Mrs. Catarrh, stepped to one side. I held Michel as the priest waved his hands and mumbled Latin incantations over the little one, but as it was all hope and love, I was fine with the saints' hearts and martyrs' flowers.

Just as he was getting to the good part, Cousin Clarence cleared his throat and crowded next to me. My heart began to pound. He interrupted the Father. "If I may," he shouted so loudly, Michel gave a start. "I cannot in all good Christian conscience, allow this charade of a christening to proceed."

Chapter 31

"Good Lord, Clarence," Elliot said, "Pipe down. Sit down. Shut up." Beau thrust back his shoulders, his hand rested on his dagger.

"What is the meaning of this?" Lady P said.

"Hear me out," Cousin Clarence said. "This baby is a fraud." The crowd gasped.

I held Michel oh so tightly. My son. I straightened my shoulders. I would protect him and his future to the bitter end.

"Go on. Unswaddle the infant. Let us all see the new lord and heir." I wanted to claw the smirk off his loathsome face.

"No. Stop," I said. "It is freezing. He will take cold. How dare you?" My face crumpled with loathing as I looked at that corpulent cretin.

"I insist."

"Brandy?" Elliot was looking at me with a queer look on his face.

I couldn't bear to look at anyone but my beautiful baby.

"Jesus wept," I heard Mrs. Catarrh say.

Elliot took the baby from me, lifted the gown, and unwrapped his swaddling. I held my breath. As a cold draft hit his little legs, he shrieked at the outrage. Oh, I understand, little one, believe me, I understand. Elliot opened his nappy. A gasp.

Three things happened. Lady P fainted. Who cares if she really did or not, or pretended to? It set off the motion of events. Elliot reswaddled Michelle, kissed her brow, and soothed her fussiness. "Shush, shush, beautiful little girl. There, there. Papa has you." That's when I began to cry.

Cousin Clarence clapped his hands and shooed the villagers out of the church. "It's over, nothing to see here. I'll be your new lord and master before the month is out." I saw him tilt his head at Malys or Calys, and she ran shamefacedly out of the church. I should have known.

"Go on," he yelled at the stragglers, trying for a peek. "It's a girl. Nothing but a female," Clarence said. "Fraud. You're lucky I don't press charges. Mondragon will be mine. My man and I will begin an inventory tomorrow, so don't try anything funny. Anything else, that is." With a sneer, he stomped away. The priest had skedaddled minutes after Lady P took her dive.

"Brandy. Why didn't you tell me? I'm her father." Elliot said, still soothing Michelle. I glanced at Beau. His arm was slung around Elliot's shoulder, and he, too, was looking into the baby's fretting face.

"I did it for you, Elliot. And for everyone. You are the rightful heir to Mondragon Manor; everyone knows it. You deserve it — all your hard work. And you love it. Every stone. Just because Michel," I amended, "Michelle is a girl, what does it truly matter? She's the exact same baby that we all love."

"It matters naught to me," Elliot said as he kissed her head. "In fact, I love her even more than ever. Unfortunately, the estate was entailed two generations back to keep it in the Pfeiffer-Mondragon line. It's unfair, but that's the way it is. Clarence now stands to inherit." He took my chin and lifted it. "Thank you, Brandy. Don't fret. Take the baby home. Er, back to Mondragon Manor. I'll meet you back there shortly. One? Will you please escort my parents out of here? Then find us. Beau? Come with me."

One helped Lady P up into her carriage. I doubt they'd ever speak to Elliot again, though, curiously, Lady P did pause to look at Michelle before she left, as if trying to remember her. Michelle, a wily girl, that one, gave up her first smile, and for a moment, I thought the old lady would relent. Instead, with a long-suffering sigh, she followed upon her husband's barked command. Even the sound of their retreating carriage wheels sounded furious.

For once speechless, Mrs. Catarrh went to wait for us in the carriage. Atsuko and I were the last to leave the chapel. "Is it strange that I want to stay and light candles and snort incense up my nose and pray my heathen heart out?"

She placed her hand on my arm. "No stranger than me wanting to gut Cousin Clarence and feed him to the pigs." We began a slow procession down the aisle toward a life where neither of us knew what to expect. "It's not your fault, Brandy. Myself, Mrs. Catarrh, and this little baby here, we were all delighted to play our part. It was worth it. You knew it couldn't last forever."

"I know. I just hoped to give Elliot enough time to make his mark. Get his patents and be well underway in finding his fame and fortune." I sighed. "He really could have helped so many people. Farmer Elliot." I brushed a tear off my cheek.

"He still can, Brandy. Who knows what will happen? Keep the faith."

We walked out of the church. As I settled inside the carriage, Mrs. Catarrh took the baby. She squeezed my hand so hard I feared I would catch her arthritis. "Well, I, for one, am glad the secret is out," she said. "I kept calling this beautiful little miss, Michelle, anyway." Our hysterical laughter subsided into tears.

We had tarried such a while in the chapel, it looked like Elliot and Beau would arrive at the manor before us. And what did we see? They were leading the townsfolk, still and all up to the manor. "What is going on?"

As Elliot helped me step from the carriage and Mrs. Catarrh handed the baby to me, the crowd broke into applause.

"Enter friends, and welcome to Mondragon Manor. Eat, drink and be merry," he told them.

"For tomorrow we lie," Beau said under his breath. "Cheat and steal, too, if we have to."

That non-event of a christening party will be stored high on a special shelf in my memories. Our misfortune, and Elliot's unfeigned joy in his daughter, and genuine generosity toward his wife, his friends, and his tenants, went a long way in kicking adversity right in the arse.

One sought me out. "Brandy, my poor little love. How are you faring?"

"Did you know?" I asked him.

"I sensed you had yet another secret," was all he would say. "It doesn't matter. Though I expect your life will be easier now."

"How can you say that? All is lost. All this. For everyone. What will we all do?"

"None of that, little one. All will be well." During the dance he insisted I share with him, I tried to believe it. I couldn't stop thinking about my treasure. I couldn't bear to give it up and give it to Elliot. But, would I dare use it to take the baby and run away with One? I wound my arms around his neck and tried to intuit the best course of action. I may have collided into the pillars of his thighs once or twice, not a regrettable action on my part. However, it was merely a reflection of my dance skills or lack thereof. I can't be expected to count steps, flirt, and worry all in one go.

The party, despite the circumstances, was a rally for David against Goliath. Our tenants let their guard down as they enjoyed libations from the Mondragon cellar along with the food, and they danced in a devil-may-care way.

Chapter 32

One walked me upstairs to reclaim Michelle. Elliot had a stern talking-to with Malys or Calys, who I had wanted to be fired on the spot. Her sister Alys intervened, and they both pledged fealty and apologized all the day long. Malys or Calys never stopped crying. And while I could hardly bear to look at her red, puffed-up traitorous face, it was the hungry bawling of our little girl that forced the issue.

With my arm slung around One's back, One carried our sleepy miss to my room. He settled her gently in her cradle, alongside her blanket from Mrs. Catarrh. She cooed contentedly, which basically made me purr — that, and perhaps those few goodnight kisses from One.

Cousin Clarence came the very next day to begin his inventory. He brought several solicitors with him to go through the manor, listing things of value.

Elliot was gobsmacked. And Beau shriveled before my very eyes. If this was the resistance, every one of us at Mondragon Manor was doomed.

"Don't worry, Cousin Elliot. I'll give you, and your," he snarled his lip as he gazed around the room, "family, over a month, until March 1st, to vacate. Plenty of time to come up with other accommodations." He and his puffed-up posse were as unpleasant as you'd expect. They clopped mud over the floors in their heavy boots, stomping throughout the hall with proprietary footsteps.

Feeling helpless, I tried to keep an eagle eye on what they were doing, noting, and writing down. It became an impossible task. Elliot ran away. Beau poured himself a whiskey, and Cousin Clarence actually had the audacity to wag his finger at him. "Tut tut, my good man. That's coming out of my collection, but on second thought, you look like you need it. Let it not be said I'm not a compassionate gentleman. Pour me one, too, would you?"

They combed the house with an eye to inventory every painting, piece of silver, and stick of furniture. I walked into my bedroom. "If you think to be opening one of my drawers in that bureau, you will leave with one less finger," I said to the shifty ne'er-do-well who hurried out of my room.

I went to tattle to Beau and found him nursing another drink in the library. "Don't furrow your brow so, darling, you're already starting to look like Mrs. Catarrh," he told me.

"Beau. Don't. Do something."

"As it happens, I am." He took another drink and set it atop a stack of papers. "It's no fun being serious sober, you know." At that, he put on a pair of spectacles. I had never seen this side of Beau. Spectacles Beau was researching cases and providing a legal tender of dispute, even though we all knew it was useless. "I am going to figure something out," he said. "Or die trying."

Cousin Clarence eventually found Elliot hard at work in his workshop in the barn. Beau and I quickly followed. Here too, Cousin Clarence was careless and contemptuous. "Playing garden again, Elliot?" He knocked a potted plant to the floor, giving leave to his clerks to do the same. One upended a tray of seedlings; another ripped several papers of Elliot's drawings and designs. One man was examining a shelf that held Elliot's prototypes of spades and digging tools. Finally, Beau had had enough.

"Halt! Hands off! You can look, but you can't touch. It's not yours just yet," he said.

"Oh, ho. And what business is it of yours?" Cousin Clarence asked.

"I am Elliot's solicitor and legal counsel. And if you and your men touch, break or even breathe on any of his or his household's belongings, whether plant or painting, I will report you to the authorities under British Parliamentary law, Feudal Rights, Section IX, paragraph 8e., pursuant to current owner tenancy ownership and obligations in lieu of transitory deed wherewith." Beau had an old navy-blue law tome with him, quite thick, and had many papers scrawled with his notes stuffed inside. "We can tie this up in the courts for years."

"You and what army?"

"The army of Her Royal Highness and the entire brigade of the peerage, who don't take kindly to their way of life being threatened. That, and we would use the entire force of the remaining Pfeiffer-Mondragon estate to sue your bilious black-guard ways that are riding roughshod over liberty."

"Bah!" Cousin Clarence waved at his men to follow him out of the barn.

I grabbed Beau's arm. "Was any of that true?" I had begun to regain my hope.

"Not a whit, darling. And as the entire Pfeiffer-Mondragon estate consists of roughly 30 shillings, that wouldn't even buy us one golden minute in the courts." He opened the book and showed me some of his notes. I had to laugh at the caricature drawing of a very fat drooling Cousin Clarence with his hand caught in a cookie jar.

Nevertheless, Cousin Clarence and his entourage were almost respectful during their remaining inventory. It detailed everything from horses, hogs, sheep, cows, and crops. Lists of tenants' names, holdings, households, rents collected and due. Furniture, silver, foodstuffs, linens, candles. He even counted the thread in Atsuko's sewing basket. What a petty man.

It was only during the tally that he exploded. Had it not concerned our very futures, it would have been quite enjoyable.

Cousin Clarence stomped his feet, banged his fists on the table, and then took his solicitor's notes and flung them toward the fireplace.

"Who threw the turd in the punchbowl?" Mrs. Catarrh asked.

"There's nothing here worth much of anything. Where'd it all go? According to my solicitor, this is nothing but a rundown manor that will need thousands of pounds just to make it livable. My family, unlike you uncouth heathens, is used to much finer things in life." He snapped his fingers, and he and his crew stormed out without a backward glance. "Don't touch anything. I'll be back."

Beau, more energized than I could remember seeing him, well, at least fully clothed that is, went to London to consult with attorneys and determine the entire situation of the estate, inheritance laws, and possible avenues of recourse.

Elliot had breakfast with baby Michelle and us. He told her fantastical tales in a sing-song voice that fascinated her. He imitated her coos and squawks. "I think she will babble even more than her mother," he said. She laughed at him, agreeing with him already. My heart felt heavy as I watched them.

This house had gotten under my skin. I loved it, from the floorboards (where my toes curled in their slippers in sheer enjoyment as I walked across the polished hardwoods) to the crown molding. From the damp, dark cellar to the ghost-story scary attic. From my hidey-hole, which included me in its secret history, to the very doorknobs, which I grasped as if I held the hand of a friend. No one knew the manor better than I. Its personality pleased me, that of a fuss-budget old spinster, lamenting her lack of funds for a pretty dress but putting on a brave face. She was my grandmother, and I loved her fiercely.

This was the first home I'd ever known, and it would be the best I ever would. Mondragon Manor loved me back. As I had spent my days snooping, my fingers would walk atop the shiny expanse of a mantle here, the bulky balustrade going up the steps there.

Two nights later, Beau was back for dinner. He held up his hand. "Not victorious, friends, but we're not in the grave just yet." We settled in to dine and hear his tale. Alys served us a delicious brisket with a gravy you'd want to drink up in a goblet; it was nectar.

Beau held court while we ate. "Cousin Clarence may not be able to pay the back taxes that are due, either," he said. "He had hoped to sell off valuables from Mondragon but couldn't find enough to make it worth his while." He pulled out some documents. "I've been trying to argue the exact point of law. Elliot, as the legal heir, is married by the age of thirty. He could theoretically name any able male as his inheritor and next in line. I've tried to justify that he could name any male as his heir, an adopted son. Nowhere does it explicitly say the heir must be birthed. Besides, we all know how despite fierce protections and a lot of looking the other way, a progenitor's line can be muddied. One day, they'll probably come up with a test that will prove we're all long-lost cousins."

Beau took a sip of wine. "So, if Elliot had a son, he would have inherited and then been given time to pay off debts, up to one year. But, since it went down the line to the next heir, which is Cousin Clarence, married with sons, the law changed a bit, and his obligation for debt fulfillment is accelerated. He only has thirty days to clear the debt and pay the taxes. If he won't settle or is unable to meet the fee, the debt would go to auction, and anyone who can afford to pay the debts and wager the highest price would win the estate."

I became silent.

"So, English please, Beau. What does that mean?" Gordy asked.

"Like most things, Gordy, Mondragon will go to the one with the deepest pockets."

Chapter 33

The worse things got, the more resolved Elliot became. He made plans, researched where we would go and what he would do. He had his eye on a farm a short distance away, though the rent was dear. It hurt my heart to see him like that. It hurt my brain to think that I could fix it all if only I gave up my treasure.

"I tried to argue the point of a legal male heir by the time of the trustee's thirtieth birthday. The magistrate was looking kindly on my point of view that a male, if adopted by Elliot, most probably wouldn't be recognized unless it was a bye-blow, some son fathered outside of marriage. Moot point anyway, since we had baby Michelle by Elliot's birthday, and no other arrangements have been made." Elliot smiled.

"Bad news, worse news. The Mondragon estate is entailed for thousands of pounds in back taxes."

"What's worse than that?" Elliot asked. "We can't pay it."

"Worse news, part B, is for Cousin Clarence. He can't pay it, either," Beau said. He sipped his wine. "That's why he was hoping to get the estate in his name, sell off everything that wasn't nailed down, and pay off the taxes. Then probably proceed to pillage the townspeople, raise their rents, lower their crop shares, and fill his coffers that way."

"So, who has to pay?"

"The law won't allow Cousin Clarence to take ownership until and unless those fees are paid first."

"So, someone could buy it out from under Cousin Clarence?"

Beau shrugged. "It appears that way, yes. Unless that oaf has some nefarious partnership with the devil to help finance him. The trouble for him is that there are not many who trust him enough to go into partnership with him. If only we could use that in our favor."

"How would we do that?" I asked quietly.

"Come up with the gold coin to buy it back."

"Thank you, Beau. At least now we know. If only I could have worked faster and harder. Two, three more years, I know we'd be making a profit with our crops, and my patents would be available to sell off. Unfortunately, I never was very good at deadlines."

"Hush. Nonsense," Mrs. Catarrh said. "Don't know that it'd help much, but what I have is yours." Atsuko, Gordy, RayRay all chimed in. I bit my lip, wishing I could be as generous.

Beau took over. "Elliot, I don't have much either, but you know it's all yours. After dinner, let's tally up what we can do."

As no one expected me to have anything to contribute, I left Baby Michelle with Elliot. I slipped out with One, and we walked down to his cottage. One placed my chair in front of Sir Stone and left me there to gather my thoughts.

Sir Stone loved Michelle as much as she loved him. Under his stern demeanor, she would calm right down if she was cantankerous. "She will be seeing you to-morrow," I told him with a proud smile. We sat there in our companionable silence, and I did my best to ignore what Sir Stone wanted to tell me.

I organized my thoughts and heard a knock on the cottage door. One escorted Malys or Calys, I never did grow to trust her, into his bedroom where I sat with Sir Stone. She gawped at him high atop his perch, and I quite wanted to slap her again. She finally withdrew her stare and bobbed a little curtsy to me. That was more like it. "Sorry, ma'am. Master Elliot sent me to find you. They need you up there." She saw the look on my face. "Baby Michelle is well. I just finished feeding her; she's with Mrs. Catarrh. It's the strangest thing. Every time Mrs. Catarrh coughs, that baby coughs right back at her, and then she smiles."

As that was one of my current favorite things my darling girl did, I begrudged a smile to Malys or Calys. "I'll be up shortly." At least this time, she stared more at Sir Stone than she usually did at One. Don't think I didn't have words of warning with him about that girl. "When I meet my end," I told One, "I require your solemn oath that she will be the last you would ever turn to."

He sealed his vow with a kiss that left me trembling. Oh, go read a romance novel; that happens all the time. Better yet, recall when you were at the ripe age that sparked your first look from a handsome man or imagined your fingers under the cover were his.

"One, please, we need to get back up, now." One tucked my arm in his, and we hurried up the path in the twilight. It was a glum crowd we encountered in the parlor. Atsuko offered up Michelle as entertainment, which no one could resist. Elliot and Beau explained how they would be forced to close up the house.

"But rest assured, I will do everything in my power to keep us all together. I think I've figured some things out, and though it may be rough going, we can do it. If you all want that, that is." Elliot picked up Michelle and held her over his shoulder with his eyes closed as if in prayer.

I hied myself upstairs. Into the linen closet, I went. I grabbed a sturdy tablecloth under one arm, lit my candle, and made my way to my stronghold. I left the passageway door and the linen closet door open. I opened the door to my lair and shook out the cloth wide on the floor.

Chapter 34

I lit the candelabra on the desk in my retreat. I looked at my gleaming treasures and knew they meant less than nothing compared to Michelle and our family.

I clunked the heavier objects down on the tablecloth first, gold and brass statuettes, candlesticks, inlaid snuff boxes, ivory fans, ornate books with hand-tooled leather and gold clasps.

Silly. Of course, I still had my very own pirate's treasure trove, discovered in the wall panel when Cousin Clarence had been after me. It was tucked in a box under the shelves for another day. Don't dare judge me. I found it, no one need know about that.

The fortune that I had harvested from the house itself was grandiose enough to save the day, or so I believed. I gathered the four corners of the cloth and pulled them together, creating an unwieldy load. I eased it up on my back, the corners held over my shoulder tightly in my hands. I left the door open and had just enough light to make my way back. It would require several trips, and I knew what to expect with this family.

The only other thing I had left to my own name was that dang-blasted tarnished silver locket. I rarely thought of my sailor. Except to imagine how fine it would be to rub his nose in my circumstances. What kind of buffoon etches his own name on a silver locket to give to a lady love? The chicken scratch of a message secreted inside was a poor excuse for any declaration of love. 'IS AZ.' Gordy would undoubtedly have something to say about that, but I had more important things to think on just then, and I wasted no more thought on what that message could even mean.

That necklace wouldn't be worth much, if anything. But still, some reason bade me keep it. It took up space yet, balled in a handkerchief in my bottom drawer. It was a small locket, perhaps the size of my big toe. Since you can't see my toe, I fear you imagine something along the size of RayRay's big toe. In that case, you would picture me bent over, weighted by such a gaudy locket you might think I kept a pet mouse inside. RayRay's feet were so big his shoes could float an armada into battle.

I stepped out of the linen closet. I huffed and puffed, gathered up my bundle once again, and went downstairs. I had been at livelier funerals. I went smack dab into the middle of the parlor and clanked my loot onto the floor.

"What in the world?" Elliot said. Everyone gathered around. I knelt and began picking up objects.

"In case things didn't work out, I thought I would put some things away for safe-keeping."

"Sticky fingers, Brandy," RayRay (of course) said. "Well done." Beau quickly began making a list, along with some ideas of what he could sell the objects for. "I actually know a great estate purveyor who would love these items."

I knew my cheeks were blushed, but it wasn't with the praise and exclamations everyone was making, in hopes of the treasures being enough. Instead, I was mortified at being caught out.

Elliot came and sat by me. "Brandy. No one here faults you." He waved his hands over the goods. "None of us knew these things were here or really saw them. Or used them or needed them. Let's just say you created a savings account for us."

Gordy, whose turn it was to hold Michelle, actually reached across and squeezed my shoulder. "Not one of us has a clean soul. You did right now, and that's all that matters."

Beau continued his tally. "Good job, Brandy." He sighed. "But unfortunately, even if they fetch high prices, it won't be enough. Got anymore?" I nodded. They followed me. It was almost like a party, like the night we had danced with our hands on each other's shoulders in a line. With all of us, we made short work and cleaned out the treasures — most of them. I studiously avoided looking under the base of the shelf.

No one needed to know about the box I had found when Cousin Clarence was chasing me. From the looks of things, it had been hidden away in that walled-up space for more than a generation. As long as I drew breath, I would make sure Cousin Clarence would never lay claim to that. I still needed some insurance for Michelle and myself.

"Dear God," Elliot said. "How did I not know this secret passage existed? I know my parents didn't know. They couldn't keep a secret to save their lives." He was examining the room and the outside corridor.

"It goes to the barn, that way," I told him. I pointed in the other direction. "And that leads to your armoire." Beau, Elliot, and I all but whistled, trying not to remember when I jumped out to surprise them.

"Hmm," Elliot said. "I bet this was for the house priest. Catholic priests were tortured years ago and had to hide." He patted the wall in the corridor. "What a great house. How many more secrets is it keeping?" I merely shrugged my shoulders.

We headed back down, and Beau continued his computations.

"I just don't know," he said. "RayRay and I will load up the wagon and take them to London to see if we can get the best prices. Elliot? What's wrong?"

"Technically, all this should be on Cousin Clarence's inventory, I suppose," he said. "Though I doubt this lot will be enough to save the house. Sadly, most of the truly valuable items were sold off by my family years ago."

"Technically, Cousin Clarence is a bigger thief than the lot of us, with a soul as black as tar. He doesn't deserve your consideration, Elliot," Gordy said. "All's fair in love and war, and this is war. He's kicking you out of your family home with glee. It's not our fault he's an addle-pated idiot. Brandy found the hidey-hole, and he could have found it. He never asked." He nodded at me. "She's the one that reaped the forgotten treasures, which the lot of you hadn't even noticed. Possession is nine-tenths of the law, you know."

"Thank you, Gordy, and all of you," Elliot answered. "That's a specious argument, my good man. I guess I am just overcome by the idea of losing our home. I need to think on it." We would have squabbled with him, the whole lot of us, but he shook his head. "Just know, you are my family, all of us gathered here, and you always will be. I've secured a place nearer town, not as many acres, of course, but a few to work with. It's smaller, and we'll need to adjust and make things work." He nodded and retired to bed.

I walked One to the front door; heavens, wooing was wearying business. I yearned for the day when One and I could officially declare whatever it was we were going to declare. One read my thoughts. "We could be married, Brandy."

"I cannot marry you."

"Though that is my heart's desire, I would be by your side however I may. Elliot would let you go; he would understand." I huddled in the shelter of his arm and listened to his deep voice that resonated in my very bones. "I want to take you to Spain and show you where I was born. It is beautiful there, and so warm. Even in the winter." I shivered.

"I fear you do not tell the truth, Sir. I cannot imagine that."

He filled my ear with whispered words of impossible dreams. "The sun is like nowhere else in the world there." His breath tickled my ear.

"What does it feel like?"

"Like a lover's kiss." Shut your gob. I, too, would have mocked that sentiment mere months ago. But trust me, those words vibrated from deep in his chest and fired a salvo across my bow.

That night I dreamed of endless summer days and sunny spirits. It was true; I was kinder under a shining sun, I thought, as I got out of bed, my poor toes pointed toward the chilly floor. I needed to see that warm land firsthand.

Elliot knew me better than I knew myself. I found him in the barn, where he claimed to do his best thinking among his plants and soils and seeds. I took the secret passageway, both for privacy from the chinwaggers of the household and to spark a smile from Elliot. I stepped through the weathered barn wood door, voila — which I believe is French for, here I am, adore me. Without even looking up, Elliot greeted me. "My Lady of Secrets." I had brought him a cup of coffee.

"Did you hear me?"

"I know you. I was expecting you. What's on your mind?" He gratefully took the cup and raised it in a small toast.

I went to the opposite side of his workbench and started sorting out soil into small pots and made them ready for Elliot's attendance. The dried herbs hanging above us, the cold grey outside reflected through the wall of windows, and the steamy warmth from the wood-burning stove, installed to keep his plants happy, conspired to coziness — another thing I would miss.

I tossed my cloak over a barrel, settled on a stool, and picked at the dirt on my nails. Elliot waited me out.

I sighed.

"Out with it, my good woman." He glanced over. "Is Michelle asleep?"

I nodded. "With Mrs. Catarrh. Atsuko is in the kitchen with Alys, and Beau has his spectacles on again."

"If only they could help him see another zero added to those figures."

A little more than a week after Michelle's baptism, Beau still wasn't able to raise enough funds to clear the debt needed to buy the estate. A pall descended, for even though we hadn't counted our chickens before they hatched, we had hoped for a feast of scrambled eggs seasoned with a soupçon of Cousin Clarence's tears.

"What's going to happen, Elliot?"

"No crystal ball, my fine girl. But we'll make do." He made some notations in his book. "We'll have enough for the rest of the year if we live simply, and we will just have to rely on our ingenuity to make it all work out. And I believe we can." He looked up at me. "It's One, isn't it? I presume he wants to marry you?"

I blushed.

"He's a fine man, Brandy. What a good husband he would be. He is, of course, welcome here. For that matter, my family and Beau's family, and many of my friends, all had families according to the legal definition, but we all experienced little more than duty, obligation, and appearances. God above, appearances of superiority before all else. You've seen my mother in action. Not a caring bone in her body, except a care for what others think."

"She smiled at Michelle in the church," I said.

"And our daughter didn't turn to stone? Praise be." He put down his pen.

"Brandy? Are you thinking of leaving us? You know our living situation is a little more mixed up than most, but perhaps that's the best kind of family to have, no? I may not know much of your childhood, but you and I, there's a recognition we share. And I'm glad we found each other. I'd like you to stay, and One, and I can't bear the thought of you taking our daughter away. But I know I can't stop you if that's what's in your heart."

"Stop being so understanding, you twat. Forbid me, or kick me out. Do something." I stood up and knocked the stool over. "I don't know why I'm crying."

"Brandy, wait. I want you to stay, and all of us to go on, just as we are. Please."

I ran back through the secret door to the manor. I had just closed the door to the linen closet when I bumped into RayRay. "RayRay. What is it? Are you looking for me?" He rocked back on his heels. His face flushed. "No. Yes. Well, I wondered if you were hungry." He widened his eyes, and I knew it took him everything he had not to whistle innocently.

"Not in the least," I said, even as my stomach grumbled. "I'll be down shortly. Elliot should be back from the barn by now and ready to eat." I waved him off. I watched him go down the stairs. He watched me walk down the hall toward my room. I couldn't trust RayRay as far as I could throw him. He was up to no good. I wouldn't put it past him to steal my ill-gotten gains. As soon as I saw the back of him, I turned and hied my way back to the linen closet.

I ran down to the hidey-hole. I lit a candle but used another unlit taper to sweep under the shelves to retrieve my treasure box. For a split second, I couldn't find it there, and I worried that someone by the name of RayRay had come back for a further search. However, the candlestick finally located it, and I swiped back and forth to slide it out.

I opened the box and took out the darkened and cracked leather pouch. Damn me. I opened the pouch and dug for that particularly gaudy, in my opinion, diamond necklace. I hefted it in my hands and considered. Time was wasting. I put the pouch with the rest of its treasures back under the shelf and tore down to the barn through the secret passageway, clutching that accursed necklace. I stopped to catch my breath and made sure Elliot had indeed gone back to the manor. I slipped inside the barn and did a quick inventory. There. That sad, drooping plant with crinkly brown leaves in the corner in a clay pot would do. I grabbed the base of the stem, pried the ball of roots out from the pot, and shoved the necklace to the bottom. I pushed the plant back in and settled the soil atop. Have I taught you nothing? Always leave yourself options.

I brushed off my hands, high-tailed it back to my hidey-hole, and retrieved the pouch with the rest of the treasures. My heart pounded, and I looked around as if it were the last time I would ever see that room. I blew it a kiss, took the candle and my fortune, and hurried back to my bedroom.

Michelle was napping with Mrs. Catarrh in her room. Somehow that baby found the crackling snores of the old woman soothing. Bless her heart. Bless their hearts.

I transferred the gold coins and jewels into a soft burgundy velvet bag and placed it under the baby's mattress at the foot end of her cradle, and tossed the blanket Mrs. Catarrh made on top. I threw the moldy bag into the fireplace, and as it burned, I smelled the regrets of lives lived before me. I waved my hands from shoulder to shoulder, not quite sure what those Catholics were about with their hands all hurdy-gurdy, but figured it couldn't hurt. Something had gone terribly wrong in someone's life for them to have hidden this king's ransom in that secret pass-through and never been able to return. Did they take the secret to their grave? I paced. I could make good use of the treasure — it would give my baby a good life. Why should it remain hidden? I, who had never had a reason for conscience before, discovered it was highly overrated. Why should I feel any obligation to share it? No one else would have ever found it. I pushed my tits up and put my cloak back on.

One wanted to take me to his parent's home. To have the security that this bounty could provide would be the answer to my problems. No one would have to know.

I knew what I had to do. I still didn't believe it could possibly be warm in winter in Spain, but damn if I didn't want to see for myself!

I followed my breath as I ran down to One's cottage. I had no thought of romance despite the flicker in his eyes. Besides, it was too soon for him to know the real me. I had stopped by the kitchen on my way and gobbled a taste of Alys's hearty cabbage stew, and thought it best to avoid a garlic-flavored burp in the middle of a passionate embrace. I ducked my head and told him I needed to see Sir Stone. He moved my chair from in front of the fireplace into his bedroom beside Sir Stone on his pedestal. He left and quietly closed the door.

One wanted to situate Sir Stone in my bedroom at the manor, but I preferred visiting my two favorite gents down at the cottage. Felt right, somehow. I liked to keep that part of my life separate.

"Sir Stone. You know why I've come. The baby is fine." I smiled. "Look at me. Would you have ever thought I'd be the mother of such a child? Yes. She already has One wrapped around her little finger. What do you think of One? You've gotten to know him. You like him, don't you?"

I sat in my chair. "What?" Sir Stone wore as forbidding a look as I'd ever seen. There was nothing noble about his stern brow. I hated when he got like that. "I know there are no guarantees; that's just what Elliot says. But that's my argument. I can't let anyone drag me down. We are all responsible for ourselves. We live alone and die alone. You know that I have to watch out for myself and for Michelle. I'm not responsible for these people."

I stood and looked away from him, out the window. "The jewels and coins were locked inside the wall for a generation, at least. I was the one who found them. Me. No one knew about them. No one can lay claim to them. Whoever put them there is dead and gone. Buried and worm food. Why shouldn't someone get the use and benefit from them? You do agree with me, right? Finders keepers."

I sat back down. "I need your wisdom, Sir Stone. I knew you would under-stand." I leaned forward in my chair, closer to him, and right then and there, he toppled off the pedestal and landed atop my foot. I screamed bloody murder, and One came running. He gently placed Sir Stone, no worse for the wear, back upon his perch. He took off my shoe and massaged my instep, his fingers strong and gentle. I may have played a swooning miss a little longer than necessary because is there anything like a gorgeous man massaging your foot? My left foot was that jealous. Long after my foot ceased aching, I pushed One away, put my shoe back on, and left. "Fuck you, Sir Stone," I whispered under my breath.

Chapter 35

"Why are you fidgeting so, Brandy?" Mrs. Catarrh said. "Atsuko, pass me that baby; she's going to drop her or give her an upset stomach."

"It can't end this way. It just can't." I passed Michelle over. "We're surely not the villains, are we?" Dear Lord. I'd never had a guilty conscience before, and I'm sure I don't recommend it. It took me three days to realize I wasn't ill. The energy to draw a full breath, inability to sleep, and the aches and pains I bore were symptoms of my miserly misery.

I would wait a few more days and see if anything could prevent us from losing all this. Or if One and I and baby Michelle would just leg it. What could I, a mere girl, do? Unbidden and unwanted, I could picture Sir Stone's visage. "Experience is the teacher of all things," he counseled me often. The answer really was simple. And I was the only one who could get it right. Experience had taught me that it's each woman for herself. But that dang-blasted family, for yes, that's what they were by then, had come along and spoiled it all. Who, but family, has seen behind the smiles and courteous manners into the dark worm-riddled torments and the shrieking pettiness that rails against the chaos of life yet still manages to accept you into their tribe? Experience may be the teacher, but family is the buffer against an unfair world. So, which would I choose?

Cousin Clarence came back right before dinner, pounding on the door. "Open up. I have the constable and his men with me, and we are doing another search of the property. It cannot be as penurious as you led me to believe. A trader in London was caught fencing a Pfeiffer-Mondragon crested ring, you thieving scoundrels."

Elliot and Beau exchanged a look. Beau shook his head slightly. I had no idea where he had stashed the money from his activities or if he had anything left to sell. Dear heavens.

Cousin Clarence stared at Elliot. "I think we'll start in the barn. Cousin?" Elliot stood from the table and led the way out the front door down to the barn. I raced for the stairs, followed by Beau, RayRay, and Gordy. Down the secret passageway we went. We arrived at the barn at the same time as Cousin Clarence and his men, but we stayed on our side of the door, peering through a crack. They were careless in their search. Flinging potted plants and tools to the floor, scattering dirt and relishing the mess they were making.

"Now see here, Cousin Clarence. There's no need for this. Do you think if I had anything of value, I wouldn't have already used it to save Mondragon Manor?" Elliot said.

The blood pounded in my ears. I could not catch my breath. I squeezed my hands. Frustrated, Cousin Clarence held up his hand to halt his men. I quietly exhaled. RayRay stepped back, and I saw him pat Beau on the back. They were ready to head back up.

Then I saw Cousin Clarence kick at a row of pots on the floor and send them crashing. With a roar of rage, he picked up a plant, dying in the corner, and smashed it with all his might. I hung my head. I couldn't bear to watch. Maybe no one would notice.

"What have we here?" Fuck me. Cousin Clarence squatted on his haunches and pulled that wicked diamond necklace from the roots. "Nothing of value, eh, cousin?" He taunted Elliot. "See, Constable? We are on the right path. Search the house."

I couldn't bear to face Beau and RayRay. Worse, Gordy turned his back on me. They knew what I had done. With my deceit, my selfishness, I had given the keys to the castle to Cousin Clarence. I ran back to the house. I was still trying to catch my breath at the dining table when a very jubilant Cousin Clarence and his men trooped back in.

Cousin Clarence stood before us, quivering like one of Mrs. Farfuddle's less successful puddings. "The jig is up." He held the dirty diamond necklace. "Thieves and liars, the lot of you. What else do you have secreted away, hmm?" I glanced up. Elliot wouldn't even look at me. Gordy's head was hanging over his plate. Beau and RayRay's faces were thunderclouds. They looked as if they hated me. RayRay curled his lip and mouthed the word "traitor" at me.

I was devastated. They had reason to hate me. They blamed me for holding out on them, and in doing so, I had cost them Mondragon Manor. My heart broke because it was true. Why hadn't I just given Elliot and Beau that damned necklace?

We were lost — all of us. I needed to make a break for it. I needed a distraction. It was time for my little one to earn her keep. She was cooing adorably on Mrs. Catarrh's lap. I reached under the table and pinched the baby on her thigh, but good — a stinging pincer on her sweet soft skin. I would spend the rest of her life making it up to her. On cue, she began a crescendo of banshee screams. I stood up and tried to make for the stairs.

"Halt, Cousin Brandy. Elliot. Stay your wife. Everyone to remain here." The constable at his side, a stern-faced man whose whiskers had gotten the better of him such that I spared a thought for his poor wife who must have to watch him maneuver food through that thicket.

I sneezed. "I've taken a chill and just need to gather my shawl. Please?" I smiled, batted my eyes, and bowed low so the gentlemen could infer my goosebumps. Baby Michelle refused to be calmed. "It's so chilly this time of year."

"Fine, ma'am," said the constable as Cousin Clarence began to bluster. "Just be quick."

"And quiet that brat," Cousin Clarence said. Atsuko glared at him. She held Michelle now, at an awkward angle, and seemed content to let Michelle air her lungs.

"RayRay, I believe I left my shawl in your room." He looked at me with loathing. He was going to refuse. "Please?" My eyes widened with urgency. That's the thing about liars. They are right quick to jump in the game.

"Of course," he said. "I meant to return it to you. My apologies. Let's go." He took my arm none too gently and made a show of quickly climbing the stairs. "We'll be right back."

Once out of sight, RayRay made to turn toward his room, but I veered him off to mine.

"What gives, Brandy? How could you do this to us? Why didn't you give those diamonds to Elliot?"

"Not now," I hissed. I opened my door and pulled him in. "Your boots, give them to me. Hurry."

He pulled them off. I kicked my slippers under the bed and raced to the baby's cradle. I pulled the velvet bag from under her mattress, shoved my hand inside, and stuffed jewels and coins deep in each toe of RayRay's boots. I lifted my skirts and shoved my feet inside his boots. I gave the bag to RayRay as we heard footsteps. He helped me slide the remaining pieces down around my ankles, shins, and calves up the sides of the boots. I dropped my skirts and grabbed my shawl, just as Cousin Clarence flung open the door.

"Sorry, it was in my room after all. Cousin Clarence, I don't know what you are expecting to find. We are quite frankly tired of this persecution. It's not our fault you don't have money to pay the back taxes. And if you're hoping to find it here, you will be sorely disappointed." RayRay stood near me, hiding his stocking feet behind my skirts.

"How do you know about all that?" He narrowed his eyes at me.

Fuck. I had the pointy side of a faceted emerald earring digging into the arch of my left foot. I hated to poke the bear, but since it was what I always did, I had to remain on point. "The tenants laugh about it every night. Surely you've heard them? What is it they say, RayRay?"

"They give toasts, I believe," he said, his eyes glinted as he held up an imaginary pint. "Cousin Clarence can barely pay rents," The bully in question glowered at us.

I managed a laugh myself, though I felt a desperate need to cry.

Cousin Clarence waved his hand at two burly men. "Toss this room. This is a good place to start. You can bet a thieving wench like this would have stolen goods stockpiled."

Touché, I thought. "RayRay?" I held my arm for him to take and help me walk. I don't know how I managed. I curled my toes and did my best to not let anything jingle or jangle. It was agony, and yet I had to sail out of there, imperiously, as if nothing was wrong. I had just about made it to the top of the stairs.

"Hold up!" That fecking Cousin Clarence.

I paused and turned my head. "You screamed?"

"Why are you walking like that?"

"Like what?"

"Like…" He couldn't describe it. Which gives you a fair picture as to how I was maneuvering.

"I am walking genteel, as a lady does. Something you no doubt, know nothing of." A toe of the boot peeked out, and I twitched to swirl my skirt to cover it back up. He banged his hand on the door jamb and returned to toss my bedroom.

RayRay caught me around the waist and lifted me just off the ground at the top of the steps, and helped float me all the way down. We rested at the bottom, and I adjusted my shawl. I clomped into the dining room, slowly dragging my heels, and made for my seat.

"Brandy?" Elliot raised his eyebrows.

I pulled my shawl close. "I feel I'm coming down with a cold." At that moment, Baby Michelle, who now was on One's lap, sneezed, breaking the tension. "Something must be going around."

None of us had much appetite. We could hear drawers being slammed, thuds and bangs, and all sorts of clamor from upstairs. I couldn't imagine what they were doing. Or what they were looking for. Or worse, what they would find.

It was my penance to keep those boots on throughout the interminable dinner. I didn't help carry plates to the kitchen, and Atsuko, with her intuition, smiled at me. "I have this, Brandy. Please, have some more brandy." Her unspoken words told me to stay and calm the gentlemen. Elliot had his head in his hands, and Beau was fidgeting. No one spoke to me. Finally, nearly two hours after they arrived,

Cousin Clarence and his entourage came down. He had a pillowcase filled with several items.

"Elliot," I nudged him. "Surely you get to see what he's taking?"

My husband, the gentleman, politely asked the constable if he could gaze upon his belongings.

"Show them," he said. "It's not our lot to appropriate one's personal belongings." Cousin Kleptomaniac protested. The Constable waved his hands to get on with it.

They had found both Elliot's and Beau's gold buttons I had given them for Christmas that they hadn't had time to have sewn onto their coats. There were a few minor, small-sized paintings in ornate frames, a gold crucifix from Elliot's room. Unfortunately, they had found some of the items Beau had planned on selling, hidden in his room, not very smartly, in his boots. I felt a sick blush creep up my chest. I pulled the shawl tightly. "What else?" I jerked my chin toward the bag. The constable pulled out my brush and comb set with a small hand mirror. And then a silver rattle that Lady P had given Michelle.

"Not that!" I stood up so fast that fortunately, the sound of my wine glass falling over disguised an odd sound coming from under the table as my boots clinked.

"That is my daughter's."

Cousin Clarence laughed and threw the rattle on the table. "Cousin Elliot," he said. "I may not be getting ownership of Mondragon Manor, and if that's the case, I'll take my lumps with great joy, knowing that you will also never be master here."

The last item out of his haul was my silver locket from the vagabond sailor. "And I'll take that." I held out my hand. "You can see it's worth nothing. It's mine."

Cousin Clarence snorted. "I should have known." I grabbed the broken chain, its locket a green darkness with tarnish. I didn't really want it, but I didn't want Cousin Clarence to have it more.

He took his cache and wiggled the diamond necklace at us with a laugh before he and his men stomped out. We heard the horses gallop off, and in the quiet, we looked around the table at each other. Elliot looked off into the parlor and then around at the walls of the dining room. "It's finally sinking in," he said. His shoulders drooped.

"I am so sorry, everyone." I gulped. "I should have just given you that necklace when I found it. I just thought there was time. I wanted to wait and see. I would have given it to you."

Beau cut me off. "Sorry, Elliot. I should have hidden the rest of those things better," Beau said. "I had an appointment to sell them on Wednesday. I just didn't think. I thought we'd seen the last of that scoundrel."

"Beau. We both know it wouldn't have made a difference. We need a heap more coin to save Mondragon Manor. Thank you, though, friend," Elliot said. He pressed his lips into as farcical a smile as I'd ever seen. "I fear I'm more attached to this old place than I'd imagined. My father grew up here, and his father before him." He shrugged. "While I do not have the happiest of memories," he looked around the table, "I find I'm quite taken with the most recent occurrences that have tumbled under this roof. I suppose, as the old priests say, a church isn't a building; it's the people, not the place. Just like a home."

"Dear Lord," I said, "If you're trying to make us weep, grab hold of your bollocks." I stood up gingerly since my feet were killing me and leaned my weight into my hands on the table.

"I apologize about the necklace. I should have given it to you when I found it. I thought it would be safe there, in the barn. I thought it was a perfect hiding place." Elliot, Gordy, and Beau looked like they needed more convincing. RayRay looked like he wanted to kiss me right then and there. His eyes sparkled. I nodded at him. "A little help?"

He ran around the table, knelt before me, and dived under my skirts. "Beau," I said. "Better get out your spectacles."

"RayRay," Gordy said. "Please. Get up. What's going on?"

I held on to RayRay's shoulder and lifted one foot as he slid the boot off. He raised it triumphantly over his head then poured the contents right onto the middle of the table. Then did the same with the next boot.

Beau stood up and went for his notebook, and everyone began to examine the loot. "That diamond necklace will go a long way toward upping Cousin Clarence's fortunes, Brandy. But it may not be enough. Let's hope not." He peered at me over his spectacles. "This, however," he was holding the strand of pearls, "yes, you are a fine girl — these jewels just might do it." I guess I'd been forgiven. "The good guys might still be in with a chance."

This family better be worth it. They cost me everything.

Chapter 36

The very next day, we could hear One shouting from his cottage down the way. I grabbed my cloak, and we all ran outside, only to see the backside, his good side, of Cousin Clarence galloping off.

We reached One. His face was red with anger, his fist clenched. "He took Sir Stone."

"What?"

I twirled to look behind me. Malys or Calys, who had just finished nursing Michelle, had followed behind us. Her eyes goggled at the look on my face. She held up her hands and started backwards before she tumbled to the ground.

"What have you done this time?" I loomed over her, ready to place a well-aimed kick at the turncoat. One caught me by the arm. Elliot stepped in front of me.

"Explain yourself." He helped her up.

She cried so hard we could barely hear her. "I was at the market yesterday, and Sir Clarence ambushed me. I swear. I didn't know. I feel ever so bad about spying for him on you all and baby Michelle, who I love as much as my own. I swear, I never gave him any more confidences. He scared me that much and threatened me."

Beau had reached us and clocked my reaction.

"Go on," I said.

"He hurt me bad and said he was going to do worse." She pulled up her sleeve, and indeed we saw bruises which I could from two paces certainly match the ham-handed sausage fingers of the brute.

"What did you tell him?"

"Nothing. You yourself know there's nothing to tell."

What did she mean by that? I hurried her on her tale as RayRay rode up on Elliot's fastest horse, eager for a chase.

"I had to give him something, so I just told him about that rock head there in the one-armed carpenter's room." She sniffed. "He wanted to know if it was gold, or silver, or better yet, diamonds."

"What's your real name, girl?" I asked her.

"Ma-Mary," she said with a whimper.

"Jesus weeps. Your name is not mammary." I cocked my head as I eyed her bosom. Well, maybe.

"She's scared, ma'am. It's Mary," said her sister, Alys, who had also heard the ruckus.

"So, what did you tell him? Who, exactly, or what, did you tell Cousin Clarence the rock was?" I asked in a quiet voice.

"Just that you seem fond of it. And that it minded me of the bloke in the picture in the book from the master's library. You were all looking at it when you were having lemonade and scones outside that day."

"What bloke?"

"That time Sir Beau was telling you not to swan about like you were Cleopatra or some such. You told him to mind his p's and q's because there wasn't a thing that women couldn't do but better than men, and Cleopatra was a dame ahead of her time and damned if you couldn't prove it." She twisted her fingers at the recitation.

"To shut you up, beg pardon," the minx actually had the audacity to say as she fumbled a minuscule curtsy, "he found a page in that book of his and showed you a drawing, and then you and he went on for what seemed like hours, having an argument over who was better. The rock looks like the bloke in the book. Julius Caesar," she said.

"Julius Caesar?" I asked. "Oh, Sir Stone." I bit my lip and turned my back in a huff on that no good tattle-tale.

"That scoundrel," Beau said. "He's going to try to sell some rock you and One found, Brandy? To some shady antiquarian or rich collector? Is it truly part of a statue of Julius Caesar? That's a story we have no time to hear right now."

"Rest assured, Brandy, we'll bring him back to you," Gordy said. He, too, joined RayRay on horseback with a pack of food Atsuko had prepared.

"No. Wait." Sir Stone was massively important to me, but I didn't want Ray-Ray and Gordy to risk their lives for him. Neither would he. "Please don't go. It's fine. Let Cousin Clarence have him." I wouldn't cry. I'd lived without Sir Stone before. Atsuko was by my side and squeezed my hand.

At a nod from Elliot and Beau, Gordy and RayRay galloped off.

"Why did you let them go? I will never forgive myself if something happens to them. You know Cousin Clarence. He is brutal. Please. Don't let this happen. Call them back."

"They will be alright," Elliot said.

Beau seconded him. "And we can't let Cousin Clarence think he's won something from us; it would never end. Besides, this rock escapade could buy him more time. Or, who knows, if he can raise more money with the diamond necklace plus that rock, he could still win Mondragon Manor. Time is of the essence, and we refuse to give up."

With bowed head, I squeezed Elliot's hand.

It was a long night in which darkness settled in earlier than normal. It was cold, cloudy, with a forecast of a sore throat. None of us had much an appetite, but brandy was to be had.

For four long days we awaited with no word. Finally, we heard the gallop of horses. RayRay dismounted and pushed Gordy out of the way to rush in first. We gathered around as RayRay flung a newspaper on the dining room table.

The headline blared, "Lord of the FlimFlam, Statue Declared a Hoax: Nothing more than a Garden Knob!"

Beau rattled the paper and commenced a dramatic reading: Lord Clarence Pfeiffer-Mondragon, of Beckham parish, had the audacity to assiduously assault an antiquarian in a nefarious fraudulent scheme. The perpetrator presented an object, purported to be part of a long-lost statue of Julius Caesar, believed to be stolen and currently at rest at the bottom of the sea. Famed Egyptologist, Sir Howard Oldengaffer, claims to have been "excited beyond belief" at the idea of the discovery of the missing head of the statue of Julius Caesar, believed to have been commissioned by Cleopatra in 45 BC, nearly two millennia ago.

Yet as the scoundrel made to reveal his "archeological artifact," for which he was hoping to be rewarded an astounding sum of money, it turned out to be nothing more than what looked like a round embellishment toppled from a down-on-its-luck gate post.

"It was no more a sculpture of the head of Julius Caesar than the buttocks of the perpetrator himself," Sir Oldengaffer decried. He wondered aloud had the gentleman in question's "fat arse" indeed been used as the impression to create the cast of the false relic, though later said he thought it too great a coincidence.

"It would have been a priceless acquisition and a truly remarkable historic event," said Sir Oldengaffer. "Our board was prepared to pay handsomely for the opportunity to acquire this rare treasure, which we could have shared with the world." Sir Oldengaffer became so distraught, he couldn't speak for quite some time. "That, that, shyster, to perpetrate a fraud of this magnitude is not to be borne."

Though Sir Oldengaffer is reported to have taken a swing at the disgraced Pfeiffer-Mondragon, the portly noble ducked to miss the aim delivered by the elderly antiquarian and tripped of his own volition, resulting in a clean break of his left leg. His personal physician adds it was the one with gout.

Pfeiffer-Mondragon threatened to file charges for assault, yet no arrest has been made. Sir Oldengaffer shook his cane in the nobleman's face and sneered, "I never touched you and wouldn't with a barge pole." He himself declined to file fraud charges, citing, "the blighter's not worth it."

Beau folded the paper and smacked it in his hand. "What wondrous news! Well done, Gordy, RayRay. You couldn't have devised a better outcome."

"He's the laughingstock of his parish," Elliot said. "If we're lucky, he'll be too ashamed to show his face around here for quite a while."

Mrs. Catarrh added, "To say nothing of his arse or broken, gouty leg."

One squeezed me in a hug. I did not want to be the peon who laughed loudest, as we all know that's the one the gods do love to target for their next prank.

"He really thought he was going to get away with it. And he almost did," Elliot said.

"Men," Beau said, "and I guess women, too, believe what they wish to see and what they wish to be true."

"Sir Stone believed that, too," I said.

Beau and Elliot exchanged a look.

"There's more," RayRay said. "Brandy. I do believe there is someone here to cock your eyes on." He bent and undid a wrap of his cloak to reveal the beloved gray and worn head, no worse for the wear. He gently placed Sir Stone on the dining room table.

I squeezed One's hand tightly. We exchanged a look while I stood back to allow Elliot and Beau to be formally introduced. I saw Beau nod his head rather vigorously at Elliot's arched eyebrows. Elliot turned to take my hand. He kissed it in a sweet gesture.

"That dog," I said. "Sir Stone and Cleopatra. Who would have guessed?"

"My dear girl, you never cease to amaze me. And as for your Sir Stone, here, it would be an honor if you would consider allowing him to reside in our family home, to guide us through the battles and bedevilments we will surely face."

RayRay poked me in the back. "So shy? Brandy? Cat got your tongue? I risked life and limb to be able to chuck this rock out of that plunker's hands." My fingers fluttered at my mouth. That's what ladies do when they are unsure of what words would be spilling forth.

"Sure, I just wanted to kill that bastard, beg your pardon, but Gordy had his eye on the prize. The fact that Cousin Clarence is getting his just desserts makes it all the more delicious." RayRay tapped his temple. "Gordy played a good game."

Gordy cleared his throat.

Dear Lord, ever since I birthed that baby, tears just seemed to seep from my eyes. "Thank you." I hugged RayRay first, who lifted me clean off the floor and twirled me because he's RayRay. And I went to Gordy and looked down into his dear face. He didn't need to hear my thank you, which was a good thing because it was stuck in my throat. He patted me awkwardly. My very own, very much alive, Sir Stone.

Atsuko came over and took Gordy's hand. Gordy swept her up in one of the most romantical kisses I'd ever seen. He pulled back and looked at us, a sheepish look on his big face. Then he knelt before Atsuko, holding her hands.

"My darling Atsuko, will you never marry me?"

Her soft laugh sounded as magical as a tune on the harp I would never master. "I would love to never marry you, Gordy." She tugged him up, and we cheered.

"But tell us, how?" Elliot demanded details at dinner that night.

"As you know, RayRay was after your kin's guts," Gordy said. RayRay smiled proudly and wielded an imaginary sword lopping a head from a torso. "We galloped off, and halfway there, we stopped to," Gordy smiled, "relieve ourselves. We were by this old ramshackle place, gate well off its hinges, weeds this high," he raised his hand. "The place was well and truly abandoned. And when I saw the wobbly post, there was a round cement head-sized stone atop, just begging to go along for the ride."

RayRay picked up the story. "Bigger than Gordy's head, it was. So, we pried it off, and the plan basically formed itself. We hied onwards to Cousin Clarence's abode; no wonder he wants this place. Peeling paint, rotting timbers, roof as saggy as Mrs. Catarrh's…" Elliot stopped him.

"RayRay, we get the idea. Cousin Clarence is not one for upkeep."

"So, we knew the bloke was there; his poor sweaty horse was in the stable. We laid low, waiting for it to get dark, and sure enough, he lit out for the local pub to celebrate. We followed him, watched him brag to all and sundry about his great good fortune, soon to be his. Gordy paid a git to keep the drinks a-coming, and we went back to his place to make the exchange."

"But, how did you get in?" I asked. "Was it hard to find Sir Stone?" We all turned to the corner near the entryway where Sir Stone was ensconced atop his pedestal, holding court. He had already taken up roost as our talisman.

"RayRay caused such a racket trying to clamber in the window, it set the hounds barking. I hauled him back just as the door was flung open and Sir Clarence's three lads piled out."

Gordy and RayRay exchanged a look. "What's their mother like?" RayRay asked. "She had already retired for the evening, so we did not have the pleasure."

Elliot wore a half-smile. "She's a beautiful little thing, silvery-gold hair, a petite little sprite. She's very fair but given to sickness. Being married to my cousin, one can hardly blame her."

"Have you ever seen the boys?" Gordy asked.

Elliot waved his hand. "Perhaps at their baptisms. Why?"

"They look like a peace treaty gone awry," RayRay said. "The oldest boy could have been Atsuko's cousin, the next one had skin dark as mahogany, and the littlest fellow, had the look of a Moorish trader, with eyes blacker than coal."

"Nice enough lads, though," Gordy amended.

"They sure were helpful," RayRay said. "See, we gabbled out that we owed their father money and needed to reimburse him. And as we were bereft that the debt had accumulated for such a lengthy time, we wished to pay our respects and clean the slate."

"Cost us a bit, too," RayRay said. "We gave each boy a coin, and they led us to the study. We asked for a quaff for our long ride ahead, and they obliged. Gordy left his bag of coins, and we pulled Sir Stone from the leather satchel Cousin Clarence had thoughtfully hidden under his desk and replaced it with the concrete knob."

"Weren't you worried the boys would tell their father of your visit?" Atsuko asked.

"Darling," RayRay said. "If those boys hadn't stolen the coins the second we left, I'd clean Mrs. Farfuddle's fingernails with my own teeth." He shook his head. "We knew Cousin Clarence would have a tight head the next morning when he was due to meet with the antiquarian. We saw the meet time and place written on a scrap of paper on Cousin Clarence's desk. It was Gordy's idea to notify the newspaper. We stayed an extra day to bring back the trophy." He pointed to the newspaper.

Chapter 37

The very next day, the occupants at Mondragon Manor were up with the sun, bent on an industrious crusade. Armed with legal documents and bank statements, Elliot and Beau made haste to the county courthouse. Atsuko, Alys, and I declared war on the housekeeping sector of our world. 'Tis humorous how the thankless task of scrubbing the floor takes precedence in lieu of eating your worries for breakfast. Mrs. Farfuddle was huddled in Elliot's barn, scheming about springtime planting, happy as a pig in a poke, nearly literally. We suspected she clawed through dirt like a miser burrowing in coin.

Malys or Calys, beg pardon, Mary, who admitted she was the one who informed Cousin Clarence about Sir Stone, thinking no great harm, wept so copiously we feared her milk supply for that ravenous little Michelle would be dried up. I took pity on her once again, vouched for as she was by both her sister, Alys and Mrs. Catarrh. Ah, Mrs. Catarrh. What was she up to during all these ongoings, you ask?

As luck would have it, it was she who answered the banging on our door a mere three days following Sir Stone's retrieval. We heard her cough, laugh, cough some more. Followed by a matched reedy-sounding voice, though of the masculine persuasion. "Come sit in the parlor, by the fire," I heard her say, like the spider to the fly. "It's cold enough to freeze a saint's piss," she said. As we were in the kitchen, we were startled to see a blur race past, then back up, and holler out, "Tea. Pronto. And some of those scones. Don't be stingy with the jam."

Five minutes later, her ladyship sailed back down the stairs, dressed as if attending her own funeral, best dress, diamond bobs at her ears, wispy hair combed high atop her head. She shook her finger at us, then swanned into the parlor. Yes, it took all three of us to carry in the tea and scones to observe.

"Set the tea right here, my dear," she grandly ordered Alys. "I'll pour." On the sofa opposite sat a right old gent, who stood upon our entrance.

"Oh, close those fly-traps, dears; you all look quite ridiculous." Mrs. Catarrh poured tea and handed the old geezer the cup and saucer, her arm shaking like a tree limb in a storm. The man executed some sort of creaky bow and resumed his seat.

"Ladies. May I present Sir Howard Oldengaffer, Antiquarian, Egyptologist, and a most astute student of the human condition." She rattled off our names as of no significance. "He came to make the acquaintance of Sir Stone. I assured him it is with our pleasure."

The zing of wrath began to boil immediately as Oldengaffer waved his small hand. "Just to say how do you do, mind, nothing nefarious. Just wanted to see him with my own eyes."

Everyone awaited my reaction. What was wrong with his eyes? Was he having a stroke? Sure, it was more than possible, as the man could have been the subject of his own antiquarian studies. His cloudy eyes still managed to glint blue sparks under his ferocious white brows. Dear Lord, was that man trying to flirt with me?

We know. Of course, we know the intent of others. Like as not, we occasionally trick ourselves as to another's purpose, either inferring scurrilous actions based upon our own shortcomings or wishing for what was not so. In my long, weary life, I believe I've learned to take the measure of a man.

"Salutations," said I. I held out my arm. "I'll introduce you myself." Mrs. Catarrh jumped off the sofa, you read that right, she leaped into the air and positioned herself on his other side. Sir Stone was suitably somber at the introduction and made quite an impression. The old gent bowed low and then, with trembling hands, lovingly stroked Sir Stone's brow, forehead, and ears. It was some time before Mrs. Catarrh managed to entice the historian back to the parlor.

Perhaps Sir Stone was our talisman after all. Through whatever legal shenanigans he could muster, Beau sold much of the loot, not all of it, paid off the back taxes, and secured Elliot's true and sole proprietorship of Mondragon Manor and the lands thusly adjoined. Cousin Clarence, holed up and hiding out, was fit to be tied and bore watching. Elliot also paid off his parents to keep their visits short — though they were never sweet — and staggered throughout the year.

Elliot was cloaked in a new mantle of maturity honed with worry and work. He treated his tenants and their families as lovingly as baby Michelle. He worked harder than ever on his farming improvements, determined to produce not only a profit but healthy food for as many folks as he could. That was his mission. Beau decided to complete his solicitor's education and was invaluable with managing the estate alongside Gordy.

RayRay, I worried about that lad. His heart was bigger than his feet, but alas, his brain was much smaller. He wanted to be important in this world; he just didn't want to be inconvenienced getting there. The world wasn't quite ready for his brand of *joie de vivre*, which I believe is French for not giving a fuck. He would have made a most swashbuckling pirate, but we are civilized now and none left of that glory but stories.

"RayRay. Stop that infernal whistling." He responded by blowing a little ditty from the underside of his tongue to captivate our little miss.

This gang of a family that I'm surrounded with has found me in possession of a conscience. It is a strange feeling, that. A burr in my side that I had been perfectly content operating without, but once uncovered, it proved to be a privilege worth honoring. I'd been tricked into it by that blighty crew — folks who I want things done right by. Gah. I've still got a backup plan or two tucked up my sleeve, don't you fear. Life isn't a bed of roses. Uncertainty is as sure a bet as there is in this life. IS AZ... Was that a clue to the note in my sailor's locket? I'd have to ask Gordy about that, and maybe one day we should all sojourn to Islas Azores.

With three fairy godfathers, Baby Michelle is blessed. Elliot brings her security and a nobleness of spirit, for which we mock him mercilessly. Beau showers her with sheer joy and curiosity and an optimism I covet. And my one-armed man,

One, bequeaths her with nothing but assurance that every breath she takes is per-
fection. Sir Stone? Well, he is the rock of certainty in a very precarious world.

As a rule, I can't say I recommend motherhood because I believe I have already
laid claim to the best baby. And heaven help us; I do not plan on going through
that again, no thank you. I adjusted the cap on my baby's head that was so bald
she could be mistook for Gordy. Other folk's children can be a trial, as I daresay
you've surely witnessed. This one would suffice. Though I couldn't wait to give a
twirl with One. I caught him looking at me out of the side of my eye. I hoped my
smile was not as sheepish as it felt.

I continue to strive to make Sir Stone proud of me. I find I can be kind for
more than two hours at a go, more often than not. Fair warning, that's mostly my
maximum. It's not my fault people are as far from perfect as Cousin Clarence is to
ever be able to eye his own parsnip again. There's always someone bound to be
stirring up trouble and aiming to throw darts in the wind — I just try to make
sure it isn't me.

In the very dastardly month of February, when nothing good happens, the
wind blew as we took turns passing the baby around and introduced her to the
whole wide world at the edge of the sea. As usual, Michelle was expedited back to
me once she began to fuss. "Shush, shush. There, there," I sang. "All is well." I
hugged her fiercely and kissed her perfect cheek. "You're with your family now,
and you'll always be safe."

The gods took that bet.

The waves crashed, and in the distance, I could see a ship. I handed Michelle
to Beau and took his spyglass. Riding high on the horizon, making good headway
toward the harbor, entering stage left, sailed The Looking Glass. The ship of my
long-lost sailor.

"Is that...?" Elliot asked me. He took the spyglass from me and looked for
himself.

"It is," I said. I narrowed my eyes. "No doubt he's coming to get his locket
back." I couldn't wait to throw it right in the rotter's face. "He probably thinks

I've been waiting here patiently, hands folded, this whole time, for his return. What do I look like, a nun?"

I straightened my shoulders. Oh, he'd get his locket back alright. And who's to say if the note secreted inside was altered in any way? Did you know the number 1 just begs to be turned into the number 4? And with a lovely flourish, a zero can become a grownup number 9. Perhaps. Just a suggestion. I'm sure I know nothing of it. Nor of the meticulous copy of the correct version safely stowed where no one would be able to find it.

My thoughts were stayed as One squeezed me in a reassuring hug. "*Que será, será,* Brandy," he told me, which I believe is Spanish for, "Vengeance is mine."

Also by Dee DeTarsio

The Scent of Jade

'Til Somebody Loves You

The Kitchen Shrink

Haole Wood

Ros

All My Restless Life to Live

Ginger Krinkles

Luellen & Lucy

HISTRIA

Addison & Highsmith

Other fine works of fiction available from Addison & Highsmith Publishers:

For these and many other great books
Visit
HistriaBooks.com